THE OTHER SIDE OF
THROUGH

THE OTHER SIDE OF
THROUGH

MARSHA D. JENKINS-SANDERS

STREBOR BOOKS

NEW YORK LONDON TORONTO SYDNEY

Strebor Books
P.O. Box 6505
Largo, MD 20792

This book is a work of fiction. Names, characters, places and incidents are products of
the author's imagination or are used fictitiously. Any resemblance to actual events or
locales or persons, living or dead, is entirely coincidental.

The Other Side of Through © 2007 by Marsha D. Jenkins-Sanders

ISBN-13 978-0-7394-8311-4

Cover design: www.mariondesigns.com

Manufactured in the United States of America

DEDICATION

To my parents who gave me life,
and Jesus, the Christ, who gave me—
myself!

ACKNOWLEDGMENTS

O God, my God, how great thou art! You are my rock and my strong tower. Your word is a lamp unto my feet and a light unto my path. To the love of my life, Jesus Christ, whose I am, and whom I serve, I thank you for carrying me when I could not walk to *the other side of through*. Your grace has been sufficient.

Dad, you are my larger-than-life hero. The older I get the more I realize what an important influence you have been. When I look back over my life, you are woven through every chapter. Your faith in me made the difference between giving up and trying again. I love you and thank you for being there and loving me unconditionally. To my husband and sons, I consider my wealth not in possessions but in your happiness. Calyn and Cailyn Abbott, I love you and you are always in my heart.

Thanks to the cheerleaders God placed along my journey: My brother, Terence "Tank" Jenkins, for remaining steadfast, immoveable and continuously supportive of me; my niece, Seanterra Burston, for your "listening ear" which helped me climb down off the window ledge; Dedra Jenkins, for always believing in me; Felicia Cromartie, Tanya Freeman and Rose March, for loving me in spite of my decisions; Judith "Judy" McAllister, for speaking life into me—I listened!; Cheri Townsend, for giving me the benefit of the doubt when everyone else bailed.

Thanks to the Angels God sent to assist me: "Magic and Cookie"—Earvin and Earleatha Johnson; "Doll and Slim"—Ruby and Robert Humphries; "Aunt Dot"—Dorothy Jeffries; "Sis"—Yolanda Branch; "Bishop and Sis"—Pastor and 1st Lady Elect Wilcox; "Barb"—Barbara Ahumada; Shirley Anderson and Randy Blackmon.

To my brother Cornell and my family members who watched, waited and prayed for me on this journey; you helped me find a strength I did not know I had. God Bless You!

Keith Washington, there would not be a book without all the heartache and pain you rendered, thank you!

Bishop Victor T. Curry your vision gave birth to my dream, thank you for keeping it REAL; New Birth Baptist Cathedral of Faith, Int'l (there are far too many of you to name), the warmth and kindness you extended carried us through some difficult times. We thank you, and Jose, you're next—wait on God; Bishop Charles Blake and Sister Mae Blake, when I was lost and couldn't find my way you reached out and guided me to West Angeles and God. Thank you, Bishop Charles Ellis, a modern-day "Guardian Angel," mere words cannot thank you enough for your guidance.

Shelley Halima and Tina Brooks McKinney, my gifted Strebor family sisters, you took a sistah by the hand and never let go. Muchas Gracias! Charmaine Parker, thank you for asking what my book was about *and thank you for telling Zane.* Zane, thank you for not making me wait another year. None of this would be happening if it were not for your vision.

Lastly, to the many haters who became my elevators—Tracy, you asked me to call you Judas; Jesus forgave him. I forgive you! To those family members, friends and acquaintances who found happiness in my tears, my heart wept for what it lost, but my spirit laughs for what it has found! God is not the author of confusion, but of peace. You were "speed bumps" and "road blocks" strategically placed by God to get me where he wanted me. What you meant for my harm, God meant for my good. Many thanks! And I am sure that he who began a good work in me will complete it! Phil 1:16.

CHAPTER 1

Katlyn Kincaid, the quintessential perfectionist, worked overtime to create and then maintain the appearance of someone who "got it goin' on."

Her current interest in interior design lent more fuel to her Type A personality, enhancing her need to ensure that the minutest detail was addressed. For example, the carefully chosen array of framed photos making up the picturescape on the end table had to be angled just so. After a good dusting, she painstakingly and meticulously replaced each photo on the table, making sure they were arranged in the original pattern. However, she couldn't figure out how to apply the same principle to her personal life, which was in total disarray. Try as she might, she could not get all the pieces to line up perfectly.

Katlyn stared at herself in the bathroom mirror; first from a distance, looking at her tiny frame. She had her mother's figure and breathtakingly youthful good looks. Upon closer inspection, she noticed tell-tale signs of her real age, the cupped praying hands that began on the outer wings of her nose and ended just above her chin, framing her mouth. For more than a year now, she'd managed to hide the creases on her forehead by tightly pulling her below-shoulder-length hair back in a ponytail. An instant face-lift, she called it.

As she stared at herself, comparing her likeness to her mother's, tears stung her eyes, forcing them to close slowly. Her mother died on Easter eve. At approximately 8 p.m., her father had answered the telephone and gasped. Nine-year-old Katlyn knew something was very wrong even before he burst into tears. He managed to call a neighbor, a close friend, to come over and sit with Katlyn and her brothers while he retreated to the bedroom to compose himself.

After several minutes passed, Katlyn's father approached the children and informed them their mother had just died of a heart attack. Being the only female left in the home, Katlyn instinctively assumed the "mother" role and immediately felt responsible for taking care of her siblings and her father. At that young age, Katlyn did not understand "heart attack" any more than she understood what a void the lack of a mother's presence and love would cause in her life. In time she'd find out how life-altering both were.

Katlyn splashed cold water on her face, and looked at her red eyes in the mirror. She knew she needed to get ready for the concert, but her mind kept replaying the telephone conversation she'd had with Justin.

"Listen, I'm running late…I'll send the limo to pick you up. Be ready by six. I love you." Justin's fitting had taken longer than expected and he would have to meet Katlyn at the concert hall. The thought of her life, a real fairy tale come true, brought tears to her eyes once more. But she pulled herself together, to dress and do her hair and makeup.

Concerts, award shows and public appearances were the norm for Mr. and Mrs. Justin Kincaid. Katlyn often joined her husband, by default, at one or the other via chauffeured limousine. Most times she went alone and was met at back entrances by his manager or publicist. Like now.

The swarm of reporters and media hounds thrust cameras and microphones in her face as she emerged from the limo.

"Mrs. Kincaid, over here!"

"This way, can you smile for the camera?"

"Any plans to start a family?"

Security pushed through the crowd, creating a pathway for Katlyn to move toward the next mob scene where reporters hovered around Justin.

"You know, it's like a dream. When my alarm went off this morning I awoke to something surreal. I'm probably still dreaming." Justin pinched himself and chuckled, the crowd joining him in laughter. "But listen," he said, raising his hand to silence them and get their attention once more. "Do me a favor, if I'm dreamin', don't wake me. I'm lovin' this." The room exploded into applause as Justin ended his brief press conference.

Eyeing Katlyn, he grabbed her hand and followed security into the green room.

Katlyn knew a few of the "bodies" that sauntered into the green room as well, each working her way to Justin's side, greeting him with a kiss on one or both cheeks. Every time one of them approached, Katlyn searched Justin's eyes to see if they revealed anything. She detected nothing.

Justin was a struggling artist when Katlyn first met him. The most gifted vocalist she'd ever heard. He had a God-given talent that no one had paid attention to, except her. Now his latest single was on top of the charts, going to number one in record time. Katlyn always knew he would be a star—and now, thanks to an excellent PR department, everyone else knew it, too!

Katlyn observed the other couples in the room who were married, shackin' or otherwise committed, and wondered which ones were truly in love and really happy. One that always seemed to be solid and very much in love now had different ideas about where their relationship was headed. The chauvinist husband was an up-and-coming actor, producer and director. His wife, a career woman, was now feeling pressure from him to become a mother first and a career woman *never again!*

Then there was the monogamous two-some who shared each other's bed, but maintained separate residences. The much older headstrong psychiatrist kept her lover's desire to be married and have a family at bay. Routinely hurt by men and well aware *she* needed to be on someone's couch she would only be with him if it was on *her* terms.

Munching on some finger food, Katlyn continued to peruse the crowd. In one corner, a gorgeous black male model, straight off the runways of Milan, was having a heated discussion with the Asian female companion he'd brought along. One drink short of drunk, she was drawing unwanted attention and with the press nearby, he could not afford that kind of attention. In another corner, four half-clad "bodies" were posing for a photographer who promised them copies of the photos in order to get their names and numbers.

At one point, Katlyn's eyes met Justin's; he winked and blew her a kiss as he exited the green room to get ready for his performance. She smiled, pretended to catch the kiss, and mouthed, "I love you." She leaned against a wall and sighed, content and in love with him and their wonderful life.

"What cha thinkin' about?" Sheree, his publicist, asked, leaning on the barstool next to Katlyn.

"How blessed I am."

"Oh yeah, how so?" Sheree asked, pulling the stool closer to sit on.

"Look around the room. Justin could have any and every one of these women in here but he's content with having just me."

"Yeah, I bet any woman in the room would kill to be in your shoes, so don't take them off, Cinderella!" Sheree knew when to exit and she also knew when to leave well enough alone. She did both gracefully as Katlyn's friend Tanya came over.

Suddenly Katlyn caught sight of the most beautiful woman she'd ever seen. She was flawless, a plastic surgeon's masterpiece whose beauty made Katlyn gawk. She caught herself staring and so did Tanya.

"You know you're equally as beautiful as that 'mannequin,'" Tanya said. "Naw—I take that back, you're more beautiful because God gave you your beauty. Trust me, she paid a pretty penny for hers."

Katlyn giggled and hugged Tanya, thankful for her support. The well-timed compliment was just what the doctor ordered. The Mannequin left her off-center; a first and she did not like the feeling.

"How's your project coming along?" Tanya asked, slicing a piece of cheese and sitting down next to Katlyn.

"Which one?"

Tanya chuckled. "I forgot you're a woman who wears many hats. I meant the decorating project for that guy who writes jingles."

"Girl, can I just tell you," Katlyn said. "His home, or should I say my work, has been selected to appear on this local morning show, ummm, I can't remember the name, but it's Chicago's most watched morning show. Can you believe it?"

"Sure I can," Tanya said matter-of-factly, nodding. "You're good at that decorating stuff. My home is a testimony to that. You ever going to get your license?"

"I don't know. I'm still up in the air about where my career is headed."

"You miss flying?" Tanya asked.

She and Katlyn had been flight attendants and roommates together in Virginia more than ten years ago. Now Tanya; her husband, Darrel; and their daughter, Lauren, lived in L.A., and Katlyn as well as Justin were glad to have friends outside of the industry. They were "real," a rarity in this town.

"Not even, but I do miss the flight privileges," Katlyn admitted.

"Yeah, but with all Justin's success, money surely is not an issue. Girl, buy a ticket, hop a flight and we'll meet you there."

"Puh-leeze!" Katlyn exclaimed. "The way Justin's tour schedule is running there's no time for fun."

"You *are* going on the road with him, right?" Tanya stared at Katlyn and waited for an answer.

Katlyn hesitated, uncomfortable with her question. She knew where this line of questioning was headed and was not in the mood to go down that road.

"Tanya, I have a life, too! Running two companies keeps me busy twenty-four-seven. If I went on the road with him, they'd suffer." Feeling somewhat pensive Katlyn added, "Besides, I think this time apart would be good for both of us!"

"Really? Are you guys okay?" Tanya asked, holding her breath.

"Not to worry, we're fine." Tanya blew a sigh of relief, as Katlyn continued, "Justin has little time for me and *us* since the new album came out. He enjoys having me around, like at the studio, or here at a concert, but we have very little time alone. Hopefully, on the road he'll miss me and you know the old adage: absence makes the heart grow fonder."

"Well you're a better woman than me. The old adage that comes to *my* mind is, while the cat's away, the mouse will play! I'm telling you, you should go with him," Tanya said adamantly.

"You know what, I don't have the time to worry about it! Justin and I have six happy years together: six happy years that have not been easy. We worked hard, together, to get where we are. I have never questioned his fidelity before; why start now?" Katlyn stated defensively. "I trust him, Tanya, just as much as you trust Darrel. Remember *him*, the one God forgot to clone before he threw the mold away?"

Katlyn always told Tanya she believed D was the epitome of manhood: handsome with a drop-dead physique, a Southern gentleman through and through and one hundred percent faithful to his wife and family. If only she could be so sure of Justin! With an inward sigh, she excused herself to go to the restroom. Upon exiting, Katlyn was greeted by Justin's head of security.

"It's time to go inside, Mrs. Kincaid."

Katlyn cringed. "Okay, Larry, let's get one thing straight: plee-ee-zz stop calling me Mrs. Kincaid! You make me feel old. Katlyn is just fine."

"Yes, Ma'am."

"Ee-uh-hh," she shrieked. "Not Mam. Now I feel like somebody's Mother! Lighten up. Just Katlyn, got it?"

"I got it. This way, please, 'Just Katlyn.'"

Katlyn laughed heartily and then motioned to Tanya and Felicia to gather the clan and go to the skybox. While her friends made their way to their seats, Katlyn had Larry take her to Justin's dressing room. Whenever she was around, she made it a point to pray with him prior to his going onstage.

"And Lord, make tonight especially blessed, let all his vocal ability be in full range and let him perform his best ever." Justin squeezed her hand and Katlyn lost her train of thought, forcing her to cut the prayer short. "We thank you for all these blessings and we ask them in Jesus' name. Amen."

Justin hugged her and Katlyn lingered in his arms. She was so very proud of him and truly grateful for God's blessings on his career and their marriage. She knew Justin was thankful for her spiritual walk and religious beliefs; since Justin wasn't sure about his own spiritual choices, he chose to lean on hers.

Katlyn hurried to her seat not wanting to miss Justin's entrance. The moment he stepped onto the stage in skintight black leather pants and a six-pack highlighted by a one-size-too-small muscle shirt, every woman in the audience lost it. The screams and applause were so deafening, Justin had to wait to sing his first note.

He worked the stage from one side to another, graciously taking roses from the near-hysterical females. At one point, a woman bolted past security and hurled herself onto the stage, then rushed Justin and held him in a death grip that literally cut his breath off. Security loosened her hold, but not before she tore his shirt off.

That sent the remaining fans who had not yet hyperventilated into a fit; it took Justin's leaving the stage to get another shirt to calm the crowd. Ten minutes later the show resumed. After two hours of swooning ballads, sexy gyrating and hormone-driven females screaming and crying, Justin geared up for the finale.

Justin Kincaid was a five-feet-nine phenomenon. His caramel-brown gorgeous skin flaunted chiseled features usually reserved for Greek gods. A head full of curly, jet-black hair, which he wore close-cut to make it wave, was more than most women could bear. They loved him, he was an aphrodisiac; you always wanted more. Four rows deep, the women lined up around the stage, throwing him roses, money and underwear. They cried, begged and screamed for the opportunity to be near him.

Justin carefully approached the crowd and leaned down to take a rose from a woman he deemed harmless, because of her small stature and controlled behavior. Not! She reached up, grabbed him in a headlock and planted her lips on his. Others in need of the same fix began to grope his body. Justin was helpless.

Katlyn stood up shocked by what she was seeing. When one of the crazed groupies grabbed Justin's oversized gift from God, she lost it! Her three-and-a-half-inch $600 Pradas slowed her attempts to climb over the three seats that blocked her access to the exit. As she finally reached the aisle, Darrel gripped her arm, preventing her from leaving the safety of the skybox.

Even though the ruckus was over in a couple of seconds, for Justin it seemed like hours. The ordeal frightened him, leaving him shaking when he thought about how dangerous the encounter was. He stood stunned for a minute or two, gaining his composure as the crowd one by one rose to its feet and began to chant the title of his latest hit, "Who's Kissin' You?"

Softly, the piano chords began to cascade through the arena. They were soothing to Katlyn. Darrel loosened his grip, realizing she had calmed down. Katlyn sat down and stared at her now half-dressed and visibly shaken husband. "Who's Kissin' You?" was a joint venture between Katlyn and Justin: he'd written the melody and track, and she'd written the lyrics. Even though it was her first attempt at songwriting, this ballad was the biggest hit of Justin's career.

"Who's kissin' you and lovin' you…," Justin crooned. Women raised their arms and swayed to the music as he made love to them with his voice. Tears filled Katlyn's eyes as she watched her husband. She'd done well in structuring her close-to-perfect life. Justin was her prince, her knight in shining armor, her fairy tale come true. People loved him; she loved him. Oh, how she loved him! Theirs was a good Hollywood marriage, of that she was sure.

CHAPTER 2

After her mother's death, Katlyn's father sent her and her three brothers to live with her aunt and uncle in the South for the summer. Katlyn was a city girl with grand ideas and big dreams, but that summer would prove to be a rude awakening. She was accustomed to a middle-class, suburban lifestyle. That lifestyle was super-wealthy in comparison to her aunt and uncle's home. What turned out to be too small a space for too large a group. The part-wood and part-tin, four-room shack sat unevenly on bricks stacked side by side and made her small home in Detroit seem like a mansion. You could stoop and look all the way under the house to the backyard.

The front porch required balance and skill, in order to maneuver around the numerous loose wooden slats. Once inside the front door, Katlyn went into shock. The entire house seemed no bigger than her bedroom in Detroit. As she stood in the doorway, she could see all the way back to the kitchen. Two steps forward, a sharp turn right and two more steps placed her at the couch: legs missing, it was anchored against the wall, which had windows opened, but without screens. Several more steps forward and she found herself in an area that closely resembled Grand Central Station—the kitchen, the busiest and most lived in part of the house.

From early dawn to dusk, this room was continuously occupied. Not a difficult task with nine mouths to feed, excluding her aunt and uncle. Katlyn's five female cousins woke at the break of daylight and drew water from the well. Then the water was boiled and poured into a tin wash-basin on the back porch, so each child could bathe.

Next the laundry had to be tackled. Huge black metal pots were placed over the fire and filled with more well water. The water was heated to a boil and a chunk of homemade lye soap was dumped in. Once the soap melted, several pieces of like-color clothing were dumped into the pot and agitated with a wooden stick for nearly a half-hour. One by one, the clothing was removed from the boiling water and rubbed vigorously on the washboard until all the dirt and stains were removed.

The rinse cycle was just as laborious. Each garment was dumped into neighboring pots of water, agitated, twisted, then fed through the wringer to remove the last drops of water. Weather permitting, the clothes were hung on the clothesline in the backyard to dry.

While two of the older girls attended to the laundry, the younger ones were chasing down a chicken for breakfast. Once the unlucky fowl was caught, one quick snap broke his neck. Then the chicken was cleaned and fried.

The younger girls busied themselves gathering eggs from the roost while her aunt made biscuits from scratch. All of this had to be done before the breakfast hour, when her uncle and male cousins—"the men folk"—rose. This routine was repeated (minus the baths) throughout the day and into the evening. Add to this the routine of gathering the clothes off the line and then folding and putting away those that did not need to be ironed.

If daylight was lost before the clothes dried, the ironing was put off until the next morning. Rising even earlier, one of the girls would lightly sprinkle the clothes with some Argo starch and then run over them until they were smooth with an iron that was heated by open fire.

Men were neither asked nor expected to do housework. The male children were waited on hand and foot by the female children. The men did their outdoor chores, at leisure, and then spent the rest of the day as they pleased. Katlyn could not adjust to a routine she viewed as chauvinistic and unfair. Her parents had been raising her brothers to be independent, self-sufficient men. With the exception of the baby, the boys did chores inside and outside the home and knew how to iron and cook things like hot dogs and eggs.

Katlyn found her aunts' pattern of spending every waking moment catering to their mates or raising what appeared to be a tribe disgusting. If they needed money for any reason they had to *ask* their husbands for the funds. Whoever was bold enough to ask was subjected to an inquisition before they were handed any money; most times they were given way less than they had hoped for. These women were totally unselfish and delighted in focusing all their time and energy on others, never once taking time to focus on themselves. For all their sacrifice and self-neglect, Katlyn saw little if any reward.

Working as hard as they did their appearance was disheveled by midday, and that disheveled appearance continued throughout the day. In sharp contrast to her aunts, Katlyn was very much a prissy girl who loved doing "girlie" things like using a pumice stone to remove dead skin from her feet or taking time to give herself a manicure. Not once did she allow her skin to carry that ash look darker skin gets when it's in desperate need of lotion. The moment she stepped out of water, lotion was smoothed all over her body. Her mother told her this was the secret to young and healthy-looking skin. She made several attempts to introduce her cousins to this pampering lifestyle, but they were either too busy to consider it or just didn't care.

That summer in the South scared Katlyn. She learned women married early and for most of their youth they stayed pregnant. Many turned a blind eye to their husband's infidelity as long as he kept a roof over their heads and food on the table. Her aunts felt Katlyn's desire to be college-educated, independent and self-sufficient was one of those foolish, uppity Northern "city girl" attitudes. "Girls are supposed to grow up and become wives and mothers," they constantly told her. Their mothers and grandmothers embedded this in their psyche and they believed it wholeheartedly. By summer's end, Katlyn realized she had almost bought into the fairy tale as well.

After returning to Detroit, Katlyn lived in fear. The examples set by her aunts caused her to be afraid of being poor and having to depend on a man to take care of her.

Her father, though he was a good man and a great provider, had his ideas of what a woman's place was that paralleled those of her aunts. He monitored Katlyn's mother's spending like a hawk even though she made the bulk of their family's income. Her pay scale far exceeded her husband's, but Katlyn's father made it his business to keep track of how she spent her own paycheck (or so he thought).

Katlyn's mother loved to shop and her dad felt she shopped too much. In an effort to keep peace in the house, her mom incorporated a shopping spree into the time she spent running errands. En route home, she'd leave her purchases at a girlfriend's home until her husband left for work. When it was safe to do so, she'd sneak the items home, remove the tags and hang them in her closet without him noticing.

Even though she was a little girl, Katlyn was well aware of what was going on. Her young mind did not fully understand why, but she found this behavior odd and unfair. She never understood what kept her mom from standing up for herself and she hated her behavior. Confused and angry, she never forgot that her mother behaved in such a manner and she never forgave her for doing so.

But what Katlyn viewed as chauvinism was really fear her father carried from his childhood. Back in the day, when he was a young boy on the farm, picking cotton, he was nearly scarred by his abject poverty. He watched his uneducated father work continuously, around the clock, for a sharecropper to provide just the necessities to keep his family alive.

As Katlyn's father grew in stature, he was obligated to work for the family living as well. Although he attended school in the day, he was forced to labor through the night to help his father meet the yield his agreement with the sharecropper demanded. Being stripped of all human rights and privileges was a hard pill for Katlyn's dad to swallow and he believed the education he was working hard to get would end that abomination.

One day Katlyn's grandfather fell ill and for days lay in bed suffering because the family didn't have the money to get him medical attention. By the time they'd begged, borrowed or stolen enough to finally send for the doctor, her grandfather was gravely ill and not expected to survive. During this time Katlyn's dad dropped out of the ninth grade and took on the responsibility of being the head of the family.

Although her grandfather survived, he was permanently blinded, leaving Katlyn's father no hope of returning to school or climbing out of poverty. He gave up on his dream to graduate from high school and college, but he never forgot it. His hope was for his dream to be fulfilled through his children. He knew education was the key to being successful and prosperous. Determined to see his offspring have a better chance in life than he'd been given, he drilled this fact into their heads daily.

Although it was her mother who did most of the doting, Katlyn was a daddy's girl; her father spoiled her. It was not something he set out to do, but that was the way with daddies and their little girls. He favored his daughter and whatever she wanted she got. But that was then.

Now time was short and money was scarce. Katlyn and her brothers saw their father for an hour or two in the evening after he awoke, prior to his departure for the midnight shift. Always in a hurry dressing, eating or preparing a lunch, he did not have time to nurture his children.

One night while praying and thinking about her life and that summer in the South, Katlyn vowed three things. She was going to be rich, she was *never* going to lose her constitution—giving up her right to decide the who, what, when and where of her life—and she was *never* going to live and breathe for a man.

In her teens Katlyn became a perfectionist and learned what to do to be the center of attention. She also mastered the skill it took to garner the praise and adoration of any and everyone she came in contact with.

Calvin, the oldest child, eventually found nurturing elsewhere. He began to experiment with physical and mental stimulants. The physical stimulants—girls—were easy to come by. High school, a playground for raging hormones, gave him all the available specimens he needed.

An attractive, dark-chocolate clone of his mother, Calvin knew his looks and quick wit were a lethal combination. From time to time he screwed some of his female schoolmates in the restroom or in an unlocked car in the parking lot. Those young girls who were left unsupervised after school brought him home to their beds.

It was one of those invites that led to Calvin's discovering drugs: half-smoked joint left out in the open on a tray with rolling papers and a cigarette lighter. He and the fifteen-year-old he was lying next to on the couch decided to smoke it.

Neither had been high before; both loved the feeling. They laughed and played like school kids, then searched the cabinets for munchies. Lost to the passing of time, they were still half-naked when the girl's mother's much-younger live-in boyfriend burst through the door.

Calvin and the fifteen-year-old grabbed their things and hid in her bedroom. Once dressed, he climbed out the window and ran home, where he slept off the remaining high.

The twenty-one-year-old boyfriend suspected the girl had smoked his roach, but did not confront her. A couple days later he caught Calvin and her together again, smoking his stash, and joined them. For months Calvin got high with his friend and her "stepdad." In time the stepdad gave Calvin his own personal stash—free of charge.

One by one, Calvin introduced those peers he trusted to this new after-school activity. One by one, they came back for more. But nothing in life is really free! Eventually the stepdad started charging Calvin. His lunch money did not purchase enough for him to share with his friends, so he too began to charge.

Calvin became the most popular kid in high school—the man. But it wasn't his good looks and quick wit that garnered him this fame. It was his drug connection that catapulted him to celebrity status amongst his peers (and some of his teachers).

Within a year he'd established and operated—exceptionally well—a booming business. He wisely chose to hide his wealth and the source of his wealth from his sister (who would have told their father), but generously shared his profits with her and his brothers.

Even though he stored his supply in the garage, no business was conducted from home. The rule was no one was allowed to come to their house. You had to buy before, during or after school.

In time, most of his clientele resorted to stealing to supply their need. A wallet missing from a teacher's purse or a fellow student's missing cell phone became recurring problems. But the school board had bigger issues to deal with and those petty crimes always went uninvestigated. Calvin graduated without ever getting busted and continued his trade. After expanding his business to the streets of Detroit, he purchased a used Mustang. He invested money into new tires and rims, but stopped short of putting anything expensive or flashy on his car, because he knew people were watching and talking. To eliminate any questions from his dad and well-meaning relatives, he enrolled in a trade school and became a licensed computer technician. But no amount of money he made fixing hard drives compared to the flow of cash he saw from peddling instant gratification.

When Katlyn received an all-"A" report card and a 4.0 grade-point average her junior year, Calvin rewarded her handsomely by giving her the Mustang he'd been driving for almost a year. He paid up her insurance for six months and gave her a weekly gas allowance. The only stipulation he gave her was her already-in-effect curfew. If she broke it she lost the car.

Her father, whom she desperately needed attention from, also took notice. For weeks he heaped an overwhelming amount of praise and attention on her, making it a point to get up a half-hour earlier than usual so he could sit and chat with his Scholar. Desperate for more Katlyn began to obsess over any and everything, ensuring it was perfect.

She was always neat, clean and organized. Their home was also always neat, clean and organized and anything she did was done in like manner. Her ability to get things done correctly and on time was unusual for teens who normally have all of life's changes bombarding them at once.

Her behavior helped fill the void left by her mother and in time her father grew dependent on her to orchestrate the everyday goings-on in the home. He taught her to write checks for the bills that were due and monitor the mail and the phone calls. Counting on her to oversee the tasks her siblings were responsible for; she ensured they would do them and do them right. The more responsibility she took on, the more time her father had to spend with her.

The gratification Katlyn felt each time her father praised her for a job well done consumed her and helped her excel. She graduated with top honors from high school and he could not have been prouder. Katlyn knew her dad was living his dream of obtaining an education through her and she felt pressured not to let him down.

A desire to be needed grew from this obsessive conduct. Like radar, she detected a need and manipulated her way into that person's life and the situation until that person was dependent on her to take care of whatever they needed. And so began the process of feeding the need: Katlyn changed who she was to what others—*especially the male species*—thought she should be.

Katlyn mastered being a chameleon and found it hard to be content with a boyfriend. Relationships and commitments seemed too hard; and changing who and what she was each time she fell in love with someone new became too tedious.

After carefully thinking about her options, she decided she was never going to marry. Instead she'd pursue a college degree from one of the prestigious universities America's upper class talked about. Of course, those degrees would be a major factor in her landing a lucrative position with a top-ten company. And with her lavish pay would come her high-rise condo on the waterfront, with her luxury car and her choice of men whose paychecks were as limitless as her choices.

But, shortly after landing her cushy $80,000-a-year (plus bonuses) position with a Fortune 500 company, Katlyn once again changed her mind about what she wanted and who she was. With no female role model to look up to, she struggled to find herself. Over the years she'd molded herself into the good girl, the martyr and the girl about town, but she still felt empty. So out the window went her pre-graduation theory of never getting married; now she wanted the stability of a family life and a husband.

Her ideal mate would be a man like Richard Gere in the movie *An Officer and a Gentleman*; a knight in shining armor who would walk into her office, pick her up and carry her away to an even grander environment than she'd created for herself. They would live happily ever after as equals, sharing the same goals and striving for the same things. And, of course, their marriage would be monogamous; two people as one, one mate, one time, for life. A standard set by her parents and a fairy tale *she did buy into*.

CHAPTER 3

The corporate world, all $80,000, plus bonuses, of it got old real quick! She wanted fun, adventure and excitement. Having researched her options, becoming a flight attendant would offer her all the above, plus some!

Katlyn first saw Felicia during orientation. Both had given up career choices, ignoring their college degrees to pursue the lifestyle of a flight attendant. Felicia was poised and very articulate. Katlyn was impressed with her extensive vocabulary. A military brat, she had been educated abroad, graduating from a high school in Germany, so she was fluent in German. Felicia was attracted to Katlyn's charm and fun-loving, outgoing personality. Her quick wit was enjoyable, not to mention she was very attractive with flawless skin and well groomed. Their recognition of each sensing a need for change in their worlds allowed them to become good friends—quickly!

After orientation, while unpacking in her room, Katlyn approached Felicia. Katlyn stood in the doorway of their adjoining rooms while Felicia, unaware of her presence, washed her face. She was surprised Felicia did not exfoliate her skin, which explained why whiteheads covered most of her face.

"Say, listen, why don't you exfoliate your skin?" Katlyn suggested.

Felicia jumped, startled by the intrusion.

"What?" she asked as she turned off the faucet, eyes shut with water dripping from her face. Groping for a towel, she bumped into the door and they both laughed.

"Hi, I'm Katlyn and I said, why don't you use one of these on your skin?" Katlyn shook her hand and showed her a buffing pad she used daily.

"What is that?" Felicia asked with a look of disdain on her face.

Katlyn ignored the expression and explained it was a buffing pad she used daily on her face to gently scrub off the layers of dead skin.

"Remove the dead skin cells and the whiteheads will disappear," Katlyn expertly answered.

Felicia sheepishly admitted she had no knowledge of exfoliating her skin or how the entire process worked. Apprehensive about trying something new on her face, she didn't readily jump at Katlyn's offer to scrub her skin for her.

Katlyn took time to carefully explain a facial to her, step by step. Feeling less concerned, Felicia agreed to a facial. The end result was quite noticeable to the eye and the touch. Her skin glowed and all the small whiteheads had disappeared. She smiled as she looked in the mirror, then rubbed her hand across her face.

"You have gorgeous skin, it just needs some TLC," Katlyn said matter-of-factly. She located a piece of paper and wrote down the steps and the products she used on Felicia's skin. Next she demonstrated on herself how to "buff" her skin without hurting it. Since all this was new to Felicia, Katlyn wrote down a list of where she could locate these items and what they would cost her.

Felicia reviewed the list and questioned if it was worth the money she would need to spend to obtain the products. Katlyn stared at her with her mouth wide open, and then pointed her to the mirror.

"You tell me, Missy!" she replied. Felicia laughed, realizing that was a stupid question. She picked up each of the bottles Katlyn had used on her face and read the instructions and ingredients. A lot of the products looked unfamiliar to her. She questioned what was a mask?

In disbelief, Katlyn grabbed Felicia by the arm and led her to the bathroom in her room. Katlyn's vanity was covered with "girlie things"—moisturizer, clay mask, toner, cleanser, tweezers, mascara, lip pencils, lipsticks, and much more. She showed each item to her and then explained why it was used.

Looking at her unruly and too-thick eyebrows, Katlyn decided to pluck them.

"Sit down, let me have at it." Reluctantly, Felicia sat down.

"Okay, this might hurt a little," Katlyn informed her as she pulled the first wild hair from her left eyebrow.

"Ow!" Felicia screamed, grabbing Katlyn's hand. "What are you doing?"

"Trust me, it'll be worth the pain."

Trust her Felicia did and they built a bond of trust that though tested throughout their years of friendship, remained true.

Like oil and water, they were noticeably different, but they gelled like peanut butter and jelly. Katlyn was the product of a loving father who raised her solo, after her mother died. Felicia grew up in a family with both parents. Her father, a stern and private person, was a dedicated family man, her mother, a dedicated homemaker.

Katlyn, though married, lived a very "free" lifestyle. If the old adage, "If you got it, flaunt it," weren't so old, one would think she'd coined the phrase. Everything that covered her body was fitted and fashionable in loud colors like lime or hot pink. Her husband loved his wife's flash and did not mind that she flaunted her body.

In contrast, Felicia liked a no-fuss appearance. She felt comfortable in the minimalist look: dark or neutral colors, mostly two-piece suits with expensive blouses or tops in white or soft colors.

Miss If You Got It, Flaunt It lived in heels, the higher, the sexier—even in the bedroom. Determined to hold on to her sexy image, Katlyn lived in the gym. Her routine of wearing her dark brown hair back in a pony-tail had its perks. After a workout, in bed or at the gym, she still looked good. And one could not help but notice her striking features, which meant she would not be caught dead without her face on.

Felicia felt she exercised enough by walking up and down the aisles of the aircrafts. In makeup all day when she was flying, Felicia wore as little as possible as often as possible during her downtime. She wore her baby soft, sandy brown hair relaxed whenever she had the time to apply a home kit. Because she was single, the "S.E.G." (Somebody Else's Guy) she'd shared her bed with for two years bailed when she fell ill and her funds ran low, she cared less about being sexy at night. And if she did decide to get some, her limit on heels, in or out the bedroom, was one inch. She had grown comfortable sleeping in sponge rollers at night, the end result of that restless night's sleep being a beautiful head of loose curls, guaranteed to go limp by day's end.

Seldom practical, Katlyn spent lots of money on things she "needed" like the same pair of $300 Manolo Blahniks, in every color, "because they were seventy percent off at Neiman's Last Call," she'd explain to Justin. Felicia, always practical, bought one pair of a more reasonably priced shoe at the same sale in a neutral color, so it could be worn with everything in her closet.

Katlyn was a go-getter, a leader who made up her mind and then did it. Felicia on the other hand, was careful, a thinker who weighed her options before making a move. But truth be told, Katlyn had often leaned on Felicia to keep her *views* of life grounded, now that she had money to burn.

Two years into their friendship, Felicia invited Katlyn to the "Ponderosa," her parents' beautiful, well-maintained and extremely comfortable ranch-style home. Now ten years later, Katlyn was inviting Felicia to her and Justin's luxurious condo, which overlooked the Hollywood Hills.

"Want some pound cake or oatmeal raisin cookies?" Katlyn offered.

Surprised, Felicia spun around, momentarily taking her eyes off the wonderful view. "You bake now?" she asked jokingly.

"Girl, puh-leeze! I have a housekeeper who bakes. The cookies are her secret recipe."

"Umm-mm. These are *too* good," Felicia said.

"I know, I'm thinking about bankrolling a business for her. She often talks about wanting to own her own bakery. I think she's sitting on a moneymaker and although I'd hate to lose her as a housekeeper, I would love to bless her with an opportunity to make her dream a reality." Katlyn thought about what she'd just said and smiled. Helping others achieve their goals was rewarding to her.

Felicia sat down in the comfy oversized chair next to the window, helping herself to the tray of cookies. Four cookies later, she took time to breathe.

"Katlyn, these are the best cookies I've ever had."

"Better than Mom's?" Katlyn posed the question, even though she knew the answer would be no. One would be hard-pressed to find anyone who made cookies better than Felicia's mother.

"Well, that's a hard one." Felicia paused for a moment to ponder the question.

Katlyn burst into laughter as she saw Felicia wrestle with her thoughts.

"I'll say they're just as good!" Felicia answered diplomatically before joining in the laughter. The doorbell rang and Katlyn rose to answer it.

"Come on in, Mamie. I want you to meet my bestest bud. This is Felicia. Felicia, meet the guru who concocted those oatmeal-raisin cookies you just inhaled."

Felicia got up and shook Mamie's hand. "You are a wonder, pure genius, my compliments to the chef!"

Mamie blushed and said nothing, excusing herself to begin cleaning.

"Wow! Things for you have really changed, girlie, housekeeper and all!"

"True, but I'm still the same person," Katlyn assured Felicia.

Felicia smiled and nodded in agreement. She thought about how Katlyn never wavered from her childhood dreams of being wealthy. Although multi-talented, she wasn't sure which one of her talents would supply the avenue to fulfill that goal, but she never stopped dreaming. Now post Justin, and watching her live her dream, Felicia was happy for Katlyn's success and glad to be in the category of "Best Buds" once again. Her eyes filled with tears.

Time and distance had separated them. Felicia still worked for the airline and finding time to get away on her days off was hard. Fatigued from working long hours to pay the mortgage on her fabulous twenty-five-hundred-square-foot home, and a new two-door Volvo, she rested whenever time allowed. Katlyn's situation was similar, so lack of available time to visit won out.

The two of them stayed up all night catching up, going over photos long forgotten and rekindling a bond they both longed for. The next morning over designer coffee, croissants and fresh fruit, they waited for Mamie to prepare breakfast.

"Girl, does your mom still make the best banana pancakes in the world?"

Felicia smiled; pleased Katlyn remembered her mom's specialty. "You remember them?"

"Who could forget them? Must I remind you, I had never even heard of banana pancakes before she introduced me to them. After I tasted Mom's homemade delicacy, I could not get enough. And for the record, *never* had any as good as hers," Katlyn said.

Still smiling Felicia told her she would let her mother know how much Katlyn loved her cooking and baking and suggested Katlyn give her a call; reminding Katlyn she was always her mother's favorite. Katlyn loved Felicia's mother. She was a bosomy woman who hugged you so tight your entire face got buried in that chest. When she finally let go of the bear hug, an imprint of your face stayed. The thought made Katlyn laugh. She knew what it felt like to be doted on; her father did it all the time. But she missed the comfort of her mother's arms and the assurance her mother offered when she wasn't quite certain of a decision she needed to make. It was painful to remember.

Years ago, Felicia was with Katlyn when she met Justin at Nouveau's, a new supper club that had recently opened in an affluent suburb of Detroit. Felicia and Katlyn, along with ten other women, attended a concert headlined by a well-known balladeer, who happened to be a close friend of Katlyn's. Four of the other women knew him, too, so front-row seating was a given. Since this was a girls' night out, the group decided to arrive in style in a super-stretch limo.

Despite sub-zero temperatures and the three inches of snow blanketing the city, the show was sold out and packed wall to wall. Standing-room crowds could be hectic on the bladder. The venue only housed one ladies room, which caused a line to extend out the door and down the long wide corridor. Many of the ladies wearing three-inch heels chose to lean on the wall to take the pressure off their feet while they waited. Katlyn was one of them.

After fifteen minutes in line Katlyn had an overwhelming urge to take off her stilettos. The cold tile felt comforting to her now swollen feet. Fortunately the rest of her wait was short-lived. Once inside the ladies room, Katlyn paid attention to the numerous characters as she waited for a stall. There were all sorts of styles and personalities crammed into the tiny space.

She chuckled at the three Destiny's Child wannabes and the sistahs who were throwbacks from the '70s in their two-sizes-too-small polyester bell-bottom halter jumpsuits. Women were packed at the mirror checking their freshly done weaves or adding another layer of color to their already well-glossed lips.

Katlyn found it difficult, if not impossible, to get to a sink to wash her hands. She reached in between two friends who were conversing and blowing smoke in each other's faces and splashed water on her hands. Attempting to reach the paper towels would be a mission in itself, so Katlyn chose to air-dry instead. Some ten "excuse me's" later, she was back in the cool corridor breathing fresh air.

Katlyn worked her way through the crowd to the entrance of the auditorium but was unable to enter. The show had already begun and the opening act, a comedian, was on stage. Frustrated, she walked over to the bar.

"What can I get cha?" the bartender asked.

"A cherry Coke with lots of cherries, please!"

"You got it," the bartender replied. Katlyn looked over her shoulder to see if the doors had opened.

"That'll be five dollars."

"For a Coke?" she snapped.

"I don't set the prices," the bartender snapped back.

"Here, take it out of this and I'll have one as well," a cashmere voice ordered. Katlyn looked up to thank the voice and suddenly lost hers. In front of her stood Mr. Too Pretty for Words.

"I'm Justin," he said, extending his hand. Katlyn reached to shake his hand but said nothing.

"And you are?"

"Uhhh…I'm…umm, Katlyn."

"Nice to meet you, Katlyn."

Justin held her hand in his, which Katlyn noticed was as soft as his voice. His gaze, the way he stared at her, made her uncomfortable. It was as if he could see right through her. The doors of the venue opened and broke the spell. Katlyn pulled her hand away from his, spun around and headed toward her seat. Justin followed gently grabbing her hand.

"Do you have a minute? I won't keep you."

"You know, I'd love to stand here and talk, but I came to see a friend perform and I don't want to miss him," Katlyn answered.

"Oh, you know Skip?" Justin asked.

"Yes. You?"

"Not well; we've played ball together. But maybe…"

Katlyn cut him off. "It's been real—gotta go!" As she turned to walk away once more, he asked if he could call her.

"Flattered, not interested." Lying, she looked back over her shoulder to see if he was following her. The truth was she found herself very interested. But he was so fine it scared her—men that fine spelled trouble.

Before Katlyn reached the door, Justin stepped in front of her, momentarily blocking her path. He grabbed her hand again; this time Katlyn did not pull away. He looked into her eyes in a way that pierced her soul. Fully captivated, she listened as he told her how he'd noticed her when she arrived with her posse. He'd calculated every move to this point but was now lost as to what his next move should be.

What he said after that rocked her world. Justin revealed to Katlyn she looked like someone he always loved, his mother. Quickly Katlyn shook loose and backed away. As she did he told her to remember his name and assured her that if she gave him a chance, she'd fall in love with him.

"Katlyn, what's taking you so long?" Felicia's timely interruption saved her.

"Gotta go." Katlyn grabbed Felicia's arm and walked inside the venue never looking back.

"Who is Dark Gable? Is he live or Memorex?" Felicia asked.

Flushed, Katlyn fanned. "Live, girl, all the way live!"

"Who is he?" Felicia repeated.

"Don't know and don't want to know." Katlyn hoped Felicia would drop the subject.

"Why? He seems nice enough."

"Too pretty. He probably lives in the mirror more than I do."

Skip walked onto the stage.

"Shhhh," came from nearby.

They both put their hands over their mouths, acknowledging they were sorry for their rudeness. Then Katlyn leaned over and whispered to Felicia she would entertain the Dark Gable subject later.

Two songs into the show, Justin appeared at Katlyn's side with a pen and paper.

"May I call you?" he whispered in her ear startling her. She jumped and spilled her cherry Coke on her dress.

"Look what you made me do," she snapped, annoyed.

"I'm sorry. I'll pay to have it cleaned. How do I reach you?" Justin slyly asked.

In support of this gorgeous hunk, Felicia kicked her girlfriend under the table. When Katlyn looked at her, Felicia motioned for her to give up the number. Katlyn shook her head.

"Listen, it took a lot for me to come all the way to the front, two rows from the stage, to ask the most beautiful woman I've ever seen for her number knowing she might turn me down in front of everyone around her. Please don't embarrass me—say yes!"

"No!" Katlyn snapped, raising her voice.

"Shhh," came from someone nearby. Justin lowered his head and exhaled. As he turned to exit, Felicia jotted Katlyn's number on a piece of paper and shoved it into his hand. "Thank you," he mouthed to her and winked at Katlyn, who pretended to ignore him.

"Remember what I told you," he said before he walked away.

Katlyn watched him leave and felt her heartbeat quicken. Her palms were sweating profusely as she thought about what he told her: *If you give me a chance, you'll fall in love with me.* She chuckled at the thought, failing to realize the enormity of what he had said.

CHAPTER 4

Most folks were in bed sound asleep at 4:30 a.m; Katlyn was one of them. The phone shocked her into a confused state of awareness. She groped for the phone. The voice on the other end was sensual and inviting; easy to listen to. Despite being angry at the nut who had just awakened her, she was equally captivated. As the voice began to apologize and explain his need to further their previous conversation, she realized who it was: Mr. Drop Dead Gorgeous, who was too short and too pretty for her taste.

Katlyn, now fully awake, sat up in bed and began to verbally beat him silly for disrespecting her by calling so late and interrupting her beauty sleep. Justin quietly took it. A momentary pause to catch her breath turned into a three-hour time-out as he capitalized on the opportunity and captivated her.

Suddenly she heard a piano playing. It was beautiful, so beautiful she asked him to play it again. It was a very melodic sound and then out of nowhere a voice began to sing. It sent shock waves through her entire body. Katlyn reclined on her bed, closed her eyes and listened to the entire song.

At first she thought that he was playing a CD. Justin told her he was singing and playing the piano, and that the song was something he had written about her once he'd returned home from the concert.

Certain this was nothing but BS, Katlyn burst into laughter and called him a liar. Without responding, Justin began to play and sing an R & B rendition of the same song, which immediately halted her laughter. It was even more beautiful than the county-western version she'd just heard.

Katlyn, a lover of R & B ballads, was stunned. The lyrics and the melody were taking her on an emotional roller-coaster ride she was unprepared for. Even though she was a flight attendant, she never thought to buckle her seat belt in preparation for this flight—and fly she did! Their telephone conversation lasted three hours. By the time Katlyn hung up, she was light-headed and completely brain-dead over Mr. Too Short and Too Pretty.

The entire month he was in town, Justin and Katlyn spent every waking moment together. Though she was very attracted to him, Katlyn was not ready to sleep with him, so she avoided spending late nights alone with him. This was not an easy feat to accomplish because he was extremely sexy, charming and fun to be with.

Justin had to perform his last night in Detroit. Katlyn accompanied him to the front-row VIP table. Several times throughout the night, he serenaded her directly. His God-given vocal ability and stage presence made women go mad. Katlyn watched him work the audience in amazement as the mass of screaming women pressed toward the stage. Security earned their keep, trying to keep one after another off the stage. Lost in the moment, Katlyn almost rushed the stage as well.

Once the concert ended, Justin joined Katlyn at his table. Throughout the night people came over to congratulate him on an outstanding performance. Many asked for autographs and some of the slick women slipped him their telephone numbers. Respectful of Katlyn, he refused to accept. This gesture captured her heart. By the time the night ended, she knew she never wanted to be away from him. He knew it, too, and made sure she would not forget him by leaning over and kissing her ever so gently.

Before departing the next day, he called her from the airport to let her know he'd miss her. Katlyn had not expected his call and kept him on the phone until the last person had boarded.

When he hung up, she cradled the receiver to her chest and smiled. He was all over her brain. In the following days she could not eat or sleep. Miss Always in Control was a mess.

Justin could tell Katlyn was different. She knew how to dress and obviously made good money. She was poised, had class and style; fly, yet elegant. Her curvaceous and well-toned five-foot-five frame housed the kind of butt men routinely refer to as "booty-licious," but she wore it long before Beyonce made it famous.

The way Katlyn spoke led Justin to assume she was well educated; and knew his own lack of education might be a deterrent, but he didn't let dropping out of school in the ninth grade to pursue a music career affect his decision to pursue her. Something about her made him lose his cool; that had never happened before. Justin had to have her. He knew if given a chance, she'd eventually fall in love with him. Eventually, she did.

Women came and went in Justin Kincaid's life. His mother set the pattern of behavior he would eventually grow to consider normal. Mentally unstable, she seldom stayed in a relationship with a man past the birth of their child. And once born, the children were treated with the same lack of affection, attention and commitment. Most times they were left alone to fend for themselves.

The youngest of seven, three-year-old Justin found this existence lonely and frightening. He loved his mother with all his heart and longed to be held and shown affection.

When he was four, his oldest sister heard him singing to one of his make-believe friends. Even then it was apparent he had true talent. Returning home days later, his sister told his mother about this discovery. Justin's mom scooped him up in her arms and playfully held him high above her head, laughing. His sister told him if he sang for his mother, he'd get some candy. He refused. She tried several more times to persuade him to sing, but failed. Repeatedly he refused, until his mother hugged him and held him tight, begging him to sing. It felt good to be in her arms and held so closely. Justin wrapped both arms around her neck and locked his hands.

That moment was short-lived. Angry he still had not uttered a sound, his mother abruptly pulled his arms from around her neck and put him down. Afraid she would never hold him again, he began to sing like a bird. His mother turned around, smiled and scooped him up once more. From that day forward he knew what would gain his mother's attention and affection and he kept on singing.

Justin never forgot that moment or that life lesson. On that day he learned how to manipulate and control women. A lesson he carried into his adult life and never failed to use.

His mother would periodically return home to hear him sing, only to leave again. Her mental condition kept her in and out of institutions. The oldest sibling knew what was happening and chose to shield her younger brothers and sisters from this shame. After her last stint in the psych ward, his mother walked away for good, with no explanation.

Justin never understood the abandonment and often wondered if his singing, or lack thereof, was the reason she never returned. Years went by before he sang again. By then he was a teenager on his own and needed to make some money, so he decided to try singing once more.

Entereing a talent show at his high school, Justin won first place—$500. He'd never seen that much money before. Rather than spend it all on himself, he fed his hungry siblings, buying enough food for the next few months.

After winning several talent shows back to back, Justin decided to make a go at singing for a living. Dropping out of school, he purchased a fake ID that made him eighteen and began to work the nightclub circuit.

For three years he made a decent living singing other artists' songs live to track. Eventually he was picked up by a local band in need of a lead vocalist. Shortly thereafter, a well-known singing group sought him to replace one of their members who'd just launched a solo act. Justin gladly accepted their offer and left Detroit for a six-month road trip.

By the time he was twenty he had no use for love and put no credence in commitment. The love he felt for his mother remained, but the wounds were deep. Bitter and confused, Justin worked through his pain, fear and frustration by looking for love in all the wrong places. Every stop the bus made on the road trip, Justin met and bedded several women. He continued this behavior for years. And although he was exceptional in bed that was the extent of his ability to be passionate, affectionate or committed—until he met Katlyn.

Katlyn made it easy to open up and let go. She allowed him to share things he could not share with anyone else. To his surprise he longed to hold her, be with her and take care of her.

Commitment, a one-on-one relationship, was something he never expected to have with Katlyn or anyone else. But this felt right. For the first time in his life he was not fearful of losing someone he cared about. With Katlyn in his life those recurring thoughts of a loved one leaving (like his mother did) never surfaced. Katlyn made him feel secure.

Justin found so much joy in knowing she was committed to him and supported him, in spite of his faults. He willingly told her some of his deepest secrets because she never passed judgment on him. Thoughts of spending the rest of his life with her made him happy. A first for him and that scared him.

Road tours had proven to be the devil's playground for him. In the past it was okay because he had no one and nothing holding him to a promise. Deep down he wondered if what he felt and hoped to build with Katlyn would last through what might lay ahead once his music career took off.

Their first bump in the road came while Justin was still in L.A. working on his demo tape. Katlyn was home alone one night when the telephone rang, unexpectedly, at a late hour. She'd already spoken with Justin, but because it was so late, she automatically assumed it was him. Caught off guard when she heard the tearful female voice on the other end of the line, Katlyn froze. The woman was threatening suicide if Katlyn did not leave "her man" alone.

Bile rose in Katlyn's throat as she listened to the woman, who was twenty years Justin's senior, explain how he had been living with her for the past six months and how she had been taking care of his every need, emphasis on *every*. Her six-year-old daughter called him Daddy.

Katlyn listened to what the woman had to say and tried to convince her suicide was not necessary. Although Katlyn knew she had fallen in love with Justin, his deception was painful. He'd had ample time to be forthcoming with her about his current relationship. Truthfully, she suspected he had someone in his life and she would have understood. As much as she loved him, she was not willing to be in a relationship that started out on a lie. She promised the hysterical female she'd freely give him up.

Katlyn never took another one of Justin's phone calls. One of the hardest things she had ever done. She changed her cell phone and home phone numbers and stayed exceptionally busy to keep her mind free of thought of him.

Three months later he showed up at her door, a free man. Full of regret and very remorseful, he begged for her forgiveness and a chance to make things right. She tried to resist him, but he was like a drug. They resumed their relationship, long distance. When they announced their engagement several months later, Felicia tried to talk some sense into Katlyn. She listened and opted to "shack" instead. Within a year they were married.

The first year of their marriage they were joined at the hip. They did everything together: grocery shopping, while racing their shopping carts in the aisle; laundry, sharing sorting and folding while they snuggled and watched TV; dinner, by candlelight and always elegantly set for two. Each considered the other's wants and desires and made a genuine effort to meet that need.

Katlyn, six years older than Justin, immediately wanted a beautiful baby girl. Justin wanted a successful career, a means to support a family. But, not one to turn down an orgasm or his wife, Justin happily obliged Katlyn's attempts to conceive. Morning, noon and night, and sometimes in between they made love. The table, the floor, a countertop, even the washer and dryer saw action. Nothing!

Finally she consulted the guru of baby making, Dr. Angel Hands: a high-profile, very expensive specialist in the infertility baby-making department. Dr. Angel Hands ran a battery of tests on Katlyn and Justin and found nothing unusual. His only suggestion was to take some time off and relax. Katlyn did. She took a leave from her job as a flight attendant and became a full-time household engineer. Three years into this hiatus and no baby, she decided to go back to work, this time for herself.

"Justin, I need to do something for myself that makes me happy. I want to start my own business," she confided.

"What about the baby?" he asked cautiously.

"I think three years of trying is long enough. I need something to take my mind off having a baby."

"Well, if starting your own business will make you happy, I got your back," Justin offered, trying not to reveal how relieved he was.

CHAPTER 5

Diva Glitz was situated in what functioned as a guest bedroom whenever Felicia, Tanya or one of the Kincaid family members came to visit. Katlyn loved having her costume jewelry company located in her home. She worked hard or hardly worked—no one decided how much or how little but her. Most of her clientele were high-profile stars, their wives or their significant others. The business had grown with little effort from Katlyn. Word of mouth and advertising of the best kind—herself—paid off. She was on a roll and everything she hoped to achieve, she had.

Today her desire to work fell on the side of hardly. After Felicia called to say she'd pop in for a visit, Katlyn busied herself preparing for a night on the town. Justin had been on tour for weeks and she'd chosen to stay home. Lately she worked long hours to keep from second-guessing her decision.

It was Felicia's birthday and she couldn't bear the thought of spending it alone. Katlyn was always fun to be with and knew anyone and everyone who was somebody. Her free spirit, despite all that flash, was something Felicia was looking forward to. The decision to celebrate her birthday in L.A. was spur of the moment, accelerated by the abrupt ending to the long-term affair she was having with a married man.

Ham Bonz, a hot new spot for dinner and dancing, was jumpin'; the line stretched around the block. Being Mrs. Justin Kincaid had its perks; not waiting in line was one of them.

"Carl, what's up, ba-bee?"

"Hey Katlyn, girl, look at choo! Loo-kinnn goo-ood. Justin wit choo?" the burly six-foot-five bouncer shouted over the music.

"Naw, not tonight."

"Aw-www, man! When he gon' grace the place wit' his face? Tell him brothas got loo-oove for him, too!"

The two of them broke into laughter. Carl grabbed the door handle with one hand as he motioned for Katlyn and Felicia to enter with the other.

"Thanks, babe." Katlyn grabbed his hand and placed a neatly folded fifty-dollar bill in his palm.

"Anything for you, Mrs. Kincaid," he said, nodding to acknowledge her kind gesture.

"Tell me you didn't just pay that throwback from the 'hood to get in this place," Felicia demanded.

"Hold up, girlie, climb back down off that pedestal," Katlyn replied. "No, I did not pay to get us in. I don't have to pay; I know the owner. Carl used to be head of security for Justin. He fell on hard times—cocaine—and Justin had to let him go. And for the record, he ain't no thro'back from da 'hood."

Katlyn had little patience for Felicia's condescending attitude toward those brothers who did not have the Harvard degree and matching stuck-up dialect.

"Oh wow. I feel so..."

Katlyn cut her off. "He's straight now, been clean for three years, but he stole to support his habit: money, jewelry, whatever wasn't nailed down. Now no one on the circuit will give him a chance to prove himself."

"Can you blame them?" Felicia said, quickly forgetting the empathy she'd just felt.

"Whenever I decide to go slummin', as Justin calls it, I come here and I make sure I bless Carl in the process. He's a good guy. I want to see him do well."

Without saying a word, Felicia reached over and hugged Katlyn tightly, thankful for her loving nature.

"You're the best. I'm sorry for questioning your judgment and his lifestyle."

"Hey, no thing. Just don't do it again," Katlyn added playfully.

The restaurant wait was more than an hour.

"I'm famished," Felicia said. "Got any pull at the dinner table?"

"Watch me work." Katlyn winked and headed toward the maitre d'. In seconds she was in a deep conversation with a strikingly handsome, very tall brother with an athletic build. When she returned, she suggested they wait at the bar.

Before the drinks they ordered arrived, they were being seated at a booth reserved for VIPs like Shaquille or Denzel.

"You definitely got pull; remind me to slap myself later for doubting you." They high-fived and toasted to the fun the night already promised. Felicia's eyes bulged when she saw one of the hottest rap artists around head toward their table. His name escaped her as she grabbed her forehead, pressing her temples with hopes it would help her remember. Before she could, Katlyn looked up and recognized Novalist.

"Baby gul—wha' chu doin' ot heah! Yo' man know you hangin' wit' da rest of us?" He laughed and leaned down to kiss her on the cheek, blinding Felicia with the bling both on his wrist and around his neck, not to mention the lights reflecting off his platinum-and-diamond grille.

"Now you know Justin knows every move I make. *I* make sure of that," Katlyn replied. "So what's new with you—hear the CD is selling off the charts. Congrats, baby! You deserve it."

A broad grin enveloped his face. He leaned down and placed another mushy kiss on her cheek. "Yeah, thanks comin' from you—Miss Songwrita of Da Year, that's a big deal."

They both laughed. Felicia could not help but notice the enormous amount of metal and money he had in his mouth. She found the sight of it repulsive and his entire persona "ghetto." Just as Katlyn was about to introduce him to Felicia, several groupies pulled him onto the dance floor.

Katlyn looked at Felicia and laughed. She knew her girlfriend well and hated that she'd missed the opportunity to gross her out by having him place one of those mushy kisses on her cheek. Though a star, he was a rap artist, and that was a genre Felicia did ascribe to. Felicia heard Katlyn laughing and knew what she had planned for her. The thought of him placing any part of that metal-filled mouth on her cheek made her quiver. As she pondered that reality, she joined Katlyn in laughter.

"Sorry, girlfriend. I was going to introduce you," Katlyn managed to get out before she burst into laughter again.

"Nuh-uh!" Felicia exclaimed, shaking her head disapprovingly. "Don't even try it. It's not like I was lined up waiting for my turn to have him lay one of those *nasty* wet kisses on my cheek!"

This time they laughed until they found it hard to breathe.

"By the way, check your cheek—you're missin' some blush," Felicia said.

Katlyn touched her face and felt something wet. She snatched a napkin off the table and rubbed the spot. They both squealed—"Eee-ww!"—then burst into laughter.

Macaroni and cheese, yams, collard greens and fried chicken is not the kind of meal you should order—let alone finish—if you're wearing a dress you had to be oiled to slide into.

"Girl, I am miserable." Katlyn exhaled slowly and leaned back in the booth, rubbing her too-full stomach.

"Me, too. This was perfect. Thank you," Felicia said, squeezing Katlyn's hand in affirmation.

"Oh, it's not over."

"Happy birthday to you, happy birthday to you..." Surprised, Felicia looked up at the group singing but failed to hear the rest of the chorus. Her eyes locked on the owner of the bodacious body now standing in front of her, holding a small cake with too many candles (according to her), smiling and serenading her.

"Hey missy, blow out the candles," Katlyn teased, poking her in the side.

Felicia blew once, twice and on the third try Katlyn blew with her. Mr. Athletically Inclined leaned over and kissed her on the cheek.

"Happy Birthday, I hope it's as special as you want it to be," he whispered in her ear. Felicia felt warm. He smelled delicious and looked edible. She extended her hand.

"Thanks, I'm Felicia," she said in a sultry voice.

"Excuse my lack of manners. Here I am, whispering in your ear, thinking about nibbling on your neck, and you haven't a clue as to who I am. Rory Dunn. I own Ham Bonz." They shook hands and he held hers in his, staring in her eyes.

"Rory, meet one of my closest and dearest friends—Felicia," Katlyn said wryly.

"I already have," he said, not once taking his eyes off Felicia.

"Well then, if you'll just excuse me…" Katlyn's words trailed off as she scooted out of the booth. She looked back and saw Rory take the vacant seat next to Felicia. The scene made her smile and reminded her of how much she missed Justin.

His tour schedule had become so hectic, when he was able to call her, he had limited time to talk. He'd been gone a month on a fifteen-city tour; at least one show per day, in a new city, every day with some venues adding additional shows to accommodate ticket sales. Katlyn was beginning to regret not going on the road with him.

By the time she returned to the table, Rory was gone. In his place was a bottle of Cristal and two glasses, already filled.

"To us," Felicia toasted.

"Nope, to you. Happy B-day!" They clinked their glasses together and slowly sipped on the expensive bubbly.

"So, what do you think?" Katlyn asked.

"About what?" Felicia said, being coy.

"Come on, don't play games, Rory, of course—Mr. Body to Die For!"

"Creamin' in my pants." Felicia smiled, but did not make eye contact with her. "Do I need to say more?"

"Nope, more info than I need." Katlyn raised her glass to toast again. The night was still young and they had more than half a bottle to go!

Several dances later and an empty bottle, Katlyn looked at her watch.

"What time is it?" Felicia asked, sounding half sleepy and half drunk.

"Time to go. I need some coffee," Katlyn answered.

As if commanded like a genie in a lamp, Rory appeared with two cups of espresso on the house. Again he said nothing, made eye contact with Felicia, then blew her a kiss as he exited. They both stared at his behind as he walked away. Having drunk one glass too many, they laughed loudly and hysterically, each consumed by her own private thoughts.

Not ready to call it a night, nothing to go home to anyway, they had the chauffeur take them over to Sunset to check out the sights. Nothing there, they headed to Hollywood Boulevard and parked in front of another hot spot that was more white-oriented.

It was loud and packed. Katlyn looked around the room. They were standing in the middle of what appeared to be little girls who had put on their mothers' makeup, clothes and shoes to play grown-up.

"There's no way any of these little trollops are in here legally, no way," Katlyn said in disgust. Felicia, taken aback by their barely-there too-short minis, declined to comment.

"Let me use the ladies room and we're outta here," Katlyn told her, motioning for her to follow.

But when they got outside they were confronted with a newly erected police barrier; their ride was nowhere in sight. Clearly, the driver had been forced to move.

Traffic was bumper-to-bumper with cruisers. Realizing that they were in for a long wait for the limo to return, Katlyn and Felicia removed the shoes from their aching, swollen feet and sat on the curb.

CHAPTER 6

Felicia loved to sit and look out the oversized picture window in Katlyn's living room early in the morning, just after a seldom-seen downpour. The view of the Hollywood Hills was breathtaking; a picturesque scene that appeared to be painted on canvas.

Katlyn had already completed her morning workout in the exercise room on the lower level, and was slowly and methodically stretching when Mamie entered the room. The three-level, four-bedroom, thirty-two-hundred-square-foot luxury condominium was built into and on the edge of a hill.

"Ms. Kincaid, is there anything special you would like me to prepare for you and Ms. Coleman?"

"No thanks, Mamie. We'll probably just munch on some fresh fruit for breakfast and eat out later."

"Okay then, if you change your mind, let me know."

Felicia appeared in the doorway, still in her pj's.

"You stop for coffee, don't you?" she said dryly, poking fun at Katlyn's much-too-disciplined lifestyle.

"Sure do. Just let me strr-ech two more minutes and I'm all yours."

Felicia sat at the bar and watched her girlfriend's swanlike movements. She was beautiful even when she was sweating, her hair flying and no makeup. Letting out a deep-deep exhale, Katlyn rose, stretched to the sky, inhaled one more time, held it, exhaled deeply—and her day was officially on.

"Listen, we have appointments at The Oasis."

"How'd you pull that off?" Felicia asked, surprised.

"I called a friend of a friend, who knew a friend…"

"Who knew a friend…," Felicia chimed in.

Felicia checked the progress of the coffee, while Katlyn twisted her hair on top of her head and wiped the sweat dripping from her face.

"So, where's my buddy—he sleeping in today?"

Katlyn was agitated by the question and chose to ignore it. Justin had not come home overnight and she'd been unable to reach him on his cell phone. Even though this was a first, he had begun to do other things that were not the norm since returning from his tour.

"Hello-oo, earth to Katlyn. Did you hear me or am I being ignored?"

"Sorry, girl, I heard you and yes, you are being ignored! Justin is already out and at it."

Felicia knew her best friend well and could tell from her tone and demeanor that something was wrong.

"Well, what time are we scheduled to be slathered with goop all over our naked bodies, then rubbed, scrubbed and wrapped?"

Katlyn turned and rolled her eyes at Felicia, who burst into laughter. "You still need some work, I see," Katlyn teased, grabbing her playfully and leading her upstairs to get dressed.

The Oasis was paradise to Katlyn. It was her secret getaway, which she made a point to get away to at least twice a month.

"Ms. Kincaid, good to see you," Natasha, the very petite, very polished receptionist, said as she walked toward Katlyn to plant two very European kisses on her—one per cheek.

"So, we givz you da usual, yes?" she asked, as she turned to get a head-to-toe look at Felicia. Natasha extended her hand to greet Felicia and guide her toward the dressing area.

"Plee-zz, you complete deez card for me. I prepare a roomz for you."

Felicia was not big on "frou-frou" and the Oasis was loaded with it. All the technicians looked fabulous regardless of their age, thanks to well-placed false eyelashes, foundation, blush, shadow, lipstick, push-up bras and girdles. A few of them could afford to shed some pounds, but even their presence commanded Felicia's attention when they sauntered by. She felt awkward, kind of like a fish out of water.

"What's the matter?" Katlyn asked her.

"You know me, I am not the one to be paradin' around, *naked* with this body in front of *bodies* like those." Felicia pointed in the direction of some of the lean and well-cut patrons that were disrobing around her.

"You trippin.' Trust me, they could care less what you look like. Now that tip envelope? Therein lies a concern. At the end of the day, they want it full. So you could be big as the table you lie on, they will make you feel like you have the body of a Greek goddess."

Katlyn dearly wanted her girlfriend to get in better shape. Felicia's body was not bad; she had beautiful full breasts that still stood at attention and equally full curves on her five-foot-four frame. In clothes she looked fabulous; out of clothes, she needed some work; everything was loose and jiggled like jelly. Though petite and shapely, she had tons of cellulite and her butt was heading south, rapidly.

Felicia sighed and reluctantly got undressed. Four hours later, she was a new person with a new attitude.

"Girlie, you're the best! This was soooo what I needed."

"Thought so," Katlyn chimed in. "Hungry?"

"Star-rrved," Felicia said, in a deep Southern drawl.

It was just early enough to beat the late lunch crowd, so they hurried over to Chan Dara, Katlyn's favorite Thai restaurant. Settling into a booth in the corner, Felicia asked about Justin.

"Where did Justin run off to so early this morning? You know, I woke up about six and sat in the living room taking in the view. I never heard him leave?"

"I was tired, he didn't wake me, so I'm not sure."

"Is everything okay with him? CD sales going as he hoped?"

"You know, Felicia, I've been married to this man a long time—almost seven years…"

"It's been that long?" Felicia interjected, shocked.

"Actually, longer; we've known each other nearly nine years!"

"What's that like? I mean nearly nine years with the same person; how do you do it?" Felicia asked sincerely.

"It's like a dream. Some days I can't believe I'm married to such a wonderful man."

"Not to mention, great eye candy," Felicia added.

That comment caused Katlyn's face to light up. Embarrassed by her thoughts, she blushed, forgetting what she was about to say before Felicia interrupted.

"Oh no you didn't—nasty girl! Did your mind just drift below the waist? Shame, shame, shame," Felicia teased.

Katlyn was frustrated. She missed her husband. Lately, he seemed distracted and overly tired. It had been some time since they had made love and she hoped he was not ill. So much of what and who she was, was tied to her main squeeze. The thought of anything happening to him left her with an uneasy feeling.

"You're really happily married, huh?"

Katlyn looked at Felicia and smiled.

"Very happy," she said.

"I mean, I always see the two of you all over each other, but I'm not with you twenty-four-seven."

"Justin and I were blessed to find each other. We are kindred spirits, brought together for a reason. He needs me and looks forward to coming home to someone he knows wants him for *him*. That's why our marriage is so good. And don't act like that's so foreign to you. Look at your mom and dad—married forever and still happy."

"Yeah, they do make it look easy, don't they? But you know, it's shocking that there are tons of people who are married and don't love their spouse, and you know I know. Mr. Man has been married more than twelve years and I was not his first affair. More times than I care to count he told me how he married her out of obligation, to avoid any baby mama drama. Yet, when faced with the decision to stay or go, he stays—not for love, but for the love of money."

"That's sad," Katlyn said, listening intently.

"I know it is. Charles worked hard to get where he is. The wealth came after he said, I do. No prenup means wifey gets at least half. Suffice it to say…he quickly learned the National Anthem of Married Men—'it's cheaper to keep her.'"

Katlyn chuckled at Felicia's wit, but found the conversation depressing. It was hard for her to imagine anyone being so callous and uncaring.

"You know, you're fortunate to be in a relationship with a man who adores you and values what he has with you. I do think you two are made for each other," Felicia admitted.

"Really?"

"You know I do. Hopefully I'll be fortunate enough to find someone who wants me, flabby booty and all."

Katlyn squeezed her girlfriend's hand, feeling the pain hidden in her words and hoping the same for her. Felicia continued, "Truth is, I ain't no spring chicken and these days men who got it goin' on only want the mannequin types. Don't get me wrong; I meet men like Rory all the time. But the moment they get the stuff, alakazam—poof—gone!"

"You're kidding!" Katlyn found Felicia's take on the single world alarming.

"It used to depress me, but I'm long over it. I figure, I make good money, enough to care for me, so I don't need no man around all the time. When I want to go out, I have certain ones for that; when I need some—for maintenance—I know who I can call; and for my emotional stability, I've got you!" she added lightheartedly. But Katlyn could not help feeling sorry for her.

"Frankly, I think it's crazy to believe a person can be committed to just one individual and realistically expect that *one* person to meet *all* your needs," Felicia added.

"You can't be serious!" Katlyn exclaimed. "There are plenty of really nice, unmarried available men."

"Like who? Name some!" Felicia challenged.

Katlyn took a moment and tried to think of guys she remembered who were not gay, and still fit Felicia's standards. The pickings were slim, but she managed to name a couple. An entrepreneur they both knew, but had not seen in years. Felicia informed her he had been incarcerated and when he got out, he wanted nothing but men. Then there was the tall, dark and handsome news anchor whom she'd already been out with and could not get to stop talking about himself. Finally Katlyn offered the jock she would have gone after if she had not met Justin.

"How about Mr. Heartthrob—Lee Walton?"

"Capital D period, O period, G exclamation point. Next!" Felicia quipped.

"Okay, what about…"

"Save it, girlfriend. I've been out there a long time. Those seven-plus years you've played house, I have been on the market. Seen many come and go; they're either gay or closet gay, into white girls, dogs or liars. Therefore, I keep several available by phone for whatever the occasion warrants."

Katlyn could see the sadness as she looked at her girlfriend and reached to take her hand as a gesture of comfort. Felicia quickly moved and picked up the dessert menu.

"Want to add some calories, something to justify the way you work out every day?" she said, attempting to lighten the air.

"No, thank you. My guess is it would look better on someone else than me!"

"All righty then," Felicia quipped. "What's the entertainment committee got planned for tonight?"

"I haven't come up with anything, but there's always something jumpin' in L.A. Or we could have a few friends over, you decide," Katlyn cheerfully added.

"I haven't kicked it with my buddy yet. I'd rather grab a bottle of something that goes down easy and watch a movie with you and Justin. Catch up with what it's like to be a star!"

Lounging in pajamas later that night, Felicia and Katlyn watched one movie they rented for the girls before Justin's scheduled arrival. They nibbled on popcorn and sipped some white wine while they waited for him to get home.

CHAPTER 7

Justin felt the same nervousness tonight that he'd experienced the first time he'd done this and that was more than fifteen years prior to this rendezvous with Nikki. He used the key Nikki left him at the front desk to enter. The room was dimly lit; a bottle of chilled wine and chocolate-covered-strawberries awaited his arrival.

Nikki appeared from the bathroom in a white lace, crotchless body stocking, fully made up and drop-dead gorgeous. Justin felt an instant rise. She approached him with the grace of a ballerina and slowly removed each article of his clothing while she gently moved her body against his in a slow grind.

The chocolate-covered strawberries were systematically fed to him as he reclined on the bed, after she held each one over her mouth and skillfully manipulated the tip with her tongue. As Justin groped for her, anxious to feel her body, she pushed his hands back and sipped wine, which she then shared with him through a passionate, deep-throated kiss.

When she could no longer keep him off her, Nikki rose from the bed and began to sensually lap dance an imaginary body in the chair she'd strategically placed near the bed in full view of Justin. He sat straight up in the bed, so hard it hurt.

He begged Nikki to stop teasing him and let him have her. She continued to tease him, now openly masturbating and moaning softly. She asked him if he wanted her. Justin got up and moved to her, lowering his mouth to the open slot on her body stocking. She sat on the chair and leaned back, raised her legs and opened them into a full V.

Within seconds her soft moans turned into loud screams of pleasure.

As she climaxed, Justin entered her and rode her until the two of them reached a level of sexual gratification neither had experienced before. Spent and exhausted, Justin lay on the bed,

holding Nikki in his arms. Looking at her, he wondered where she learned to dance like that. He'd seen that kind of action before at the nudey booty bars he visited before hooking up with Katlyn. He wondered if Nikki was a former nude dancer, but was respectful enough not to ask.

Sensing what he might be thinking, Nikki rolled over on top of him and stroked his ego. She told him she found him extremely sexy, and the provocative way she'd just seduced him was a result of him turning her on in ways no one else had been able to. His ego grew as big as his manhood.

Nikki knew what to say and how to say it. No stranger to satisfying men, she had mastered the art of making love. Her former stint as a dancer and all that went with that territory helped her.

Justin was late, very late. The limousine pulled up to the front door, but he opted to go in through the garage instead. Reaching into his car trunk, he pulled out his extra cell phone charger. After checking his messages, he turned his phone off, put it on the charger and plugged it into a socket in the garage. Then he opened the glove box of his Mercedes, placed his pager inside and locked it and the Benz before entering the condo.

The garage entered to the laundry room and the entertainment complex. Justin could see lights glowing from the main level. It was obvious Katlyn and Felicia were still up. Justin followed the sound of the TV, which led him to the den off the living room.

"Baby, heyyyy, you're home." Katlyn walked to him and hugged him warmly. Justin held her tight.

"Whuz-uuup, playah!" he said playfully to Felicia, who was curled up in her favorite chair.

"Hey, party pooper. You sure know how to blow a good time," she responded just as playfully.

"Yeah, sorry about that…"

"So, what happened?" Katlyn pulled away from his embrace and waited for an answer.

"I got tied up at a meeting; it ran over, you know." Justin sounded like he was fishing for words and he knew it. "Um sorry, okay?" He pulled her close again, avoiding looking in her eyes.

"Aw, forgive the big lug so we can watch the movies," Felicia shouted, trying to lighten the tension lingering in the air.

"Hey, I see you got videos. Whose selection is up first?" Justin asked as he walked away from the chill coming from Katlyn.

"I don't care," Felicia responded.

"Listen, you want something to eat? Felicia and I had pizza, but I can fix you something," his wife offered. Justin told her no thanks and said he ate while he took care of his business matters.

Felicia remained quiet, mentally taking notes. She could tell Katlyn was extremely upset and hoped she'd keep her cool.

"I'm gonna get out of these clothes and take a shower. Don't start without me."

Justin ran upstairs to the bedroom as Katlyn burned a hole in his back with her gaze.

"Look, girlfriend, lighten up. He's a busy man, in demand. It goes with the territory."

Katlyn turned and stared at her like she could slap her. "He doesn't have time for me anymore," she confided in Felicia, holding back tears. "I don't believe Justin ever came home last night. If he did, he never came to bed. It's been weeks since he's made love to me and he seldom spends quality time *alone*, with me. Once we are alone, he's fast asleep. No romance!"

Dabbing away her tears, Felicia listened as she held Katlyn's hand. She assured her it was nothing to worry about, and told her to trust her man. "He'll come around, he worships you." But she hid from Katlyn what she really thought: *There is more to this story.*

CHAPTER 8

Katlyn waited in front of the skycap stand for Felicia to pick her up. Her flight to Atlanta landed early, otherwise her always-on time 3G's (good, good, girlfriend) would have been there. At eleven a.m. sharp, Felicia rounded the corner in her new convertible Volvo C70.

"Nice, very nice," Katlyn said approvingly as she carefully rubbed her hands along the lines of the car.

"Like it?" Felicia asked, not sure if Katlyn would appreciate the style and class of a Volvo, since she was a Mercedes-Benz sellout.

"Love it!" Katlyn purred. Felicia smiled, glad her buddy approved of her decision. She stared at her girlfriend, who was dressed in an animal-print cropped top that showed plenty of cleavage and skintight black knit pants with strappy animal-print sandals. She smiled.

"That's my girl," she said under her breath.

"Whaaaat! You think I'm overdressed?" Katlyn asked, not the least bit surprised by Felicia's reaction.

"Try underdressed." They both laughed.

Katlyn had agreed to attend an outdoor fund-raiser for a new prenatal wing of a hospital where Felicia was a volunteer. She glanced at Felicia's outfit as she cruised through traffic. A simple sleeveless black top and white linen pants fit her perfectly.

In her opinion, Felicia was too conservative and if she was hoping to land one of those doctors or moneymen who would surely be in attendance at the fund-raiser, she was going to have to loosen up.

They stopped at a light and Katlyn turned to admire the cream-colored Bentley Azure next to them. The driver saw her openly staring and nodded.

"Hi!" Katlyn said as she pinched Felicia.

"Ow, what is your prob—" Felicia didn't finish her question. She could clearly see what Katlyn's problem was.

"Oh gir-rrl! Look at him!" Felicia said just above a whisper.

"You know him?" Katlyn asked, still staring.

"No, but I'd like to," Felicia whispered, looking forward again.

"Girl, he's staring at you!"

"So!" Felicia snapped nervously.

Katlyn continued her quest to get her friend to take the time to find out who he was. "Pull over, now, before he pulls off!"

"Duh, that's not how it's done."

Genuinely unsure of what she meant, Katlyn pressed the issue. "How what's done? If you're interested, don't you tell him?"

"You really have no clue, do you?" Felicia said sarcastically. "It's a new century. Women do not play their trump card first."

"I see, so you just let him ride off into the sunset?" Katlyn asked mockingly.

"Sure do. If he's interested—he should act like it," Felicia explained.

"Okay. Have it your way. But he nearly stared a hole through you. That was a clue if you ask me!" Katlyn sighed and sank down in her seat.

Angry at her persistence, Felicia clenched her teeth and gripped the steering wheel. She took a moment to regroup before asking Katlyn to drop the subject.

"No problem," Katlyn said dryly.

Just as the light changed, Mr. Bentley Azure spoke up.

"Excuse me!"

Katlyn pinched Felicia again, as she turned to see what he wanted.

"Can you tell me which way I turn to get to Alpharetta?"

"No problem. Take I-285 and exit at the second off ramp. That will dump you right in the heart of where you need to be," Felicia said, pointing toward the freeway.

"So, how do I get to 285?"

"That's on my way," Felicia said, motioning to him to follow her. "He's married," she concluded, checking him out in her rearview mirror.

"How do you figure?"

"I just know. He's too wonderful to be available!"

"I think he's available," Katlyn stated matter-of-factly. Curious about her reasons, Felicia asked Katlyn why she thought he would not be committed.

"The car! It's a ho-getter. A married man wouldn't drive something like that!" Katlyn explained.

"So then what's the difference? A ho-getter is not much better than a married man who gets hoes; either way, I ain't no ho!" Felicia responded, offended.

Approaching the entrance to I-285, Felicia pulled over and pointed to the freeway entrance. Mr. Bentley Azure also pulled over and got out.

"Thanks for your help." He smiled and extended his hand.

"I'm Terrel, Terrel Sanders."

"Nice to meet you, Terrel. I'm Felicia Coleman and this is my dear friend, Katlyn."

"Hello, Katlyn." He leaned past Felicia to shake Katlyn's hand. "Nice to meet you."

Terrel smelled sexy. The fragrance he was wearing was soft, fresh, yet masculine; the kind of aroma that lingers in your nostrils. Felicia was aroused. All that loveliness was up close and personal. She worked hard to ignore it and him.

Returning to his car, he paused momentarily, then approached Felicia's side again and handed her his linen-white colored, heavy stock business card. She read it out loud. "Denmor Investments and Holdings, Inc. Terrel Sanders, President and CEO." Although she had not heard of the company, the title "President and CEO" caught her eye. She was impressed.

"President and CEO, Denmor Investments and Holdings. Well, I can see you do well, Mr. President." They all laughed as Felicia eyed the Bentley again.

"So, Ms. Coleman, do you have a card or a number you feel comfortable giving out?"

A number you feel comfortable giving out. Felicia liked his approach. She answered yes, but did not offer the number.

"What, you gonna make me beg?" He laughed, aware of the cat-and-mouse game she was playing.

"Not even!" She fished around in her purse for a pen and paper. Katlyn handed her both.

"I'm giving you my private number, don't spread it around."

Again he burst into laughter and stood curbside laughing until their car was out of sight.

"Okay, do tell…what was that about?" Katlyn demanded.

"What?" Felicia answered, playing dumb.

"You know what!"

Felicia knew Katlyn was about to give her a piece of her mind, so she braced herself. She didn't have to wait long.

"I cannot believe you! If you react that way to all men who are obviously interested, it is no wonder you are A-L-O-N-E!"

Felicia felt hurt by Katlyn's brutal honesty. "He wasn't all that!" was the best she could do in an attempt to muster a defense.

"Says who?" Katlyn said in disgust.

"Says me—you got a man, remember?" Felicia snapped.

"Are you telling me you're not interested?"

"No! I agree with you. He may be available, but he's got to be dating numerous women."

"Annnnd?"

"Katlyn, please! A man like that—driving a current model Azure, wearing an Italian designer suit with matching shoes, and a tie that cost more than some folks make in a week—probably has females slingin' it at him all day!"

"Felicia, I know you're not worried about becoming another notch in his belt buckle. Girl, please, you are not the average female. And since when did you back down from a challenge?"

Katlyn was right. Men had never intimidated Felicia before. But now she was genuinely afraid of Mr. Sanders and not yet ready to share that with Katlyn.

"So what if he calls?"

"He won't," Felicia responded dryly.

"Felicia, what are you afraid of?"

Katlyn's question hit a nerve and Felicia snapped, "I'm not afraid! Stop insinuating I am!" Neither said another word and the silence lingered until they reached the fund-raiser.

"I know you mean well." Felicia spoke first, hoping to ease the tension between them.

Katlyn replied, "I love you and just want to see you happy. Let me say this, then I'll leave it alone. Call the man, see what happens!"

"And say what?" Felicia asked apprehensively.

"You'll know," Katlyn assured her. "Just call."

After the fund-raiser, which turned out to be a huge success, Katlyn and Felicia sat and sized up the day's events. There were zillions of handsome, wealthy and available doctors, lawyers, CEOs, etc. Not one held Felicia's attention. Katlyn suspected it was because Terrel Sanders had already done that.

Katlyn called Justin at the studio. His engineer said he hadn't been in all day, but they were expecting him any minute. Katlyn felt uneasy as she hung up the phone.

"What's up, baby girl?" Felicia asked concerned.

"Um, nothin', I guess." She sat and thought about her last conversation with her husband.

"You know, I'm almost certain Justin said he had to be at the studio *real* early and would not be available by phone. He gave me the studio number if I needed to reach him. Problem is, he's not there!"

"Well, maybe he's been there and left to get something to eat," Felicia offered.

"The engineer said they were waiting for him. Actually, they were expecting him any moment," Katlyn explained, sounding worried.

Sensing Katlyn's concern, Felicia checked her watch. It was still early in L.A.; there was a three-hour time difference to consider. No early riser, Justin could have easily overslept. In an attempt to calm her, Felicia pointed those facts out to her and suggested that he might have stopped to grab a bite to eat en route.

Katlyn knew Felicia was trying to minimize her concerns and appreciated the gesture, but there was something odd about the whole scenario. She just couldn't figure out what it was. She tried more than once to reach Justin by cell phone, but kept getting the message: "the cellular customer you have called is unavailable." And he had yet to answer his pages. The wheels in her head started turning.

In her pre-Justin days, Katlyn had seen this game. Truth is, she'd played it herself once or twice: uncertain she was still happy with her current guy, she'd kick it with someone on the side. Whenever the first man called and she was with the other guy, Katlyn didn't answer. She knew how and why people played phone tag, which made her mind want to probe why Justin was playing more deeply. Afraid to go there, she forced herself to drop it.

Sometimes life drops us little hints that we consciously choose to ignore. Katlyn felt the twinge, she'd felt this before when she realized her mother's death meant permanently losing someone she dearly loved. This time the permanent loss she faced could be the man she could not bear to live without. She chose to dismiss the feeling—her fear.

❀❀❀

Terrel enjoyed his single lifestyle. As he settled down on the chaise in the guest bedroom of his best friend's home, he thought about his day. After twelve hours of continuous driving from Boca Raton to Atlanta, even in a Bentley, he was tired. His boy had already let the cook leave for the day, but he made sure she left a plate out for him.

Felicia came to mind the moment Terrel's head hit the pillow. She was intriguing, obviously intelligent and sassy. Not your typical airhead with a nice body and a pretty face. She made him laugh and that was a good thing. Anybody who could make him laugh could be fun, and Terrel was all about F-U-N!

Marriage was the furthest thing from his mind; the thought of it gave him chills. His mother and father shacked, had him and never married. Eventually his father moved on to a younger woman, leaving his mother bitter. Aware of the pain his father's departure inflicted on his mother, Terrel chose to stay uncommitted. He never wanted to hurt a female the way his father had hurt his mom.

Mrs. Sanders, an extremely hard-working, religious woman, gave her son a good life. She kept him from the things the neighborhood bad boys were doing by carting him off from one Little League event to the next, every waking moment of his childhood. Year-round he played every sport available, and played them well. He was an exceptional athlete whose skills did not go unnoticed.

By high school he was in newspapers all over America. In the tenth grade he was the most sought-after high school athlete. But his mother refused to let him drop out of school to play professionally. In his freshman year at USC, he signed with a professional baseball team located in Oakland. He did well contractually, but he did even better off the field.

Terrel had a knack for Wall Street. In his down time, off-season, he played the stocks. Two years into his professional career, he was quite secure financially and launched Denmor Investments and Holdings Inc., his now multimillion-dollar real estate investment company.

After a long hot bath and a nap, Terrel pulled Felicia's number out of his wallet and called. No answer. He left his cell phone number and asked her to be sure to call him, tonight.

Katlyn rushed in the door from the garage and headed straight to the bathroom off the kitchen.

"Ooo-oo, I nearly peed my pants," she joked, trying to sound like Julia Roberts in the opera scene from the movie *Pretty Woman*.

Felicia laughed and checked the messages. She saved Katlyn's message from Justin, who said he'd be in the studio all night and would call her tomorrow. Then she played the remaining six messages, the last of which was from Terrel. She listened to it four times.

"Should I call?" she asked Katlyn apprehensively when her friend emerged, uncertain for the first time what to do with a man.

"You askin' me, Miss Thang? Thought I was out of touch with how things are done. Besides, I thought you weren't interested in him," Katlyn teased.

"Katlyn, please! What should I say?"

"Oh, so *now* we've decided to call?" Katlyn laughed and avoided an answer again.

"Katlyn, don't do this to me. I can't think, should I call or—"

Katlyn cut her off. "Listen, call him and tell him you're returning his call, then wait to see what he says. Not hard, is it? And I thought I was out of practice."

Felicia picked up the phone and dialed the number. He answered on the first ring, before she could hang up.

"Terrel here."

"Hi, Terrel, it's Felicia, returning your call?"

"Heyyy. Glad you did. How's it going?"

"Ummm, things are—"

Terrel, anxious to set a date, unconsciously cut her off.

"The reason I called was to convince you to spend the day with me tomorrow. I'm leaving the day after and I'd really like to spend some time with you."

"Can you hold a minute?" Felicia asked.

"Sure."

Hands shaking, she laid the phone down and pressed the mute button. Grabbing Katlyn's hands, she jumped up and down while telling her what he wanted. They giggled like schoolgirls as Felicia checked her flight schedule and returned to the phone.

"Tomorrow is good," she said calmly, masking the excitement she felt within.

"What time—you an early bird?"

"Sometimes…"

"Tell you what, let's do breakfast and we'll take it from there," Terrel suggested.

Felicia agreed to breakfast at 9:30 a.m., which would give Katlyn time to drop her off at the restaurant and use Felicia's car to get some shoe shopping done.

"That works for me—anywhere in particular?" Terrel asked.

"Yes, I simply love the menu at Duets, in the Ritz-Carlton."

"You're no cheap date!" Terrel teased. "See you at nine-thirty."

"I look forward to it," she cooed. Katlyn, seated on the sofa, stared at Felicia, amazed at her level of excitement.

"Don't say it. I know I'm out of control, but it feels good." Spinning on her heel, she turned and sauntered up the stairs to her bedroom. Full of excitement, she tossed and turned for hours before falling off to sleep. When the Sandman did arrive, she slept soundly, waking refreshed and anxious to rendezvous with Terrel.

Duets, a five-star restaurant in the Ritz-Carlton in Buckhead, did not offer prices on its menu. If you needed to ask, you could not afford to be there. Terrel and Felicia sat on the patio, which was charming and comfortable. He stared at her as she sat across from him. He liked her style, fashionable with old-money class. His staring made her uncomfortable, so much so she almost began to squirm. Looking up from the menu, she met the challenge and returned the gaze.

"You're very pretty."

"Thank you for noticing." She smiled, remembering she stole that line from Katlyn.

Terrel poured them both mimosas and handed a glass to Felicia.

"Cheers." They clinked glasses and smiled, staring into each other's eyes.

"So, what is Ms. Coleman all about?" Terrel asked, sincerely.

"Well-l-l, I'm originally from Fayettenam…"

"Fayettenam?" Terrel laughed. "Where's that?"

"Fayettenam is an inside airline term for Fayetteville, North Carolina."

"Ohhh, you're a military brat, huh?"

"You know it!" Felicia responded, surprised he knew Fayetteville was a military base.

"So, what is your association with the airline industry?"

"I'm a flight attendant."

"Really, how long?"

"Dinosaur years," she said and they both burst into laughter.

"You planning on retiring as a flight attendant?"

"Sure do, but I plan to deal in real estate afterward," she said, smiling with pride.

"I see," Terrel responded, smiling. It pleased him to know she had ambition post-retirement.

"And you, where did you go to college?" Felicia asked.

"USC."

"What did you major in?"

"I didn't, I went pro in my first year."

Felicia was shocked. He appeared to be a scholarly individual and she assumed he was college-educated. But she played off her initial reaction.

"I'm impressed. Pro what?"

"I played baseball for ten years and built my company, Denmor, in the process. After I retired, I dove full-time into developing my company and securing my future."

"And exactly what does Denmor invest and hold?" she asked, wittily.

"Good one. I like that about you, quick wit and humor." Felicia smiled, pleased with what he said. "To answer your question, real estate."

A broad smile came over her face. "You've got to be kidding," she said enthusiastically.

"Small world. So right off the bat, we know we have something in common," he said approvingly.

The waiter interrupted. "Ready to order?"

Terrel motioned to Felicia to order first. She exhaled softly, relieved he didn't try to order for her. That irked her—a lot! After the waiter left they continued to get to know each other.

"So Terrel, where are you from?"

"Bone and razed in 'Bama. Bummingham to be exact!"

Felicia laughed at his overly exaggerated Southern accent. "Yeah, I can tell you're a Southern gentleman, but not because of the accent. I hadn't noticed it until now. Do you live here in Atlanta?"

"Naw. Been in Florida for years."

"That's right. I did notice the Florida plates on your Azure. What part of Florida?"

"Boca."

"Woo-ooo! That's high rent; congrats!" Felicia said, resting back in her chair as she looked more closely at this "too good to be true" specimen of a man seated across from her. She found his company soothing, like a cool glass of water on a scorching hot day. He was easy to talk to and fun to be with.

Saying nothing, Terrel made the same mental notes. But he was still unsettled with his thoughts on her present career as a flight attendant. He'd dated a few in his day, and found them to be shallow, pretentious and loose.

"Tell me about your life as a flight attendant. I mean you're on the go a lot, right?" he asked in a feeble attempt to broach the subject.

"Let me put it this way: I've been everywhere I have desired to go and if I choose, I can go again. But, the majority of my travel on my days off is to visit Katlyn, who lives in Los Angeles. However, I don't quite believe that's what you wanted to know. Am I right?"

Surprised by her frankness, Terrel grinned a bit lecherously and looked away. He sipped on his mimosa in silence. Felicia's ability to read his mind caught him off guard. Few women were able to do that.

"Hey, you still here?" Felicia asked, smiling slyly.

Terrel smiled and changed the subject. "Your friend Katlyn looks familiar. Should I know her?"

"Don't know—should you?" Felicia looked at him suspiciously.

"Oh, hold up! It ain't like that. All I meant was her face looked familiar." He looked away, trying to keep a straight face.

Felicia giggled at the sight of him squirming. "Truth is, she's a successful songwriter who just happens to be married to Justin Kincaid."

"You're kidding me, right?"

"Not even, why?" Felicia asked.

"I just played in a celebrity golf tournament with that brother in Orlando. Cool guy. Real down to earth."

"Yeah, they're very happily married and doing quite well for themselves."

"You know, he shared with me how well his new CD was doing. So, did Katlyn write anything on this CD?"

"Sure did. 'Who's Kissin' You?' is hers."

"Get outta here!" his voice boomed. "I bought the CD just for that tune. Aw man, she's good!"

"Yeah, she is; that's my girl." Felicia smiled as she thought about her best friend.

Terrel stared at her lips. They were full and sexy—he liked that.

After breakfast, Terrel dropped the top on his Bentley and jumped on the highway. It was a humid, yet comfortable, overcast morning; perfect for a convertible. Felicia was thankful she'd pulled her cotton-puff hair into a bun. The humidity would have guaranteed an Afro.

"Is the air okay?"

"I'm loving it, thanks for asking."

"I know you sistahs got a thing about your hair. Just thought I'd check—make sure I wasn't acting presumptuous."

"So, your reference to sistahs...you have much experience with other ethnicities?" Felicia asked, curious to know if he "skied" (dated white) like most brothahs do when they make it.

Well schooled, Terrel approached the question cautiously. "I've had some encounters with women who were not African American. It was a learning process when I was in the pros."

"And?" Felicia threw out, wondering where this was going.

"Never married one and never took one home to Momma."

That pleased Felicia. At least he wasn't one of those who made it and sought out the plain Jane, bleached blonde he had to sober up, then dress up, to move up to the east side.

They chatted throughout the rest of the drive down the coastline and back to Felicia's home. The evening ended with both expressing a desire to see each other again.

Katlyn had crawled up on the sofa and was half-asleep, listening to some of Felicia's old CDs. Felicia startled her when she entered.

"Hey girl, you have a good time?" she mumbled, still drowsy.

"The best!" Felicia answered, going into the kitchen for a cold glass of iced tea.

"We drove to the coastline and spent the day hanging out near the water. When the sun set, we walked on the beach."

"Wow, lucky you. A man who knows about romance."

"Yeah, an added bonus to all his other wonderful qualities."

"Like what?" Katlyn asked, now wide-awake and propping herself up on the pillows.

Felicia, wanting to be alone with her thoughts, changed the subject. "So, what did you do all day?"

"Shopped at 'Needless Mark Up' (Neiman Marcus), then hit Saks, next Loehmann's and finished at the DSW Shoe Outlet."

"Any good sales?"

"Tons. I went over my limit," Katlyn admitted, laughing. Felicia knew she was serious. When things were not going right, Katlyn went shopping. Justin's inattention and inability to respond to his wife's phone calls was all the excuse she needed.

Felicia looked away in a daze, thinking about Terrel. Katlyn interrupted her moment.

"So spill it. What's he like?"

"Um, he seems to be a together brother. A Southern gentleman who is unattached, or so he says, and fun to be with."

"That spells trouble for you," Katlyn said lightheartedly.

"Yeah, he is definitely doable."

"You planning to see him again?"

"Yeah, before he leaves."

On the surface, Terrel appeared to be everything Felicia wanted in a man: secure, confident and fine. Her best friend was right. He definitely spelled trouble for her. She wanted to be in love and she wanted to be loved, but neither seemed to come her way. There had been numerous men and she'd made lots of mistakes. Dating a married man, exclusively, for several years, was one of those mistakes. Now older and wiser, she was a little gun-shy about jumping into any kind of a relationship, especially one that could eventually carry labels.

"Yep, you've slowed your roll for sure."

"What does that mean?" Felicia asked, agitated.

"You stumble upon Mr. Right and then choose to play hard to get..."

"For the record, it's not like that. He seemed interested, but who knows where he's coming from!"

"Never stopped you from doing a one-nighter before!"

"Yowww." Felicia made a sound like a cat striking in defense of itself.

"Put your claws away. Where is this coming from?"

Katlyn realized she was being a B and in the process hurt Felicia's feelings. "Sorry, I'm PMSin'."

"Yeah, well, don't unload on me."

"I like him, Felicia. He brought you home at a respectable hour, and I'm guessing because it's only two a.m. he didn't try to get the booty and then ask to see you before he leaves. My kind of guy!"

"Then you go meet him for breakfast," was Felicia's sarcastic response. Katlyn giggled.

"I'm serious. Anyway, you catch up with Justin? Everything okay?"

"No," Katlyn answered shortly.

"Okay, sorry I brought him up. Did you eat?" Felicia asked, changing the subject.

"Why, did you bring me something?" Katlyn's question was full of sarcasm.

Felicia picked up her shoes and purse and headed off to the shower without another word. Tonight she was much too tired to be Katlyn's punching bag.

CHAPTER 9

Justin was hung over and tired. He lay in the bed next to Nikki, who was still asleep. Katlyn was not due back until tomorrow, which made his decision to see Nikki one last time, easy.

Nikki was good, the best he'd ever had. Sure, he loved Katlyn, but love had nothing to do with this. Nikki did him like Katlyn never had! The thought of him all over and all in Nikki caused the sheet covering his manhood to form a tent. That rise was short-lived—his cell phone rang.

"Hey, baby. Yeah, I'm fine, just a little hoarse," he whispered, trying not to wake Nikki. Carefully he climbed out of the bed and tucked himself away in the bathroom. "No, baby, nothing's wrong. I spent the night at the studio. We worked all night and I was too tired to drive home."

Katlyn, always sweet and considerate, let her husband know she was concerned for his well-being. It made him feel like a louse.

"Aw baby, um sorry. You're right; I should've called you to let you know I was staying here all night. But, I figured since you were in Atlanta and three hours ahead, you wouldn't be concerned. By the time you got up, I'd be home. Sorry I worried you, baby. But, listen, I need to get back in there to see how Jerome is coming with the mix. Love you, too."

"Justin, you in there? Unlock the door, I gotta pee!"

Justin grabbed his head. Nikki pounding on the bathroom door made his already throbbing head ache more. He swung open the door and pushed past Nikki. He felt guilty for lying to Katlyn and even more guilty for actually enjoying his affair. Until Nikki, he had only thought about cheating. A flirtatious dinner here, some heavy bumpin' and grindin' there, but never had he gone all the way. No one had captivated him like Nikki—no one. All he could do was hope this too shall pass!

As he waited for Nikki to rejoin him in bed, he thought about his wedding night. Katlyn was good in bed, a passionate lover. She knew his body, every inch of it, and she was skilled. But the passion and need for sex he once felt for her had faded. Life with her was no longer exciting. Instead, their nights of passion and days of carefree nothingness had been replaced with things like responsibility, schedules and expectations for success.

Over time, Justin began to enjoy being a solo act. He spent days away from home and Katlyn, and only had regrets when he slowed down long enough to wrestle with the reality of his situation. He was married, but he wanted to enjoy his fame alone, without the pressure of commitment and vows.

That was how Nikki ended up in his bed. No pressure to be where he didn't want to be. No demands, no expectations, no commitments and no vows. All she wanted from him was what he wanted to give her, a high hard one, over and over again.

"Hey baby," Nikki purred as she crawled under the sheets and went to work. Justin knew he had to get back to the studio, but not just yet.

Returning to the studio three hours later with two new messages from Katlyn waiting, he realized he had a problem. Nikki had to go today! She was becoming a habit he could not break. Continuing to see her was a risk, a big risk. One he had never taken before—then again, he'd never met anyone like Nikki.

By the time she reached Justin, Katlyn was very annoyed.

"You know, Justin, this is getting old. I call you at home, no answer. I call you on your cell, no answer. I call the studio where you say you'll be, you're not there. I page you, no response. So you want to tell me what is going on?"

"Bay, you trippin'!" Justin tried to sound sincere.

"Oh, I'm trippin'? Guess again. I'll be home tomorrow, Justin. I'd appreciate you being considerate enough to be honest with me. Your BS is not working—understand?"

"Like I said, baby, you tri—" The line went dead.

"Man, you really messed up this time," he mumbled to himself. The cell phone rang again. Justin answered, hoping it was Katlyn calling back.

"Hello."

"Heyyy baby," Nikki purred in a sensual tone. "I can't stop thinking about this morning. I need to see you."

"Not now, okay?" Justin snapped, angry with himself. "I gotta get this mix done."

"You don't want to see me?" she asked, sounding like a pouty brat.

"Listen, Nik, I ain't in the mood and I got work to do!"

Ignoring his outburst, she continued. "Tell me, you ever had it in an elevator?"

The visual was instant, as was his hard-on. Justin could not believe what he was hearing. Nikki explained in vivid detail what he would be missing if he did not show.

He listened, pin drop silent, clinging to her every word.

"Meet me at our spot in thirty minutes. Wait for me at the elevator." She hung up.

Justin stood there, hard as a rock, contemplating what to do.

"Yo Lisa. Tell the engineers I'll be right back, I need to get me a quick bite to eat. Be back shortly…" His words tapered off as he exited the studio from the rear door.

Nikki wore a micro-mini with a halter top and pumps—no panties. They entered the express elevator and before the door closed he pinned her against the wall, reaching under her skirt for her button. They kissed hard, her hands reaching to free his hardness. Sucking on a nipple, he pumped fast and hard. Within seconds he shot his load and exited her. They quickly fixed their clothes and hair and then waited for the elevator to stop. The doors opened on the restaurant level at the top of the building. Nikki went to the ladies room to regroup and Justin returned to the studio.

Concentrating on his mix was impossible. His mind kept replaying the elevator rendezvous over and over again. As he listened to the track, his mind drifted to the first time he saw Nikki.

The moment he laid eyes on her, he knew he wanted her. They met at a Hollywood A-list fund-raiser. The venue where the fund-raiser was held had two levels. Access to the second level was via either the elevator or the grand spiral staircase. Wanting to stand out from the many femme fatales present, Nikki chose the stairs.

She paused on each step to ensure that those watching (which included everyone) got a good look! When she entered the room at the top of the stairs, men and women stopped to stare. Flawless, she strutted with a slight model's sashay across his path. Justin froze! Her barely dressed, well-chiseled body commanded attention. She was stunning and she knew it.

Men tripped over themselves trying to get the chance to say hello. Women pulled their dates and husbands closer when she walked by. Men could not and women would not take their eyes off her. She knew how to work a room and she did that well.

Not usually intimidated, Justin found himself unsure how to approach Nikki, so he followed her around the room. When she finally approached him to introduce herself, his knees buckled; he found himself tongue-tied and at a loss for words—a first for him. They exchanged numbers and now they were exchanging much more.

CHAPTER 10

Recently signing with a new record label placed Justin in a higher tax bracket. Reportedly, he'd inked one of the most lucrative recording contracts for a solo R & B artist in the history of JAMZ. The executives at this trend-setting music conglomerate felt signing him for $20 million was a steal. Before this five-year pact ended, they knew they would recoup that and more.

Sherwin, his new manager, was a heavyweight in the entertainment industry. He had a roster of mega-stars that stopped short of God. Everyone who was anyone (and those who wanted to be someone) sought his representation. A short, stodgy, gray-haired Jew, he'd discovered and launched the careers of nobodies, taking them from flat to fluffy, for twenty-seven years. At seventy-two, he'd spent the last fifteen years taking those who were already stars to mega-stardom.

Married for forty years to the same woman, he respected Justin for being married and staying out of the tabloids. No small feat when you're a star, which told Sherwin a lot about Justin. "Smart" was the word of choice. It took brains to hold it all together in Hollywood. Lose your brains, lose your fame. It was just that simple!

Justin was punctual for his press conference. He met Katlyn and Sherwin there. This was Sherwin's first time meeting Katlyn. Unlike days past, Katlyn and Justin were no longer always attached at the hip. As a matter of fact, Katlyn didn't know Justin was changing labels until it hit the local news at noon.

"Hey…baby, can you meet me at JAMZ?"

"JAMZ? Uh, sure, but…Justin why didn't you tell me you were making this move?" Katlyn asked, hurt by the obvious slight. Momentarily silent, Justin replayed who he had discussed it with. Remembering it was Nikki, he lied.

"I—uh—wanted to surprise you."

"Well, you did." Her response was dry and sarcastic.

"So-ooo…can you meet me, like, now? I've got a press conference and you know I want my baby by my side."

The press conference was scheduled to begin at 11:30 a.m. It was 10 a.m., giving Katlyn very little time to get glammed up. She briefly thought about telling him no, but decided to make an appearance. Despite her hurt feelings, she was not a fool. Photo ops announced to those females seeking her spot that it was not vacant.

"Sure, give me a minute to get cute and I'll be there."

"Thanks, you know I love you." Justin hung up realizing that he barely made it through that near-disaster. He needed Katlyn to be there, she was always an asset to his public image and she knew how to handle the press. Her pleasing personality greatly complemented her striking good looks. His popularity hinged on the public's impression of him and they loved him. Image was everything and his image was a happily married man. When Katlyn arrived, looking gorgeous as usual, Justin softly exhaled and smiled; thankful she did not let him down.

"It's great to finally meet the renowned Sherwin Ingber," Katlyn said, as she shook his hand vigorously.

"Nice to meet you as well. Glad you could be here," he said, motioning for her to join Justin on the platform.

"Am I late?"

"No, we were just about to start."

Justin leaned over and kissed her lightly on the cheek as she stepped up. The flashes from the cameras blinded them momentarily. Katlyn grabbed his arm to steady herself.

"Hey bay, you look great," he whispered.

"You look tired," she whispered back through smiling lips and clenched teeth.

"I am, we worked all night."

She felt a meltdown coming but continued to smile for the cameras, not saying another word. This was neither the time nor the place to question why he was absent when she stopped by the studio at 2 a.m., after her flight landed—something she never does.

Although she was tired and jet-lagged from her early-morning arrival from Atlanta and the press conference, Katlyn waited up for Justin She hoped he'd be home in time to watch the news with her, but he'd called and said he would be late. His noon press conference was the lead-in on all the networks. After the news went off, time seemed to crawl, so she fought off sleep by working on the manuscript she'd been leisurely writing in her spare time.

"Wow, you still up? What's cookin', good lookin'," he said when he finally came home, trying to be funny and much too casually to have been away from her for more than a week.

"I decided to wait up. I missed you." Katlyn crawled out of bed, making sure Justin noticed her barely-there teddy.

"What's this about?" he asked as she slowly and seductively wrapped an arm and a leg around him.

"Try 'I missed you' or 'I'm glad to see you,'" she whispered softly as she rubbed his chest.

"Me, too. Let me unwind a minute," he whispered in her ear. Pulling away, he retreated to the shower.

When she heard the shower stop, Katlyn lit the candles on the night-stand and lay across the already prepped bed. Still wet, Justin lay next to her and rubbed her forehead as he looked in her eyes. Katlyn fought back tears. She missed this; the way things used to be.

Justin kissed her as he gently caressed one of her breasts, rubbing ever so softly. He moved his mouth to her nipple, circling it with his tongue. He worked his way down her stomach, stopping just below the navel. Hungry for more, Katlyn arched her back, beckoning her husband to continue.

Gently he kissed her soft pubic hair through the teddy. Katlyn gasped and grabbed his head. She lifted it and stared into his eyes. Justin shared her gaze for a moment. Sensing her urgency, he lowered his head and continued. Within minutes Katlyn began to shake violently. While she climaxed he entered her and joined the ride to euphoria.

Katlyn sensed something was not right, but for now, she did not want to know what was wrong. Her desire was to enjoy this and Justin as long as she could. She knew how to please him, and for the next hour, please him she did.

He was up early the next morning. Katlyn, who had been awake from the moment he rolled out of bed, met him at the door. Surprised to see her, he jumped.

"Sorry, didn't mean to wake you."

"Why not? Don't I get a good-bye smooch?"

"Of course." Justin hurriedly pecked her on the lips. Before he could dart out the door, she grabbed his arm.

"Justin, what time are you coming home?"

"Uh, I don't know, baby, why?"

"I miss you. It would be nice to spend some quality time together. Maybe take in a movie or something."

Justin stared at her. She was about to cry. He hugged her and she held on for dear life.

"Hey, what is it, babe?" he whispered.

"It's us. What is happening to us?" She cried and buried her head in his shoulder. Justin said nothing for a few minutes. His cell phone ringing drowned out the sound of her crying.

"Baby, I need to get this, could be the studio," he said, pulling away from her. Forgetting to check the caller ID first, he answered. It was Nikki.

"I'm wet and waiting. Where are you?"

"Okay, I'm on my way," he blurted out before he flipped the phone closed and stuffed it in his jeans, praying Nikki would not call back. His heart racing and palms beginning to sweat, he turned to leave.

"They're waiting, gotta go. I'll try to break away early—see you tonight—love you." Justin blew her a kiss and left.

Katlyn watched him back out the garage. She stood there, going over the thoughts in her head. Something was different between them, but what—and why? Tears formed and, one by one, slowly trickled down her cheek, dangled from her jaw line, then cascaded to the floor. In need of some girlfriend time, she called Felicia in Atlanta.

"Katlyn, whuzz-uup, girl?"

Katlyn tried to tell her without crying, but she burst into tears before she could get one word out.

"Hey baby girl, what's wrong?"

"I'm sure it's someone else. Justin, he's…" Katlyn dissolved into tears again.

"You sure? What makes you think he is seeing someone else?"

"Us! It's all wrong! Las—last night he did just enough to keep me quiet. I've been gone for more than a week. I-I-I was so horny, climbing the walls but he could take it or leave it!"

"He's been working long hours at the studio, maybe—" Felicia began.

"Save it. I stopped by the studio when I got in. Two o'clock in the morning, Felicia. They hadn't seen him since 10 P.M."

"What? Did he call?"

"Sure, after I got home. Said he had just left the studio, but was going back to finish a mix."

Feeling stronger, Katlyn continued. "And get this: he changed labels. Can you believe that, he changed labels and never told me?"

"Well, how do you know?"

"He called to tell me after I heard it on the news. The news, Felicia. I'm his wife and I have to hear about this on the news!"

"Did you ask him why he didn't tell you?"

"Claims he wanted to surprise me."

"You don't believe him?" Felicia asked.

"Not in the least."

Concerned about her state of mind, Felicia asked how was Katlyn planning to deal with this revelation. Katlyn screamed and began crying again. As good girlfriends do, Felicia shut up and let her cry. Once she calmed down, Felicia made an attempt to smother the fire.

"Listen, you have no proof of him f-in' around. Justin loves the ground you walk on; he'd be lost without you. Think he'd risk losing what he has?"

Katlyn didn't answer.

"Look, there's a lot going on right now with both your careers. Take a deep breath."

Katlyn inhaled deeply through her nose.

"Now exhale." Felicia could hear her blow out the air slowly. "Better?" she asked.

"I guess so," Katlyn responded. "You think I'm imagining all this?"

"I think you're tired and need to rest. Let your head clear."

"You're right. Things will be fine. I'm just tired. So whatcha doin' today?" Katlyn asked, trying to sound upbeat.

"I was about to call Terrel to thank him for the info he sent me regarding real estate classes."

"Oh, how sweet." Katlyn let out a long sigh.

Sounding quite content, Felicia responded, "Yeah, he's definitely not the norm."

"Well, go call him and call me later."

"Hey, it'll all work out, okay?"

"Sure. Later." Katlyn hung up the phone and sat thinking about what Felicia had said. Was it all in her head, a figment of her imagination? Time would tell.

CHAPTER 11

Justin was two days behind on his project. He needed to focus, but could not get the last couple of nights and days with Katlyn out of his mind. Making love to her again was good, but he could take it or leave it.

"Yo Justin, where's your head, man? You gotta focus. We need to have this mix wrapped by tomorrow," Keith, the engineer, admonished. Justin threw up his hand and waved in acknowledgment.

"Aw right then, let's do this." Keith smacked him on the shoulder and pumped up the volume, hoping he would get a full day's work out of Justin.

They successfully completed three-quarters of the remaining mix before Justin's cell phone rang.

"Mr. Kincaid, wut uupp?"

"That you, Chuck?"

"Yeah man, I'm in town; got time to show a brother L.A.?"

"You know it. How long you here?"

Chuck checked the time. "A quick minute."

"Okay, cool. Give me another hour or two and I'll swing by and scoop you. Where you layin'?"

"Same place. La Mirage, you know how we do it," Chuck boasted.

"Yeah, see you in two," Justin agreed and turned his phone off to finish his mix.

Happy to hear from his best friend and anxious to hang, Justin totally forgot he'd agreed to meet Nikki later. The next time he thought about her, she was standing in front of him, pissed off. Justin tried to get rid of her, but she was not having it. Concentration blown, he led her by the arm to her car, explaining he had a close buddy in town he was meeting at La Mirage. He gave her money to get gas and a bite to eat, and promised to meet her at their spot by nine.

Chuck was already one draft ahead of Justin when he arrived at the hotel bar. He rose and hugged Justin, motioning to the waitress to bring two more drafts.

"Hold up, I gotta make a call." Justin pulled out his cell phone and dialed home. While he checked in, Chuck detoured to the restroom.

"Baby, it's me. Listen, Chuck's in town. I stopped off to see him. I won't be long, just a couple beers and I'm all yours. Okay?"

"Sure Justin, see you later," Katlyn said nonchalantly.

"So, you call my girl?" Chuck asked with a huge grin on his face when he returned.

"Yeah."

"How is she? Everything okay, man?" Before Justin could answer, Nikki walked in with a girlfriend and proceeded to a table.

"Whoa! You see that?" Chuck whispered, pointing.

"Yeah, I saw it." Justin's dry response made Chuck take his eyes off Nikki and her friend momentarily. He studied his friend's face, looked at her, then him again and put two and two together.

"So, you hittin' that?" Chuck asked. Justin took a long swig of beer and didn't answer.

"Yo man, this is me. I know you. That's got your name written all over it!"

"You're way off base, Chuck."

"Who's foolin' who, Justin? It's me, Chuck. What's up?"

Chuck knew Justin well, and he also knew what a nose wide open looked like. He'd been there. Left his African American wife for the Asian woman he was now happily married to.

"Chuck, I've messed up, man. Bad—don't know what I've gotten myself into. And the scary part is I like it!" Justin admitted.

"Let's do the math," Chuck said. "You and Katlyn been straight for about five or six years, right?"

"Right! It was bound to happen. That old seven-year itch is right around the corner. Marriage ain't easy."

"Tell me 'bout it," Justin said, feeling down.

Nikki walked over to the bar and ordered drinks for her and her girlfriend, never once acknowledging Justin or Chuck. She knew they were looking at her; every man in the bar was. As Justin watched her, Chuck watched Justin. His boy was sprung, that was obvious. He could lie to himself, but eventually the truth would come out. Chuck shook his head and ordered another round. "You thought about what you doin'? I mean the consequences?"

"Think about it all the time," Justin admitted.

"Booty that good?" Chuck chuckled, trying to lighten the conversation.

"Come on, Chuck, it's about more than just the booty."

"Is it? Like what more? You got up in this girl's head? Know what she's about?"

Justin was silent.

"Thought so!" Chuck quipped. "When it's all said and done, it *is* about the booty and the booty rules. When it's hot, it's hot!"

Chuck reached his hand out for Justin to slap him five, but Justin was too busy staring at Nikki to notice. Two guys had joined the women and Nikki seemed to be very interested in the fly one.

"Yo man, you gon' leave a brotha hangin'?"

"What? What was that?" Justin answered absentmindedly, still focused on Nikki.

"I was sayin' marriage has a better chance of working if your woman is working you right in the sheets; less chance to stray."

Justin heard him, but did not respond. Fly Guy was now leaning close enough to Nikki to comfortably put his arm around her shoulder, and she was letting him. Justin felt his temperature rise. As he began to get up from the bar stool, Chuck grabbed his arm.

"Justin! Hey man, what you doin'?" Justin snatched his arm away, but Chuck, much larger and stronger, grabbed him again, this time like he meant it.

"Chill, man! You trippin'!"

"Let me go, man." Justin wrestled with him trying to get free. But Chuck was relentless. Not able to free himself, Justin finally calmed down.

"Um cool, man, let me go."

"You sure?" Chuck asked, loosening his grip.

"Yeah, now let me go," Justin demanded. He sat down, straightened his clothes and grabbed a napkin to dab the sweat off his forehead.

"Check yourself, man. You walkin' on thin ice."

"Save it, Chuck, I don't need the lecture," he snapped.

Chuck snorted. "If she can push your buttons like that, you're in serious trouble. Not only are you sprung—she's in control!"

Justin looked at Chuck as if he had slapped him. Not because he didn't like what his friend was saying, but because what he said was true—and the truth hurt.

"Slow your roll, playah, she ain't worth it! She's playin' mind games, working you like a puppet on a string," Chuck continued.

Justin downed the rest of his beer and ordered a shot of cognac. Chuck stood up and began to jerk and turn in circles with his arms flailing. "Danger, danger," he joked. His poor rendition of an out-of-control robot from the movie *Lost in Space* made Justin laugh. One drink away from being inebriated, Justin's laughter became contagious and they both laughed until tears ran down their faces.

With a sudden urge to use it, Justin hurried from the bar to the men's room. When he returned, Nikki and the Fly Guy were gone. Seconds later her girlfriend and her date left as well; a sobering moment for Justin. Any high he had left!

"This is f-d up. I got a good woman at home," Justin muttered.

"Yeah, Katlyn is all that," Chuck agreed.

"Naw man, you ain't hearin' me. I knew I loved Katlyn the moment I laid eyes on her. Not only is she beautiful, she's intelligent, classy and a good person: a total package. Man, she's everything I ever wanted in a woman—until I met Nikki," he said softly.

Chuck reared back and stared at the spot where Nikki had been sitting. "Know this; there's a reason you creepin'. Chew on that!" Checking his watch, Chuck stood up and downed the last of his beer, then patted Justin on the shoulder. "Let me know if I can help—I got your back." He stared at Justin, waiting for him to rise so he could hug him.

Justin was too deep in thought to realize Chuck was standing, arms wide open. *Smack!* Chuck playfully slapped him on the back of his head, like they used to do to each other growing up. Any other time it would have made Justin laugh. Not this time.

"Yo, what s your problem, man?" Justin snapped.

"How you gon' leave your boy hangin'?"

Justin realized Chuck was waiting to embrace him. "Sorry, man, my bad." Justin stood up and hugged him; sad he had to go.

"As always, it's great when we get together. Love ya, keep in touch, all right?"

"Yeah, I will. Later, Chuck." Justin sat back down. He was feeling real low. Chuck was right; he was in deep—way deep. Nikki had him strung out on her stuff. No booty should be that good, but hers was. Not ready to go home, he ordered another beer. Sipping the head off the top, his mind wandered.

Chuck had done it. He'd left his wife for the woman of his dreams. Could he live with Nikki? Was what he was feeling for her all physical? He tried to put it in perspective. "Nikki is just somethin' to do," he said out loud.

Katlyn was his rock, his security blanket. They'd grow old together. She'd loved him for who he was long before his name became a household word. She had his back, he trusted her. She deserved better.

His cell phone broke his train of thought. "I'm waiting."

Hearing Nikki's voice made him angry. He thought of her and Fly Guy. "So what are you callin' me for? Where's Fly Guy?"

Nikki could detect jealousy and she loved it. That let her know she was all over his cranium, and that was exactly where she wanted to be. She decided to play more mind games with him.

"What fly guy?"

"Don't play games, I'm not in the mood," Justin commanded.

"Yessuh, mastah, whatever ya'll says," she said, laughing and hoping to piss him off some more.

"I don't have time for some dizzy chick who likes to mess with one head by way of the other." Justin hung up on her and headed home.

Ten minutes from the safety of Katlyn's arms, the phone rang.

"Aahh, do it good to me, ooo-mmm. Justin, I need you, pleez do me like only you can do me!" Justin turned the car around as he listened to her soft sexy voice.

"Don't you want me to take it in my mouth and stroke it, slowly up one side…"

"I'm pulling up now, what's the room number?"

In an effort to hide his hard-on, he grabbed his jacket from the backseat and carried it in front of him. He stopped at the front desk and got the key Nikki had left for him and rushed to the elevator. The elevator door had just opened, which was perfect timing for a man who could barely walk.

Nikki lay facedown, spread-eagle and totally nude across the bed. She heard him open the door.

"It's waiting on you, daddy," she whispered seductively as he entered the room.

Justin did not take time to undress. He loosened his belt, unzipped his pants, dropping them just enough to free his unmanageable hard-on. Nikki looked back and saw his erection and crawled up on all fours. She was noticeably wet. Justin rammed his hardness in her as far as he could.

"Oh-hh, baby! Harder, do it harder," she panted.

Nikki was hot and tight. Justin pumped frantically; he needed to release some tension. In moments he climaxed. Nikki pulled away and rolled over, reaching out for him. Spent and tired, he lay in her arms and they both fell asleep. His cell phone awoke them. Justin reached to answer it and realized where he was. Looking at the clock, he sat straight up. He was late. Very late. The caller ID indicated it was his home phone. Before he answered, he put a finger to his mouth, motioning to Nikki to keep quiet.

"Hey baby," Justin said, trying to sound upbeat and composed.

"Where are you?" Katlyn asked, barely above a whisper.

"I had more than one beer with Chuck, then I felt a little sick so we got a bite to eat."

"I've been calling. Your phone just rolled to voice mail," she told him.

"Maybe I didn't have a signal while I was in the bar at La Mirage." Katlyn's silence made him feel guiltier. "Sorry I worried you, I'm on my way." Katlyn began to cry. Justin held the phone, feeling like a butthole.

"What is going on, Justin? You owe me the truth!" she finally said through her tears.

"The truth about what, Katlyn?" Frustrated with the whole scenario, Justin worked hard to control his temper. "Nothing's going on." Katlyn continued to cry and then hung up the phone. Disgusted with himself, he sat on the edge of the bed, silent.

"Everything okay?" Nikki asked, breaking the silence.

"I've gotta go," he said dryly as he pulled up his jeans that were still draped around his feet. .

"Okay, I'll leave, too." Nikki gathered her clothes and went into the bathroom.

"You got gas money?" Justin called to her.

"I'm straight, thanks."

Justin stopped at the door, turned and looked at Nikki, who had just come out of the bathroom.

"The last thing I want to do is put you in the middle of my mess," he explained. Justin felt lost.

Nikki walked up to him and placed her index finger on his lips. "Shhh!"

"Nik, I need time to figure this out."

"Take all the time you need. I'll be waiting," she whispered in his ear.

Justin hugged her and held her tight. His mind was far too busy trying to sort out what part of the day's events he'd share with Katlyn to really pay attention to Nikki's words.

"I'll be waiting" meant far more than the mere words said.

CHAPTER 12

atlyn always found comfort in music. "No More Tears," an Anita Baker classic for those sistahs who finally "woke up," was cascading through the house. Sitting in Felicia's favorite chair by the picture window, watching the moon, Katlyn said nothing when Justin came in.

The moonlight created an eerie feeling for him. Katlyn always wore her emotions on her face. Problem was, he could not see her face or her hands and that made him uneasy.

"Did you eat?" he asked, taking each step carefully, as if he was walking on eggshells.

"Sit down, Justin," Katlyn said softly. He slowly sat in the chair across from her.

"If you've ever loved me, you'll be honest with me." The calmness in her voice sent chills down his back. Katlyn leaned forward, out of the darkness, so the moonlight could illuminate her face. Her eyes were red and swollen from crying, yet her entire demeanor seemed calm—too calm.

"I won't ask you who. I only need to know why and what now. If you need time to think about your answer, take it. But I only want to hear the truth."

Justin knew from her tone and the look on her face that she was not playing. Everything about her at this moment scared him. He could not remember if he'd ever seen her like this. It reminded him of that scene in the movie *A Thin Line Between Love and Hate* when Lynn Whitfield, the lied-to girlfriend, nuts up on Martin Lawrence, the cheating dog.

"Katlyn, listen, I…"

"Justin, I only want the truth. Save the melodrama for her."

Justin's heart was pounding so hard he could not hear himself think.

"Okay, listen. There is nothing and no one who could make me leave the person I love more than life…"

"Cut to the chase; I know you love me. Are you sleeping with someone else?" she asked pointedly.

Justin thought fast and quickly weighed his options. "When all else fails, lie" was the unspoken motto amongst the brothas who had traded in their playah's card for a marriage certificate.

"No, Katlyn, I love you too much to do something like that."

Katlyn had a sinking feeling in the pit of her stomach. She exhaled—long and hard—but said nothing. Unable to read her face for the first time, he got up and approached her. Katlyn raised her hand to him in that "talk to the hand, the ears ain't listenin'" position.

Justin stopped dead in his tracks, U-turned and retreated to their bedroom to pack. He had a three-night engagement in Detroit and was looking forward to the time alone.

Katlyn stretched out on the chaise next to the window and stayed there until morning. She knew Justin was lying. Now she needed to talk to Felicia to decide what to do. Unable to reach her she called her girlfriend Tanya. With her husband, Darrel, out of town she had some free time and accepted Katlyn's invitation to lunch.

Tanya was happy Katlyn called. A first-time mom, she looked forward to talking to someone she could understand. The soul food gospel brunch at the well-known restaurant, Aunt Kate's, was a casual enough environment for a new mother who was still learning to juggle things.

"Hey girl," Tanya greeted her, pushing a stroller the size of a car.

"What's that?" Katlyn asked, pointing and laughing at the monstrosity as she held the door of the restaurant open.

"Girl, a shower gift from some coworkers."

"Did you have to get a license to drive it?" Katlyn said, still laughing. Tanya joined in the laughter as she hugged her.

"Nope, no license needed, but I did need a course in how to use it. It has really proven to be worth the money they spent on it."

"Expensive, huh?"

"Hel-lo! I could have bought a car!" They laughed and hugged again before being seated, happy to see each other.

"Glad you could make it, girlfriend. I wanted to spend some time with you and my goddaughter, since Justin is out of town."

"He on tour?" Tanya inquired.

"Just a few dates."

"And you didn't go," Tanya asked, looking at her as if she were green.

"Don't start, okay?"

"Any-wayyy!"—Tanya obliged Katlyn's request and changed the subject— "since I'm not with the airline anymore, Darrel is working all he can. My only adult conversation is when he's on his way to sleep, getting up or on the toilet. So suffice it to say I was thrilled when you called."

"So how is D?"

"My huzz-band is great as ever," Tanya answered in a way that made Katlyn believe she was thinking about a recent sexual encounter that made her toes curl.

"Uh-huh! You two keep that up and you're going to have a little brother for Miss Lauren."

Tanya chuckled and reached down to pick her up. "Keep what up?" she teased.

"Yeah, play dumb. Remember I warned you."

Tanya smiled. "By the way, you still trying?" she asked, looking away from Lauren long enough to make eye contact with Katlyn.

"Somewhat," Katlyn answered, looking away.

"How can you somewhat try to get pregnant?"

Katlyn did not want to have this conversation with someone who was so happily married she could win the Mother of the Year award. She made an effort to tiptoe around it as best she could.

"What I mean is, I'm not taking fertility drugs anymore, but we are still making love sometimes."

She tried to stay composed, but failed. Tears fell one after the other. Tanya, busy with the baby, didn't notice immediately. When she heard Katlyn sniff, she looked up again. The tears frightened her. She'd never seen Katlyn like this.

Standing, she approached Katlyn reaching with one arm to hug her, while she cradled Lauren in the other. "What is it?" she asked. "Talk to me, what's wrong?"

"I feel so out of it. Justin is always gone and seldom shows any interest in me."

"Well, Katlyn, he is working on finishing his new project, right?"

"So he says." Katlyn shrugged out of her friend's embrace.

"What, you think he's doing other things?" Tanya asked in disbelief.

"I don't know what to think!" Katlyn shouted, slamming her hand on the table. *Temper tantrums are so not Katlyn's style*, Tanya thought, trying to calm the baby before putting Lauren back in the Rolls-Royce stroller.

"Listen, how long have you been off the drugs?" Tanya inquired.

Katlyn gave her a bewildered look. "What's that got to do with anything?"

"Maybe everything. You know those fertility drugs mess with your hormones."

"I hadn't thought about that," Katlyn admitted, calming down.

"You should go see your doctor. I bet this is physical." Tanya patted her hand trying to reassure her.

"I'll do that," Katlyn lied. She had no intention of seeing a doctor. She knew Justin was having an affair and she also knew her hormones were not the reason.

Suddenly, Katlyn regretted arranging this outing. If only Felicia had not gone to see Terrel. In need of a body to keep her company, she'd called her only other dearest friend. Big mistake! How could she talk about being unhappily married to someone who was the only happily married person on the planet?

Katlyn changed the subject by bringing up Tanya's family members. There always seemed to be a story to tell when you mentioned her siblings. Tanya was the oldest and most responsible of the lot and she rescued them often.

Today she entertained Katlyn with her failed attempts to help her sister who had wound up in a marriage to a good man, but could not see it for pining for her baby's daddy. "Only so much you can say when a person is stuck on stupid," she admitted. That subject reminded Tanya of an earlier point she'd wanted to make.

"That's the norm now. The person you'd die for doesn't even know you exist, which is why you love him so much."

"What are you talking about? Where did you get that from?" Katlyn asked.

"It's true. Think about all our unhappily married friends. Thank God Darrel and I are not the norm. But neither are you and Justin," Tanya added, trying to lift Katlyn out of the funk she was in.

Still half asleep, Lauren began to cry. Tanya gently pushed the stroller back and forth, successfully quieting her. "It's almost time for her feeding."

"You still breast-feeding?" Katlyn asked.

"Of course," Tanya said, lifting Lauren to her exposed breast. "So where was I?"

"Ummm, I can't remember." Not wanting to continue talking about happy marriages or lack of, Katlyn lied.

All she wanted to do was leave. "May I burp her?" Katlyn reached for Lauren.

"Auntie Kay-Kay wants to hold mommy's little angel, yes she does." Katlyn took Lauren from Tanya and held her in the air, talking to her in baby talk.

"Yook at auntie's yittle girl…"

"Doesn't she look like Darrel?" Tanya asked.

"A little. I think she looks more like you."

A broad smile came across Tanya's face. "You really think so?"

"Definitely, look at her nose and dose yittle bitty eyes, yes you do look like your mommy." Lauren was smiling and cooing back at Katlyn. Holding her made Katlyn feel sad; that desire to be a mother surfaced. She wanted a baby, but not now. Not if what she suspected about Justin was true.

Tanya, observing Lauren's facial expression, knew she was in the middle of or done doing her business. Katlyn could smell her and got over the mommy moment real quick.

"Here, I think she needs her diaper changed." Katlyn, holding her breath, passed her back to Tanya.

"Oh, so now we're done playing auntie?" Tanya laughed as she reached for a diaper. On the short walk back to the table after changing Lauren, she remembered her train of thought and picked up where she left off.

"Anyway, as I was saying, there are so many more people who went into marriage with the wrong conception of what it really is."

"What do you mean by that?" Katlyn asked, not really wanting to know.

"Marriage is not about money and it is not all sex and passion. Women don't marry the man they love. They marry for security and stability, and a good lay." Katlyn listened intently.

"If you marry for the sex, that fades and you look for that feeling elsewhere." As Tanya continued all Katlyn heard was "blah, blah, blah." Her thoughts shifted to Justin. Had he married her because the sex was good, or did he really love her?

Tanya, unaware Katlyn had tuned her out, continued.

"Trust me. I know what I'm talking about. Now that I'm a stay-at-home mom, everyone calls and dumps their drama on me. Trust me, no one is happily married."

"You make their marriages sound so hopeless." Katlyn sighed, reflecting on her own situation.

"I don't mean to sound that way. But the truth is I no longer see love and marriage the way I used to."

"So, I gather," Katlyn said, still wondering if Tanya was talking about her own marriage. "Now that you've brought it up, I suppose I have lived the 'fairy tale come true' life…at least I thought I had." Tears welled up in Katlyn's eyes again.

"Hey, what's still eating at you?" Tanya asked, reaching for her hand.

"Like you said, it's probably physical…the drugs."

Tanya stood up, placed Lauren on her hip and with the free side leaned in and hugged Katlyn. Letting go of her embrace to tend to fidgety Lauren, Tanya squeezed Katlyn's shoulder as she sat.

"I'm all ears if you need to talk." Based on today's conversation, wisdom told Katlyn as much as she needed to talk this over with someone. Her problem with Justin was not a topic to be discussed with Tanya. She watched Tanya juggle Lauren from leg to leg while maneuvering her fork to her mouth, avoiding Lauren's reaching little hands.

"You want me to hold her, since I'm done?" Katlyn offered, getting up to take Lauren. Hungry, Tanya gladly handed Lauren to her so she could finish eating.

"Umm-mmn, thanks! This omelet is so good," Tanya managed to say with a mouth full. Lauren began cooing and reaching for Katlyn's ear-rings, which sparkled in the sun that shone through the window. Katlyn observed Tanya, who appeared to be happy and content. She envied her for having it all: a devoted husband and a beautiful daughter. A lack of both in her life left her feeling disheartened and ready to go. Moments after Tanya took her last bite, Katlyn suggested they leave. A little tired from handling busy Lauren, Tanya happily agreed.

While waiting for the valet, Tanya hugged her girlfriend and thanked her for brunch. Katlyn leaned down and kissed Miss Lauren, who was fast asleep, and waited for Tanya to get them situated in their car before she climbed into her two-seater Benz. She blew Tanya a kiss and pulled out of the lot.

The message alert on her cell phone, which she intentionally left turned off, beeped. For safety, Katlyn pulled off the shoulder and checked her messages. Justin had called three times and Felicia had called twice. Not wanting to deal with Justin, she speed-dialed Felicia.

"Hey girl," Felicia answered lazily.

"Caller ID, what a blessing," Katlyn kidded trying to sound normal.

"You called…sounded like you were crying. Everything all right?"

"No, but I'm driving. You gonna be home later?"

"How much later," Felicia asked, not wanting to wait to find out what was bothering Katlyn.

"I'm en route to my house now. Maybe thirty minutes, that is, if Justin is gone!"

"Sure, I'll be here. But listen, my second call was to let you know I'll be there in the morning."

Katlyn gasped. She really needed to see her girlfriend.

"Great! What time should I pick you up?"

"Slow down, girlie. Terrel is picking me up."

Momentary silence.

"Terrel? What's he doing in L.A.?" Katlyn replied, annoyed.

"Business," Felicia answered.

"Are you staying with him?"

"That was my plan," Felicia answered cautiously.

"So let me get this straight. Will I see you or are you penciling me into your schedule with Terrel?"

Katlyn sounded hurt, making Felicia feel guilty. Throughout all her numerous relationships-gone-bad eras—Katlyn was there. Felicia knew her best friend needed her now, but she wanted to spend this time with Terrel.

"Tell you what. I'll spend as much time as I can with you, but I committed to this a week ago. I'm sorry…"

"Not a problem," Katlyn retorted. "I'll call you later," she managed to get out before she burst into tears. Felicia felt awful. She sat holding the phone trying to weigh what to do. In the end she compromised: she'd stay with Katlyn and still keep her agenda with Terrel.

CHAPTER 13

Say When had grown from a handful of has-been entertainers and athletes to a roster of hundreds of A-list types. African American celebrities past and present agreed to lend their time and names to raise money to benefit programs that helped to mentor and educate African American children with incarcerated parents.

Terrel had always wanted to participate, but had never found the time. His New Year's resolution was to make time. This celebrity golf tournament he was participating in was his first event.

Pebble Creek was the course everyone who was anyone dreamed of playing. Aware that the publicity surrounding this event would boost his company to another level, Terrel paid $100,000 to have his logo and name on banners that would be strategically placed along the golf route.

He sat on the ottoman and opened the overnight package he'd just received from Say When. Inside were photos of the banners, the roster, and his itinerary and airline tickets. Studying the photos from previous events, Terrel concluded his money had been well spent.

The lineup was exciting. He recognized all the names on the roster, four of which he'd played ball with. Turning his attention to the itinerary, he noticed they had him on a tight schedule, which left little time to play. He hadn't anticipated having to attend press conferences or radio and TV appearances.

"These people really got their act together," he said, looking over the scheduled events. Placing the package down, Terrel thought about the all-day, everyday pace they'd laid out for him and realized it would be difficult to spend time with Felicia.

"Fuh-lee-sha," he said, enunciating each syllable slowly, then smiled as he thought about her. He knew the real estate packet would score big. "Yeah, kind of reinforces the 'I applaud your choice to be a career woman, independent and self-sufficient idea,'" Terrel mumbled, slouching down in his overstuffed recliner. Raising the leg rest, he kicked off his house shoes and got comfortable. Felicia had potential, major potential. She intrigued him and he got off on her style.

"She'd look good on my arm, maybe as a permanent fixture." He chuckled at the thought of settling down. It was something he planned to do—one day.

Terrel replayed the day they met in his head, savoring the image of her. He liked her full lips and button nose. And he hoped her head full of curls was not a weave. He hated them. She knew how to pull together that long-money, rich-girl look, which went well with her I-got-it–all-together attitude.

"So Miss Coleman, you buckle your seat belt, 'cause you're definitely in for a ride." He laughed as he picked up the remote and began channel surfing.

❂❂❂

Horny and ovulating, Katlyn sat staring out the window, brooding over her situation; she had everything she'd ever wanted. She and Justin were meant to be together. He was the cream in her coffee and she was the yin to his yang. Surely Justin would not risk losing all they'd worked to build.

"There would not be a Justin Kincaid if it had not been for me," she proclaimed. When Justin asked Katlyn to marry him, they'd been shacking for nearly a year. His efforts to land a record deal had stalled in the first year of their marriage. Katlyn took out a loan with her credit union to finance a studio for Justin. In order to accommodate the equipment she had to expand the luxury condo she'd purchased for them. She enclosed the sun room and deck, had it sound-proofed and *voila!*—a studio for

Justin. Once Justin had completed his demo tape, she purchased the B'Mer and the wardrobe he needed to pull off "the look."

Katlyn's $50,000-a-year salary as a flight attendant carried them until he got his big break. In the fourth year of their relationship, third year of their marriage, Justin landed a record deal. But it was not until the world heard "Who's Kissin' You?" that his stock rose.

"Surely my sacrifice and support means something to him," she mumbled.

Katlyn's ability to pen what a woman wanted to hear from Justin Kincaid made him who he was: a star. With all she had sacrificed and worked so hard to build, why would she walk away? Why turn him over to someone who would come in and benefit from her hard work and sacrifice, sweat and tears? Katlyn felt lost. How could she ever *think* of leaving him? *Besides, I really don't know if he's sleeping around*, she thought, even though her intuition told her differently.

"And if he is, so what? I'm Mrs. Kincaid and no one is going to sit on my throne, until I choose to give it up!" He *belonged* to her, "'til death do us part."

❂❂❂

Justin lay on the chaise in the bedroom watching BET. It was *106 and Park* and he wanted to see what position "Who's Kissin' You?" had landed in. The ballad was number three with a bullet on the Billboard Music Charts and #10 internationally. It had wound up in the fifth position on the countdown.

"Next week it'll be number one," Justin said confidently. As he lay there watching the other videos, he thought about his dilemma. His mind drifted to Nikki, naked. He loved everything about her body. The smell, her copper tan, the taste and most of all the way it felt. He had tried to convince himself she was merely a repeat booty call but deep down he knew he was fooling no one but himself.

European, Nikki had always dated brothers. The one she had married was a drug-crazed actor who, in a rage one night, put her face through a wall. Her wealthy family had paid for a quiet divorce and her new look.

Joel Steinberg, "The only one to choose when you are in need of a new you," had re-created her. She had custom-ordered her face, teeth, breasts, waist-line, butt and hips. Her fabulous legs were hereditary, as was the long healthy mane. The makeover was so perfectly crafted, only she and the sum she paid the doctor for her privacy would ever know.

❀❀❀

Katlyn continued to explain to herself why she should ignore what she knew. Try as she might, she could not ignore it. Frustrated and tired of it all, she called Asa, her personal version of the tabloids.

"Your dime," the ultra-hip, ultra-fly gossip queen said, answering on the first ring.

"What's up, girl?" Katlyn responded in kind.

"Katlyn? Katlyn Kincaid? Uh-oh! Let me move; I know lightning's get-tin' ready to strike." Asa's sassiness always made Katlyn laugh.

"How are you, missy?"

"In shock. Let me do the math. It's been about a good year since I've heard from you, right?"

"Not that long, but close," Katlyn reluctantly admitted. "You okay?"

"Blessed, highly favored and seasoned with grace."

Katlyn was caught off guard. She'd never known Asa to be religious.

"Oh-hh-kay, I'll bite. Where is this coming from?" Katlyn asked, poking fun at Asa's spiritual response.

"You late and lost, I see," Asa burst into laughter. Katlyn didn't. "I have been committed to serving God *and* happier than I've ever been in my life, for the past year. Does that tell you something?" Asa asked sarcastically.

"Yep, I need to do a better job of staying in touch."

"You got it, Ms. Forget Where You Come From, now that you've moved on up to the East Side with George Jefferson and Wheezie." They both laughed.

"So, tell me about this serving God thing and being happier than you've ever been."

"Well, remember when I was pregnant. I was at my lowest point, no baby daddy in sight and about to lose my job. I could not fix my circumstances. Then someone told me about God. He sounded like a sure thing, so I bet on Him. And can I just tell you, it has truly paid off." Katlyn was intrigued and wanted to know more.

"Oh, so now you go around totin' a Bible and tellin' all of us sinners we're going straight to hell?"

"Not exactly. I tell you about the goodness of Jesus Christ and how He died for your sins and all you have to do is receive Him as your Lord and Savior. The rest is on you. So, girlfriend tag, you're it! Any questions?"

Katlyn was dumbfounded. There was no way something that simple could make such a drastic change in Asa. Katlyn was no stranger to religion, but she felt a need to know more about Asa's Jesus experience that seemed to make her so happy. Asa's phone beeped and she put Katlyn on hold.

"Listen, girl, I need to take this call. Can you call me back?" Asa asked hurriedly.

"Sure, but wait a minute. Remember your friend in the music industry? Is he the same guy who wrote those soft drink jingles?"

"Who, Terry? Lives in Alpharetta?"

"Yeah, that's him. Listen, will you see what he'll tell you about a good friend of his named Terrel?"

"Well, uh yeah, but you need to know I don't do that gossip thing anymore. I'll get the facts: age, single or married, profession, baby mama drama." They both laughed and agreed to talk the next day before hanging up.

Katlyn lay in the dark, thankful for the stillness in the room. The change in party-girl Asa was mind-blowing. In her day no man, especially not your man, was safe from her claws. She knew everyone and she was extremely connected. She lived the single life and loved it. As long as you were on her "in" list, she loved you and you loved her. But get on her "out" list? You'd be better off dealing with a mother eagle protecting her nest. And gossip! Mrs. Clinton would have known about the intern long before the press if she'd been on Asa's "in" list.

Jesus had to be something else to pull off a transformation like that. Suffice it to say, Katlyn thought this might be the cure she needed for what was ailing Justin.

Asa's review of Terrel left Katlyn with mixed emotions. The upside—he was safe, not married, no babies and no axe murderer skeletons. The downside—he wasn't the marrying kind. To his credit Asa didn't label him an outright dog, but he did have difficulty remembering which dog-house he called home.

Katlyn was sorry she'd gotten involved in her girlfriend's business. Now she was faced with the dilemma of whether she should warn Felicia, who was pretending to be just casually interested; or whether she should let it run its course. She knew Felicia really did want to be married and have kids. And if she was reading all the signs correctly, in her mind Terrel was the one.

Knee-deep in thought, Katlyn did not pay attention to the phone or the fact that Justin answered it on the first ring.

I'm going to be straight up with Felicia, tell her I learned this info from a conversation with Asa, Katlyn decided, having already made the choice to omit one pertinent detail: that she asked Asa to dig into this man's background.

As she picked up the phone in the kitchen to call Felicia, she heard Justin and a woman talking. Bile rose to her throat and her legs felt like noodles. Katlyn leaned against the refrigerator, trying to grasp what was happening. She broke out in a nervous sweat and her heart beat wildly as she covered the mouthpiece to shield her rapid breathing. She had never listened to any of Justin's telephone conversations. What a breach of trust but then, he'd already broken that contract.

"Hey, sorry to call you there, but I didn't hear from you yesterday," the female voice said.

"It's cool. I got tied up and forgot to get back with you."

*Oh no, his woman is calling my home. The nerve...*Katlyn's mind was racing.

The female caller continued, "I need to know where we stand. What have you decided to do about our situation?"

What situation? Katlyn nearly shouted.

Justin told her he had given it some thought and truthfully he felt it was best they part company. No response from the female caller made Katlyn feel sick. Her husband was letting this hussy go and even though she should feel a sense of relief, she did not. She was sickened to finally know he was out there and she wanted to know with whom before he cut if off.

"Really, I'd hoped you would have a change of heart. This isn't at all what I expected." Katlyn surmised whoever she was, she sounded remorseful and disappointed.

"Well, Lynn, you knew the rules," he said coldly.

The rules; this S.O.B. has rules the ho has to follow? Well, rule number one, never call my house 'cause my wife might answer she obviously forgot! Katlyn was fuming while trying her best to remain silent.

"Justin, listen—it was a mistake. I'd hung out the night before and overslept. Please give me another chance," Lynn begged.

"Sorry, Lynn. You put me in a bad position when you no-showed. I lost time and money searching for someone to replace you. I'm already behind on the project."

Katlyn's head began to spin. She felt dizzy and worked her way to a chair. This was a business call, regarding one of his backup singers. She felt like a complete idiot for losing it! Maybe this was all in her head; maybe she was wrong to be suspicious of Justin. Maybe, just maybe he really *was* working long hours trying to finish his project. The only thing Katlyn knew for sure was something had to give.

Shortly after Justin hung up the phone, she returned the handset to the mount in the kitchen and stepped onto the balcony to regroup.

What am I doing? This is out of control, no, I'm out of control. The reality of what she'd done frightened her. Ms. Perfect, who is always in control, would never stoop so low. Feelings of guilt, helplessness and vulnerability consumed her.

Justin looked up from the refrigerator and saw Katlyn on the balcony. He poured himself a glass of orange juice and joined her.

"Hey, whatcha doin' out here? You all right?" he asked, taking in the view.

"Yeah, why?" she asked barely above a whisper.

"Well, since I didn't get in from the studio until a couple hours ago, I'd hoped you'd handle the phone."

Embarrassed by what she'd done, Katlyn avoided looking at Justin. She didn't know if she was busted, and she knew her face would give her away.

"The phone? What are you talking about?" Hoping he was not baiting her, she played dumb.

"You didn't hear the phone ring?"

Katlyn waited to answer, trying to figure out if this was a trick question.

"Baby, you hear me?" Justin tapped her on the shoulder to get her attention. Katlyn jumped and looked at him. "What's wrong with you? You feeling okay?"

"Um, no, I'm not. I was in the kitchen about to fix me some breakfast and I began to feel faint. Dizzy—you know, and then I made my way out here for some fresh air and that's probably why I didn't hear the phone. I'm sorry," she said, fighting back tears.

"Hey, it ain't that serious. I got some z's and you know me, I can sleep anywhere. Forget about it, okay?" Justin reached out and pulled her close to him. This was not the Katlyn he once knew. He was worried, maybe something was wrong with her physically.

"Babe, listen, you haven't been yourself lately. Why don't you make an appointment to see your doctor and make sure things are fine?"

"Yeah, Tanya said the same thing. Maybe I am out of it. She thought it might be the fertility drugs!"

"I thought you were no longer on them," Justin said, puzzled.

"I'm not and she thinks that's the problem: hormones going in every direction."

Justin stared at her. She looked tired. He knew she was not resting at night. How could she? The chaise was good for lounging, not sleeping all night. He wanted to reassure her he would not leave her, not even for Nikki, but he knew to leave the dead buried.

"Go on back to bed," Katlyn told Justin, faking a smile.

"Okay, but promise me you'll call your doctor."

"Sure Justin—today."

He went back upstairs to bed, leaving Katlyn to deal with her guilt.

Katlyn felt off center and slowly walked back into the kitchen. Locating

Dr. Surulli's number and called for an appointment. The earliest opening was Friday; today being Monday, she had a few more days to wait to have a doctor tell her what she already knew, that nothing was physically wrong with her.

Not wanting to be alone and still feeling light-headed she went upstairs and lay next to Justin on the bed. Without thinking, she blurted out what was bothering her.

"Justin, I still think you're having an affair." His back was to her and he thought about pretending to be asleep. But, no better time than the present to address this issue and bury the dead—again. He turned over and looked in her eyes.

"You are way off base. Listen to me, I'm here; when I'm not, I'm at the studio. What more can I say to convince you you're wrong?"

Katlyn began to cry. "I don't know. I'm just feeling so lost," she said, wiping her tears.

"This is it, crunch time, baby. This new project comes on the heels of our biggest wave. 'Who's Kissin' You?' is going to be hard to top! I gotta put in the hours and stay focused," he explained, apologetically.

"I understand that, Justin. But it doesn't make what I'm feeling go away."

"So what is it you're feeling?"

"Distance. Justin, we're drifting apart!" Katlyn sat up because her nose was beginning to feel congested. She grabbed a tissue, blew it and gently wiped her eyes.

Justin hated to see her cry. He felt lousy and was sorry he didn't fake slumber. He sat up and pulled her close.

"I'm sorry, baby. I know I haven't spent much time with you. I'll do better. This will be over soon and we'll go away on a much-needed vacation—just you and me. Deal?" He kissed her pixie nose and smiled, then blew his morning breath in her face. Katlyn pulled away laughing and fell back on the mattress.

"Eww, Justin," she squealed. "That's nasty!"

Justin grabbed her and pulled her under the covers; holding the covers in place he farted and held Katlyn in his arms so she couldn't break free.

Katlyn laughed, struggling to free herself. Justin grabbed her again and wrestled her back under the covers. In their folly he landed on top of her. Katlyn could feel his hardness and she desperately needed him to make love to her. Fulfilling her wish: they made love passionately, like they used to.

This time Justin's thoughts didn't drift to Nikki and neither did Katlyn's. Justin fell asleep after they were done. Katlyn, feeling much better, got up to work. She was behind on her jewelry orders and had not picked up her book manuscript in weeks. As she entered the office she turned on her favorite radio station. It was 2:30 a.m.

Not long after organizing her paperwork, she was disturbed by a loud, vibrating sound. Stopping what she was doing to locate what it was, her attention was drawn to Justin's cell phone hopping around on the windowsill was like an insect. She tried to ignore it, but it continued to hop forcing her to get up to turn it off. The first button she pushed did not work so she studied it some more. Pushing the small button on the right at the top didn't stop it, either. However, when the next button was pushed, the hopping stopped and revealed his message.

"I'm wet and waiting, where are you?"

Katlyn didn't know how to make the message appear on the screen again. In desperation she began to push all the buttons. Similar messages dated weeks and days prior appeared one after the other. Completely shaken by what she was reading, Katlyn fell to her knees and threw up. Vomit splattered everywhere; on his phone, on her, the walls and all over the carpet. She used her top to clean his phone and placed it back on the windowsill. Just as she did, Justin appeared in the doorway.

"Are you okay?" Justin rushed to her side. Katlyn did not answer or look up. She sat there, shaking. Justin reached down, put her arm around his neck and lifted her to her feet. Then he picked her up and carried her to the bathroom and gently sat her on the commode. Katlyn was still unresponsive, so he ran cold water on her facecloth and wiped her face. After removing everything from her face and hands, he ran the shower, undressed her and stepped in the shower with her to make sure she didn't collapse.

The water was warm and felt good against her skin. Katlyn slowly reached for the soap and began to rub her body with the bar. Excited to see life in her, Justin took it from her and gently washed her back. Giving it back to her he grabbed the shampoo and poured a small amount in his hand. Gently he massaged the shampoo into her hair working it into a lather. An hour later, clean and exhausted, Katlyn exited the shower, wrapped a towel around herself and went to bed; never uttering a word.

Justin was at a loss as to what to do next. He felt he needed to go to bed with her just in case but the vomit smell was permeating through the house. Cleaning the house won out. He got a mop, a bucket of water, rubber gloves and disinfectant and went to work in the office and then the bathroom. It had been a long time since he had been so attentive to his wife and even longer since he had paid any attention to their beautiful home. He felt good; pleased he was there for her and surprised he could still respond to her like he did.

When Justin awoke the next morning, Katlyn was not at his side. He found her in the office again with the radio on, humming to herself and moving things from one pile and then placing them back on the original pile without realizing what she was doing. This was a definite indication his wife was in trouble and he knew why. It was his fault and he needed to stop what he was doing, but he could not. In way too deep, he didn't know how to help her because he didn't know how to help himself. Seeing her like this was too much for him. He needed some air, a change of scenery. Justin waved his arms to get her attention but she did not notice him. "Katlyn," he shouted.

She jumped and turned toward him. "How long have you been standing there?"

"Long enough to notice you rearrange that pile three times."

She looked at him as if he were an alien. "I didn't do that," she answered matter-of-factly.

"Maybe you didn't know you did," he said pointedly. "I've got to get going. I'll try to be back for dinner."

Katlyn cut him off, knowing he was blowing smoke up her butt. "Call me later," she mumbled, turning her back to him.

"Okay. See you later," he said nervously, wondering what she really thought. No sooner had his Benz pulled out of the garage and around the corner, than he reached for his phone to call Nikki. He couldn't find it. Pulling over he searched the entire car, then stopped to reflect on the last time he'd used it. Panic slapped him upside his head when he remembered he left it in the office. The same office Katlyn was now sitting in and the same office she threw up in last night. He wondered if that had anything to do with her getting sick.

"Nawww! Katlyn would never check my phone," he murmured confidently. He turned his car around and pulled up to the front door. Katlyn was standing at the door with his phone. She handed it to him and shut the door without saying a word. Suddenly he wasn't so sure she wouldn't check his phone. He looked at it as he walked to his car. It was off, but that was because the battery had no charge. Relieved, he felt certain his wife didn't check his phone, even if she wanted to, because it was dead.

Once again he dialed Nikki. He got her answering machine. They had spoken over the last couple days, but he hadn't seen her. She had been angry because he was still sleeping with Katlyn (something he was stupid enough to admit to) and he was mad at her for demanding he make a choice between the two. When he didn't choose in a timely manner, Nikki decided to expedite things, thus the 3 a.m. phone call. She hoped it disturbed any lovemaking that was transpiring and caused problems for Justin in the process.

"Nikki, I miss you, baby. I need to see you. Call me as soon as you get this." He hung up and dialed again, this time paging her with 9-1-1.

Nikki, home the entire time Justin was frantically trying to reach her, had received all his pages and messages. She reclined on her bed, smiling. "So, Mr. Kincaid. You outta jail and want to see Mommy, huh! I think not! I'll teach you to put me on the back burner." Nikki hadn't answered her phone, pages or the door all day.

Unable to get with Nikki and not wanting to go home, Justin reluctantly went to the studio. It took a while to focus, but he finally did and managed to get another mix completed. Pleased with himself, he wanted to celebrate. He dialed Nikki again.

Checking caller ID, she smiled and answered, pretending to be winded. "Hello!"

"Nik, where you been?"

"I just got back in town," she lied.

"What do you mean? Where you been?"

"Anyway, I was feelin' lonely and needed some company."

Justin knew he had no right to be jealous, but he was.

"What, you and the Fly Guy went somewhere?"

"Hold up, boyfriend! Do you hear me asking what you and the Mrs. been doing in the days you've been noticeably absent?"

The last thing he wanted to do was make her angry. "Sorry, baby, it's just that I missed you and…"

"Whose fault is that?" Nikki asked in a nice nasty tone.

"Mine, and I am sorry. Let me make it up to you, pleezz, baby."

Nikki knew what he wanted; she wanted the same. But things were going to be different now. Justin was whipped, and Nikki loved the power this gave her. "I don't play second to no one!" Soon Justin was going to be forced to make the decision he had put off making; Nikki would see to that.

Nikki's new condo was immaculate. Her housekeeper had just left. She lit some candles and then ran a bath, adding her new scent, D&G. Soft music wafted through the dimly lit split-level condo. She looked through her dresser and found her most revealing negligee and laid it on her bed. Next she unlocked the entry from her garage, left a provocative note for Justin to join her upstairs and settled into the tub with two glasses of wine—hers and his.

Justin felt relaxed the moment he parked his car in Nikki's garage. The note on the door gave him an immediate erection. Her home smelled feminine and sensual. Anticipating the moment, he unbuttoned his shirt while walking up the stairs to the bedroom. By the time he reached the bed, he had stripped down to his underwear. The sight of her negligee on the bed made his need to climax more urgent.

Nikki looked up and smiled as he stood in her doorway, naked and hard.

"Is that for me?" she whispered.

"So is this," he said, pulling a rose from behind his back.

She motioned for him to come closer. Candlelight made her features more pronounced; she was beautiful and sexy. Her hair was pinned on top of her head; curly ringlets framed her tanned face. Sweat beads rolled down her face, but her makeup was still in place. Justin walked over and stood in front of her sunken Jacuzzi tub. Nikki handed him a glass of wine and then slowly poured some of hers on his manhood that was standing at attention. It was cold, but he didn't lose his focus. Her warm tongue removed any wine that remained, while Justin moaned and enjoyed the sensation.

"Nikki, don't tease me. I need to feel you," he begged.

"Not yet," she said, sounding like a well-rehearsed version of Marilyn Monroe. She worked him professionally until he couldn't stand it. Shaking all over, he shot his load in her mouth, balancing himself against the tub. Opening his eyes, he mouthed, "I love you." Nikki motioned for him to join her in the tub. He did and made love to her doggy style.

Waterlogged, they got out the tub and retreated to her bed. Nikki slowly spread fragranced body lotion over her frame, another turn-on for Justin.

"Let me do that," he said, reaching for the bottle of lotion. Nikki leaned back on her elbows and spread her legs. "Baby, I missed you," he moaned in her ear between kisses. She threw her head back as Justin softly kissed her neck, and then arched her back as he moved down her chest to her cleavage.

"Nikki, I love you." She moaned and slowly rotated her hips, receiving all of him.

"I love you, too, so much so much," she purred, digging her nails into his back and wrapping her legs around him. They enjoyed each other for hours before falling asleep. Justin woke first and lay there watching her.

"I have to have you in my life. I can't go on like this," he whispered. Nikki heard him and opened her eyes, shocked at what he was saying.

"Justin, you have a wife."

"I know; I'm working on changing that."

Nikki felt a rush. What she heard was music to her ears. The thought of becoming Mrs. Justin Kincaid excited her. "How do you plan to do that?"

"I'll figure it out; just hang in there with me, baby."

Nikki sat on top of Justin and looked at him. He reached up and squeezed her breasts, then moved his hands along the outline of her body.

"Come with me on my next three concert dates."

"Oh, Justin I'd love to but…"

"Shhhh." He placed a finger on her lips. "Let me worry about the details."

Raising her body, she slowly lowered herself onto his hardness.

"Ahhhh, baby," Justin murmured.

"You want me?" Nikki cooed.

"Always."

As she rotated her hips and thrust her pelvis in a motion that made him take short breaths, she kissed him gently. Justin rolled her over and they locked in an embrace as they moved faster and faster. Climaxing, Justin let out a groan and held her butt in place. They were both drenched in sweat. Lying on his back, Justin hoisted Nikki onto his stomach.

"I've never known anyone like you," she sighed.

"You're incredible," he managed to say in between breaths.

"No, you," Nikki said, tickling him. He laughed and pushed her off him.

"Want to get something to eat?" Justin asked.

"Sure, I can order pizza."

"No, baby, get dressed. Let's go out."

Nikki knew he was not thinking straight, but she was not about to remind him of his responsibilities. Although she wished he would, he seldom spent time with her in public, on his home turf. She wasn't exactly sure when Justin began to consume all her thoughts, or when she began to fantasize about how wonderful it might be to spend the rest of her life with him.

She usually dumped her married lovers after a few months of sex and tons of trinkets because they always wanted to leave their wives for her. "No commitment" was the ground rule she laid and they agreed to. When they broke that rule, she left. But not this time; Nikki wanted Justin to leave his wife. She realized she was in love with him.

Not wasting one moment of this opportunity, Nikki got as gorgeous as possible, making sure to wear something sexy. She looked so beautiful, Justin thought about going back to bed, but the hunger pains were growing more and more intense.

The meal was exceptional as was the company. During dessert, Justin looked at his watch.

"Aw-www, do you have to go?" Nikki whined.

"No, but I should make a phone call." To his surprise and delight, he got the answering machine. He left a lame excuse and retreated to the restroom. Before entering, he caught a glimpse of Nikki, seated at their table. She was so sexy. He knew every man envied him and wanted her. Looking at her he knew he could no longer live without her.

This was it; what Chuck meant. He knew he wanted her, for the rest of his life.

Although he loved Katlyn, he loved Nikki more, in an entirely different way. Sure, he had the safety of Katlyn's undying love, but the entire life he was living was a fake. One big lie! He had done it all for the wrong reason: security. The wife, the lucrative career, the fabulous house and cars and the happily ever after, was all BS. Nikki was what he had always wanted, of that he was now certain.

CHAPTER 14

The throng of media and fans was massive. Hollywood was well represented; actors, directors and wannabes all present and accounted for. The support for this year's Say When Celebrity Golf Outing was overwhelming.

Terrel knew it would be impossible for Felicia to find him. He decided to call her on her cell phone. "Hey, where are you?"

"Keep your shirt on. I'm pulling up now."

"Don't get me wrong, I'm anxious to be graced by your presence, but I'm calling out of concern."

"What's wrong?" she asked, alarmed.

"Chill—everything is fine. It's just that this place is packed. I don't know that you'll readily find me."

"What do you suggest?"

"Uh, let's see, what do you have on?"

"Pale blue T-shirt and matching capris." She'd learned in one of their phone conversations blue was his favorite color. Terrel smiled.

"Blue, huh? You're good, girl. I'll look for you."

"I'm coming in the main entrance now."

Terrel found this hide-and-go-seek moment exciting, so he continued to talk to her on the phone. Spotting her, he walked up behind her. "So glad you could join me," he whispered in her ear.

Felicia smiled and turned around. Terrel leaned over again and pecked her on the button nose he was fond of.

"Terrel, you little bugger," she said, poking him in his rock-hard abs. "Nice six-pack," she noted.

"Like that, huh?" Terrel chuckled and winked at her. "You look great. How was your trip?"

"Hectic. We were two hours late and I had to drive like a bat to get here."

"But here you are and I'm glad," he said, taking her hand in his.

"Back at cha," she said, relaxing her hand in his grip.

The press had not yet recognized Terrel, which put him at ease. He'd never welcomed media day when he was a pro—nothing had changed. He and Felicia stood by the bar making small talk. One of his former teammates recognized him from across the room and rushed over to greet him.

"Terrel, Terrel Sanders? Aw man, whuzzup?"

Terrel immediately recognized Jeff, they embraced and let out a loud yelping sound. People in the room turned and stared: they ignored them.

"Man, where you been, whatcha doin'?" Jeff asked all in the same breath.

Felicia noticed the Trinket hanging on his side and figured she was his trophy for the day. Him sporting an obvious diamond wedding band and her finger bare, helped to confirm her suspicions. The Trinket tried to smile and look less like a fish out of water, but she didn't belong and it showed. Felicia decided it was not her turn to baby-sit and left well enough alone.

Perusing the room, Felicia caught a scene that caused her alarm. She turned and faced the direction of the crime to make sure she was seeing what she thought she was seeing. Most of the men in the room had begun to watch the bombshell who had just entered the room. She was drop-dead gorgeous, exotic and erotic—all in one package. But, that wasn't what caught her eye. It was the body she was attached to that caused Felicia concern—Justin Kincaid.

"Hey baby, let me introduce you to an old buddy of mine." Terrel pulled her in his direction, interrupting her spying. "Meet Jeff, we played ball together, but more important we's be frat brothers." Again they made the loud yelping sound and burst into laughter. Felicia briefly peered over her shoulder, trying to keep an eye on Justin. He and the femme fatale were gone.

"Felicia, is it?" Jeff asked, extending his hand.

"That's me; nice to meet you, Jeff," she responded, shaking his hand. Turning to the date who could easily be his daughter, she said hello as well.

"Oh yeah, sorry. Terrel, Felicia, meet Natalie." Without extending her hand Natalie smiled and said hello. The moment was awkward and before anyone could speak cameras began to flash.

"Terrel, Jeff...over here," the press shouted.

Felicia grabbed Natalie by the arm and pulled her out of the mob. They stood by the bar watching the reporters shout questions at their dates.

"Wow, this is kind of exciting, huh?" Natalie exclaimed, looking like a kid on her first trip to Disneyland.

All air, Felicia thought. She'd been there, done that and knew who was in way deep—Natalie was, Jeff wasn't.

The golf tournament was about to begin. Once again Felicia looked around the room, hoping to get another glimpse of Justin and the femme fatale. No luck.

Terrel worked his way through the crowd to Felicia's side. Natalie stood off in a corner, hoping Jeff would come rescue her.

"Listen, my tee time is up and I need to run. Looks like I'm here for the duration," Terrel explained, hoping she understood. Felicia stared at him as if he was invisible. She was angry because she thought he'd spend some of the day with her, but she played it off.

"So, you think you'll be done, say in a couple hours?" Terrel found her question humorous; it showed how little she knew about the game of golf.

"No baby, more like eight or nine tonight. Wanna meet me for dinner?"

"Eight or nine tonight," she repeated. "We'll see," she answered dryly, attempting to stay composed.

"Okay, cool, let me know." Terrel kissed her forehead and hurried off. Most of the women lingered in the clubhouse; the femme fatale was one of them. Felicia stood off in the distance with her sunglasses on, hoping to catch Justin with her. He never reappeared. After an hour of watching her and no Justin, Felicia decided to leave.

Spending the day with Katlyn in her crazed state of mind was not something she was looking forward to. Felicia returned to her rental car and dialed Katlyn's number. She got the machine and started not to leave a message, but opted to say hi.

"Hey girl, I'm here. Call me when—"

"Felicia, where are you?" Katlyn screamed, full of joy.

"You screening your calls?"

"Yep! You nearby?"

"I'm en route," Felicia lied, looking at her watch.

"Nuh-uhh! Say it ain't so!" Katlyn shouted. Having someone so excited to hear from her made Felicia smile.

"My flight should be landing in about an hour. Pick me up curbside, okay?"

"See you then. Are you on USAir?"

"Of course, dah-ling," Felicia said, feigning a European accent. They laughed and hung up.

Katlyn ran around the house like a woman who'd just heard from a new lover. She carefully chose her outfit and fussed over her hair and makeup incessantly.

En route to the airport, Katlyn tried to organize the numerous thoughts she had dancing around in her head. One thing she decided was not to tell Felicia what she'd learned about Terrel. After careful consideration of her girlfriend's feelings, she felt it would all work itself out. Besides, she had a full plate and needed to tend to that.

Non-rev'ing—airline lingo for employees who fly free—had its down side. Today was one of them. The three scheduled flights to Los Angeles were overbooked and Felicia would not be making the trip to see Katlyn after all. She tried to reach her at home; no answer and no machine. Katlyn's cell phone kept telling her "the cellular customer you've called is either away from the phone"—in other words, she couldn't be reached.

Frustrated, Felicia got back in the rental, paid the parking fee and hopped on the Interstate headed to nowhere in particular. She noticed an outlet mall twenty minutes from the golf course and decided to kill some time there. A movie she'd wanted to see was playing in the theater across from the outlet, so she decided to go there instead. After using the restroom, she tried both Katlyn's numbers again. This time she left her a message on her home phone.

That done, she bought a box of popcorn and a drink, turned her cell phone off and settled into a seat. She and four other people paid to see a dud. Now highly frustrated and extremely bored, she decided to window shop. Before exiting the theater, she turned on her phone; there was one message.

"Yo babe, Terrel here, call me."

"Call him? He should be knee-deep in grass and golf balls by now!" She dialed his cell. "Hey Terrel, it's Felicia. What's wrong?"

"Rain delay, can you believe it?"

"Rain? I'm only twenty minutes from you and I don't see…" The moment she found her car, the rain began to fall. "I take that back, I'm in the rain."

Terrel laughed. "So where are you?"

"An outlet mall."

"You hungry, want to blow this place?"

"Don't you have to stick around?" she asked, genuinely concerned.

"Says who?"

"All righty, then, I'm on my way."

Terrel arrived at the golf tournament in a limousine, so he drove them to a restaurant on the beach in the Lincoln Felicia had rented. "You bring some flip-flops?"

"For what?" Felicia asked.

"The beach, baby. The B-E-A-C-H." Terrel smiled, knowing there was no way she forgot about *the beach*. They shared their first kiss on the beach in Georgia and it was some kiss. Neither forgot and both were looking forward to another.

The Dunes was crowded, a good sign as restaurants go. Several of the celebrities from the tournament were there. The wait for a table was forty-five minutes, just enough time to have a drink and unwind. The maitre d' recognized Terrel.

"Mr. Sanders, glad to see you again, sir. Table for two?"

"Yeah, Vic."

"Just a short wait, sir, I'll come and get you." He motioned them toward the bar area.

Terrel was accustomed to the attention he garnered. Folks stared; some knew him and called him by name, others thought they knew him and called him by the wrong name. Women smiled and sat up straight, ensuring their breasts were pointing north instead of south. Thanks to Katlyn, Felicia had been exposed to this environment and knew how to handle herself.

Dinner was more than she had hoped for. The food was excellent; the service, supreme. Terrel knew from previous dates that Felicia would enjoy the ambiance and the meal.

"So my lady, shall we walk?" Terrel guided her by her hand as if she were royalty being led to the dance floor. Felicia laughed, curtsied and followed his lead. He guided her to a bench, removed his shoes and helped her remove hers. Placing the shoes in one hand, he placed her hand on his free arm and headed toward the water.

Two minutes into the sand and wonderful ambiance, the sky opened up. Hail the size of golf balls fell to the ground. Terrel grabbed Felicia by the hand and then dashed back for the safety of the Dunes. People were running from every direction to the safe haven of the only restaurant on the strip.

"Wait here, I'll go get the car."

"Gladly," Felicia said, winded and trying to salvage what curls were left in her hair.

Terrel returned to get her in the two-door Lincoln. With the adverse weather conditions, the only thing left to do was go to his place. Felicia doubted she'd be able to drive to Los Angeles, so she assumed she'd stay with Terrel. In his mind, her staying with him was never a question.

No stranger to northern California, Terrel was well prepared for this rendezvous with Felicia. He'd contacted a business associate and negotiated a night or two in a luxury condo the man owned near the golf course with access to the beach and an ocean view. The entrance was plush and impressive.

"There's no place like home away from home," Terrel said, walking into the front door. Felicia followed and was instantly captivated by the view of the ocean from the living room window.

"Like it?" Terrel asked, already certain the answer was yes.

"Whoa! Like it? I love it. Is this place yours?"

"Only when I want it to be," he said honestly.

"And that means?" Felicia probed, not letting go of her need to know more about this man.

"Time-share," Terrel answered, taking her by the hand and leading her to a balcony on the opposite side of the condo. Lounge furniture and a chimney decorated the area.

Somewhat tired, Felicia rested on the edge of the chaise closest to the entry and yawned.

"Not allowed," Terrel kidded.

"Oh, I'm fine. Time difference and jetlag kicking in; it's been a long day and—". Her phone rang; it was Katlyn. "It's Katlyn, mind if I take this call?"

"Naw baby, I'll get us some drinks." Terrel left her alone on the balcony and shut the sliding glass door behind him, allowing her privacy.

"Hello."

"What happened to you?" Katlyn said with an attitude.

"Didn't you get my message?"

"Yeah, I got it. I still hoped you'd drive in and spend the night with me."

"Katlyn, that was my intention, but the weather is really bad here: hail the size of golf balls." She could hear Katlyn crying. "I can tell you're upset, I'm sorry."

"I'm tired, call me tomorrow, okay?" Katlyn hung up, not waiting for Felicia to answer.

Felicia sat staring at the ocean. She flipped her phone closed and turned it off. Now that Katlyn had successfully ruined her wonderful mood, she could do without any additional bad news.

Terrel watched from the kitchen. He could tell her conversation with Katlyn did not go well. As he opened the balcony door, Felicia turned to look at him.

"Come here." She stepped in the doorway and he sat her in a side chair.

Reaching down, he removed her shoes and massaged her feet. Moved by this timely gesture, she sat back and sighed.

"This is just what the doctor ordered."

"How'd it go with your friend?" he asked concerned, hoping not to be perceived as dippin'. Although he knew Katlyn, Felicia did not often share their business with him.

"She's upset. We'd planned to get together tonight."

"Oh, I didn't know that," he said, surprised, ego a little bruised.

"Yeah, my plans were to spend the day with you and drive to L.A. and spend the night with her. She's really disappointed."

"Let me grasp what I'm hearing. So, your being here with me tonight is by default? Man, you know how to beat up on a guy's ego," he joked.

"Wait, see it's not like that, I..." Unable to explain, she began to laugh. Terrel kept squeezing and rubbing her feet. Her laugh was cute and contagious. It pleased him to see her laugh and forget about what had just happened with Katlyn.

"Ready for your tour?" He stopped massaging and stood up, as if she'd requested to see the place.

"Sure."

"Follow me, madame." He bowed and pointed to the kitchen. It was huge, with a walk-in pantry, marble counter-tops and matching floor. As Felicia admired the unusual design of the island, Terrel hoisted her up onto it, placing her eye to eye with him.

"Wow, how tall are you?"

"Six-one... I like you in this position," he said, moving her legs apart and leaning into her. Felicia chose to remain silent, savoring the feel of his arms around her. She raised her arms, which he had pinned to her side, and folded them around his neck. Then she laid her head on his, which had found its home on her chest. Terrel listened to her heartbeat as she gently rubbed the top of his clean-shaven head.

"Careful, you're entering dangerous territory," he teased. Felicia giggled; she knew all men enjoyed having their head massaged, both of them.

Terrel looked up, stared in her eyes and kissed her deeply, with his eyes open; a major turn-on for both of them. He carefully chose what to touch, avoiding all her sensual spots. She had a soft, shapely body and he loved the way she smelled. Working his way to her head, he hesitated, afraid to go any further in case it was a weave. Felicia clutched his face with her hands and pulled him in, hoping to get even more tongue.

Her kisses were good; she was a skilled kisser and probably a skilled lover. Not thinking, he moved his hand further up and landed in a mound of soft, cottony-feeling curls; they were hers. Thankful, he kissed her harder. With things clearly getting heated between them, Terrel decided to ease up; the night was young.

Breathing hard, Felicia was thankful for the chance to regroup. Terrel helped her down and they continued the tour. There were three bedrooms, all with a fabulous view. The master bedroom was something out of a magazine: a raised bed, sunken sitting area and a Jacuzzi were tucked away in the rear of the room. The bathroom had an all-glass, octagonal shower, with a private toilet area. The living room was the most impressive; its smoked-glass ceiling revealed a beautiful sight. As Felicia looked up, so did Terrel. A shooting star went by and they both shouted, "Make a wish!"

"Can I get you something else to drink?" Terrel offered, as she sat down on the eggplant-colored ultra-suede sofa.

"Something noncarbonated would be nice."

"Juice or herbal tea?" he asked.

"Herbal tea sounds great."

"Your wish is my command." He backed out of the room, bowing over and over again, pretending to be a genie. She laughed heartily, enthralled with his sense of humor.

The smooth jazz playing in the background was relaxing. Felicia reflected on how comfortable she felt with Terrel, in his company and especially in his arms. He returned with a pot of hot water, several different teas and some snacks. Sitting down next to her, he laid everything out neatly on the coffee table and dug into the peanuts. His hand full of nuts, he turned his attention back to her.

"You havin' a good time?"

"Wonderful, you're a fabulous host," she told him. Terrel smiled.

"I think you're one heck of a female, definitely different from what's out there."

"How so?" Felicia angled her body and leaned back on the sofa, allowing her to look directly at him.

"No kids for starters. And you enjoy your independence, doing things for yourself…not lookin' for a man to take care of you. Yeah, rare…" His conversation tapered off as he got lost in his thoughts. After a second or two, he added, "I could really get into you."

"Ditto," she chimed in, as Terrel scooted closer to her. She looked at his face and tried to imagine what he looked like as a boy.

Terrel reached over and gently touched her chin, then softly rubbed the side of her face.

"You're beautiful." He kissed her on her chin, and then moved to her mouth. This kiss was an abbreviated version of the one in the kitchen; for this she was grateful. Terrel felt her tense up and decided to forego any hot and heavy romance.

"Don't worry. Your panties ain't comin' off—at least not tonight." She laughed, not because his bluntness was funny, but because he caught her off guard. She suddenly felt naked, as if he could see right through her. His ability to read her so well so soon, made her uncomfortable.

"You got my attention and I know I'm here." He pointed to her head. "Thing is I want to be here." He lowered his finger and poked the area just above her breast.

"You mean that?" she asked apprehensively.

"I choose to be here and this ain't about a booty call."

Felicia was speechless. His frankness was refreshing. She was not used to a man being so open and honest. But his cockiness frightened her.

Terrel wanted to make love to her, but knew she was wondering if that was *all* he wanted. Not wanting to play games, he decided to call it a night.

"I'm beat. I'll see you in the morning." He got up and kissed her on the forehead. Felicia, excited about the prospect of sleeping with him, looked startled and lost.

"I put your bags in the guest bedroom down the hall on the right. Fresh towels are in the linen closet in your bathroom."

"Okay, well, I guess I'll see you in the morning," she responded, disappointed.

"You need me to set a clock for you?" he asked.

"I have my own. Flight attendant—remember?" she said, making small talk, not wanting to part his company.

"What time is your flight?"

"Noon," she said. "Yours?"

"Tomorrow evening. I'm going to get in a few rounds of golf." His answer hurt. Knowing he was going to bed early to get up and hit some golf balls was a slap in the face.

"I'm definitely losing my touch," she said to herself.

Terrel stuck his head out of his room. "You talking to me, baby?"

"No, good night."

"I'll probably be gone when you get up. Sleep well." Terrel walked over to her doorway, kissed her lightly on the lips and walked away, leaving her standing there wanting more.

When the limo arrived the next morning, he slipped a note card under her door before leaving. Felicia awoke, well rested, hoping he was still there. She got up, checked her appearance in the mirror, washed her face and brushed her teeth, fixed her hair a little and tipped into the hallway. She was alone. Returning to her bedroom she noticed the note card and sat on the bed to read it.

Hey babe,

Your gracing me with your presence is just the jump-start I need to a difficult week ahead. I'll be in Georgia next week. I'd love to see you.

Felicia lay back on the bed, confused. *Was he into her or not?* He was unlike anyone she'd ever known. Because she cared for him, she was glad they had not slept together. *The anticipation had better be worth the wait,* she thought as she headed off to the kitchen. Teapot heating, she took a quick shower.

Her breakfast consisted of two slices of toast drowned in butter and a cup of herbal tea, which she enjoyed on the balcony as she basked in the morning sunrays. She thought about calling Katlyn, but decided against it until she was actually on the plane.

CHAPTER 15

Hawaii was not new to Nikki, but taking it all in with Justin Kincaid was. They checked into a five-star hotel on the ocean. Their suite had a king-size bed, sunken Jacuzzi tub and a contemporary living room attached, both with breathtaking views.

"Justin, this is so perfect," Nikki exclaimed, well pleased.

"Just like you. I only want you to have the best," Justin told her, settling down in the armchair next to his luggage. He knew he needed to call Katlyn, to let her know where he was and how to reach him. Later, he decided. Right now he wanted nothing to spoil his good mood.

"Hey Nik, I can't take you with me to the interview, but I'll be back as soon as I can. You need anything?"

"No, I'll probably kick it poolside."

"Well, if you want anything, charge it to the room, okay?"

Nikki walked over and hugged him. "Annyyy-thing?" she replied with a sly grin. "Within reason," he clarified. She laughed and kissed him passionately. Justin felt a rise in his pants and gently pushed her away.

"Come on, Nik, not now!"

Justin headed toward the door. He looked back, and felt lucky to be in Hawaii for three whole days and nights with the most perfect creature on earth. The thought of having her whenever he wanted made him hard again. She stood looking at him, knowing he was contemplating making love to her. Nikki lifted her skirt, reached under her lace thong and began to play with herself. Justin shut the door and joined her. They did a quickie, then he freshened up and left her asleep.

On the way to his first press conference, Justin called Katlyn. No answer at home, he tried her cell.

"Hey babe," he said, sounding upbeat.

"Oh hey," Katlyn replied, sounding down.

"Tried you at home, no answer."

"I left early," she said, really not interested in the conversation.

"You okay?"

"Oh yeah fine." Her line beeped. "Hold on…"

Justin waited for three minutes, then hung up. He'd call her later. Besides, he wasn't feeling her depression.

The ride to the radio station did wonders for his head. He managed to push Katlyn *and* Nikki to the back of his mind. The station was bombarded with screaming, partially clothed females, all trying to see or touch him. Once inside, he was ushered to studio A for a live, on-air chat. Nikki tuned to the station on her Walkman so she could listen to the interview poolside.

Katlyn, now upbeat after receiving a call from Felicia to pick her up at LAX, tuned her car radio to her favorite station for her morning laughs with "The Fly DJ" and his morning show crew. Just as she pulled up to the airport and parked curbside, she heard him announce the interview with Justin.

This morning they were doing a live feed from Hawaii to cover the kickoff of the second leg of Justin's tour. Katlyn was excited to hear him live, but wondered why he hadn't told her about this interview. As his wife, she could have gone with him on this trip. Justin didn't ask. She felt a twinge of pain when she thought about it, but got over it quickly, reminding herself she didn't want to be around him.

Felicia waved and Katlyn motioned for her to hurry. Winded, she threw her bag in the backseat and sat down.

"Shhh, listen!" Katlyn said excitedly.

"Listen to what?" Felicia asked.

"Listen. It's Justin."

The radio crew introduced him and made small talk for a moment.

When they played "Who's Kissin' You?" Katlyn and Felicia high-fived and pulled off. Justin kidded with The Fly DJ and his crew about his career. They teased him about white women and groupies, something Katlyn did not find funny. She thought about Justin being with other women, especially white women, and dismissed it immediately. He always told her he only wanted sistahs and she believed him.

The first ten minutes of calls went exceptionally well, as did his interview. However, after the third commercial break, with only fifteen minutes left to the one-hour interview, the bottom fell out. A dozen red roses with a card attached were delivered for Justin. He read the card, but kept what it said to himself, tucking it into his shirt pocket. By the time they were live again, in spite of Justin's pleas to not mention the roses, the female host broached the subject.

"So Justin, do tell, who are the roses from?" Justin, disgusted, ignored her. Moving in for the kill, she continued, "Ladies, what you don't know is this—during the commercial break, a dozen red roses were delivered to Mr. Kincaid. And they came with a card. If you care who sent them, call in *and* if you could care less, call in anyway. Let us hear what you have to say to this heartthrob." The lines lit up!

Justin sat there numb, thankful he'd never told Katlyn about the interview. Nikki sat poolside, pleased with herself for sending the roses, which she'd charged to his room. Katlyn, shocked by what she'd just heard, turned to look at Felicia in disbelief and nearly crashed the car before she was able to pull onto the shoulder.

Sitting roadside, the car running, Felicia turned the radio off and sat there trying to think. Katlyn was a basket case and in no shape to drive, so Felicia made her move to the passenger's seat and drove them to Katlyn's home. Once there Felicia helped Katlyn to bed and turned on the teakettle. This was a nightmare and she was at a loss about how to help her friend get through it.

"Here, some herbal tea will go a long way. Take a sip." She extended the cup of warm tea to Katlyn, who stared at the wall. Felicia set it down on the nightstand and left the room. Twenty minutes later, she checked on Katlyn. Her posture and position had not changed: she was still sitting up in bed, staring at the wall.

"Listen, I saw a note on your refrigerator. You have a doctor's appointment in two hours. Rest for a while and I'll wake you in time enough to make it."

There was no eye contact, no response, no reaction. Felicia left the door open and allowed Katlyn to be alone with her thoughts.

They both knew Katlyn did not send the roses to Justin. They also knew his refusing to say who had meant only one thing—the woman he was sleeping with had sent them.

Katlyn's worst fears, those suspicions she'd managed to downplay as a "figment of her imagination," had risen from the recesses of her mind and become a reality. Justin had now changed the standards of their life, without her permission. Plotting how she'd make him pay, Katlyn fell off to sleep and had a really bad dream. She woke in a sweat, her bed linens soaked.

Felicia appeared moments after she woke, in time enough to see her best friend falling apart. Katlyn looked frightened and lost. Sensing her fear, Felicia climbed in the bed with her and held her as she cried.

On the way to the doctor's office, Katlyn found her voice.

"Felicia, I haven't been feeling well, dizzy spells. At first I thought it was nothing, but then they started to become frequent."

"Is that why you're going to the doctor?"

"Not really. Only you and I know about the spells. This visit is because Tanya thinks my hormones are out of whack, causing me to imagine Justin was f-in' around."

"Well, you still don't know for sure he is," Felicia chimed in trying to be supportive.

"Whatever! I'm no fool."

"For now, Katlyn, let's focus on why you're having these dizzy spells. Justin is thousands of miles away and will be gone three more days. We have time to deal with his butt; let's just deal with you now, okay?" Felicia hugged her before they walked in the doctor's office.

Katlyn hadn't seen her doctor since she stopped taking the fertility pills.

That was eight months ago. Her doctor cautioned her about her physical state, making sure she understood she could get pregnant, even though their attempts over the past couple years

had been futile. She also informed Katlyn she could experience numerous physical and emotional changes.

Dr. Surulli had been Katlyn's OB-GYN for a while, so the visit with her was a routine exam: a Pap smear, a pelvic exam, bloodwork and a urine test. Katlyn and Felicia were back at the condo within two hours.

They were sitting and discussing Justin's demise when the phone rang. Katlyn checked her caller ID to make sure it was not Justin. Worse: it was Dr. Surulli's office. Katlyn was immediately on edge. They only called if something was wrong.

"Hi, Trisha," she said in an upbeat tone.

Nurse Trisha informed Katlyn the doctor needed to speak with her and placed her on hold. Feeling faint again, Katlyn sat down in the chair closest to the phone. Felicia, concerned, moved closer to Katlyn.

Dr. Surulli came on the line.

"Hello, Katlyn. I have your tests results back and congratulations are in order."

"What do you mean?"

"You're pregnant. You can't be that far along because I could not tell on the exam. But all urine and bloodwork confirm a pregnancy."

Katlyn was squeezing Felicia's hand so tight it went numb.

"Does that explain my dizziness?"

"Probably. I ran additional bloodwork and we'll know more in a couple days."

Katlyn mouthed to Felicia, "I'm pregnant." Felicia's eyes began to tear.

"Now there is another concern," she warned her.

Katlyn's heart dropped. "What concern?"

"You have an STD."

"What?! STD! Wait a minute, you mean a Sexually Transmitted Disease?"

"Yes. Chlamydia to be exact. I'm calling in a prescription for you. Be thankful we caught it so soon. I don't anticipate it causing any problems with your pregnancy, but getting treatment in the next few weeks will be important to you and the fetus."

Katlyn hung up the phone and stared at the wall. "That S.O.B. gave me Chlamydia," she said in disbelief, bursting into tears.

Felicia, having heard it all and been there before, cried with her. Felicia knew Katlyn's pain: she'd been pregnant by someone she loved, who happened to be married. She contracted Gonorrhea from him and wound up in the hospital, because he failed to tell her. She lost her baby and the ability to have one. The disease left her with severe scar tissue—sterile they called it! Her ongoing female problems led to a partial hysterectomy.

Katlyn never knew about this painful time in Felicia's life. It happened at the only point in their twenty-year friendship where they lost contact. Hurt by what she felt was abandonment on Katlyn's part, Felicia kept a stiff upper lip, grinned and bore it; then buried the whole ordeal. Watching Katlyn live it exhumed Felicia's pain; causing reflection on a very difficult time.

It's hard to think when you're hurting. When you realize your world you have lived in happily, for so long, is threatened and on the brink of falling apart, every inch of you hurts. Your mind is blank and your heart is dying. The intense pain you feel cannot be corrected with the popping of a pill, or even a good cry. You are forced to face truth, and for Katlyn her truth is her husband has made decisions that will forever change the life they've made together. Felicia hoped whatever the change, her dear friend would be able to handle it.

Katlyn found it difficult if not impossible to fathom how Justin could put her at such risk. He knew to use a condom; no way could she believe he'd come to the point in their marriage where he could care less what happened to her. She felt as if her heart was dying.

"Well Felicia, you said I have no proof he was f-in' around—got some now."

"Katlyn, I'm so sorry."

"Yeah…me, too!" Katlyn blurted out before bursting into tears.

Felicia drove them to Katlyn's pharmacy. They went inside together to lessen Katlyn's humiliation.

At the corner of La Brea and Sunset, Felicia stopped and got their favorite Chinese food to go. Once in the safety of her home, Katlyn took off her dark shades and opened the antibiotics. They were huge.

"Horse pills." She sighed.

Felicia handed her a bottle of water. "Maybe you should eat something first," she suggested. They both had zero appetites, but Katlyn managed to get a little something down before she popped the pill. She called a cab to take Felicia to the airport.

Chlamydia was proof enough for Katlyn that her husband was sleeping with some hoochie—unprotected. She lay in bed, staring out the window, ignoring the ringing phone. Felicia promised to call when she got home; that was another two hours away, so Katlyn surmised it had to be Justin trying to reach her and she let it ring until the answering machine picked up.

The revelation of Justin's deception left her feeling hopeless. The only life left in her was in her womb; something she should be joyously celebrating with him. Instead, she was trying to figure out how she would handle motherhood solo.

Midday came and went. By evening she had managed to move to the living room. Felicia called and they both held the phone: Felicia not knowing what to say and Katlyn having nothing to say. Before hanging up, Felicia assured her she was there for her if Katlyn needed her.

Katlyn held the handset until the noise became unbearable. When she rose to hang up the phone, she ran to the bathroom and threw up. She was not sure if it was the antibiotic or the baby making her sick. Still nauseated, she looked at the calendar, and realized she had two more days to decide what to do about Justin. Right now she needed to sleep.

The next morning Katlyn woke up running to the toilet. She had dry heaves, which hurt, and she needed to eat, but was too weak to feed herself. Lying down on the bed again, she dozed off and began to dream.

In the dream she saw her mother, who looked pretty, standing in the doorway dressed in white from head to toe. She sat down on the bed and rubbed Katlyn's hair. As she did, an unbelievable peace came over her. Her mother whispered, "Step out of security and into significance" and then disappeared. Katlyn awoke, sat up in the bed and looked around the room. Her mother was not there, but she knew she had been.

Katlyn felt stronger: strong enough to eat. She fixed a can of soup and a peanut butter and jelly sandwich. Something her mother would have prepared for her, she thought, and managed to smile.

After she ate, she went in the bathroom and stared at herself in the mirror. The "oulda" family decided to join her. You know…Shoulda, Woulda and Coulda. Katlyn proved to be a great host.

First they discussed what she shoulda done when she first thought Justin was messin' around: "You been around long enough to know, when he would not answer the phone or return your calls, something was wrong. You shoulda checked his phone messages."

The Coulda family members decided they could top that one. They reminded her how she coulda caught him when he started getting sloppy. "When he was always MIA at the studio, you coulda waited for him to leave and follow him. You'da definitely busted his slick butt then."

Last but not least, the Wouldas decided she missed a golden opportunity to get her revenge when she reconsidered her plan to clean out the bank accounts and the condo and leave. "After all the lies he told you every time you asked for the truth, you woulda been justified in taking what is rightfully yours. You don't owe him a thing and he owes you everything! Dump the dog and move on."

"Someone will love you for you, Katlyn Kincaid," she assured herself, slowly taking note of every feature, blemish and mole. She lay soaking in the oversized tub, no lights and no noise. Again Katlyn heard her mother's words…"Step out of security and into significance," and she wondered what that meant.

One thing was certain; she knew she could not stay in this place. The pain was too much to bear and only intensified when she contemplated how wrong she had been about something she was so certain, Justin's love.

It is human nature to want to avoid most, if not all, of the difficulties that go with just being alive. Oftentimes, change, voluntary or because "God shoved you," is not welcomed with open arms. No one likes pain and change is painful.

"Through" is a painful and frightening place you are forced into by your actions or choices (or because someone changed the rules and forgot to tell you). It is a dark place where you are bounced around, squeezed, pushed and prodded. You are stretched beyond limits you or someone else, set for yourself.

To leave this place, to make it to the other side, movement is necessary; not haphazard, left to right, lateral movement, but forward movement. Unfortunately many never make it to the other side of through. Some choose to stay where they are, suffering in silence, because it is safer than moving beyond their familiar, "cushy surroundings."

Katlyn's journey had begun, but she was not alone. "Drama boosters" like confusion, loneliness and heartache showed up to slow her progress. Not to worry, Life's Super Heroes: strength, faith and patience were there strategically placed on the sidelines at various mile markers, to cheer her on and hand her that cool sip of water, just when it was needed.

The last day of her reprieve, Katlyn woke up feeling like her old self. The queasy feeling was still there, but the vomiting had subsided. She searched for some peppermint tea in the kitchen and made a cup, settling down in her favorite chair to think.

She was scared; her decision to walk away frightened her. She had not been on her own in a long time. Being out there with no one to count on but herself was foreign to her.

Katlyn once believed she had grown up an independent, self-sufficient woman who never needed a man. It shocked her to realize she was nothing like that. Truth was Justin had become her whole world, her life and her reason for living. She had no life of her own because she had lived her life for and through him. Now she had to find a way to move on for her life and the life inside of her.

CHAPTER 16

Justin tried to find a comfortable angle for his head. The flight attendant had already given him three pillows, but nothing helped. He was tired: he and Nikki had made love all night, their last night together, uninterrupted. He knew he needed to get some sleep and be well rested to deal with what lay ahead.

Always one to make careful decisions, Justin thought he'd figured it all out. His marriage to Katlyn was planned, a move he'd calculated like a skilled chess player. When it was time to move to the next level, marriage, you married a Katlyn. He knew the life he'd planned for himself needed a "security blanket." Katlyn became that and more. But he got bored, very bored with his "safe" life and needed a little somethin'-somethin' to do.

Having been there before and never been caught, doing Nikki was supposed to be easy. Hit it and quit it. But somehow, even with all his experience, he miscalculated. He double-dipped—went back for more. *Bad move*, he thought.

Going back for more got feelings involved. Now his perfect, mundane world was topsy-turvy and he no longer felt content being married to Katlyn, day in and day out. With Nikki, he felt a connection that he'd never had with his wife or any other female. He could not see life moving on without Nikki and he no longer saw his life moving forward with Katlyn.

From time to time Justin would have a recurring nightmare. Each time he was headed to a place unknown. The journey was difficult and he never made it far. He was surrounded on all sides by layers of fog. There was always a limited time to make a decision to move: each move had to be right, left or forward—back was never an option. Every step forward resulted in the space behind him disappearing. Fear of the unknown stifled him, so Justin would opt for the safe route and stay where he was. Never once did he finish the journey and he always wondered what was on the other side, if he made it through!

Pre-Nikki, Justin knew someday that things with Katlyn would come to this. For years he had lived a lie. Not long after he married Katlyn he began to creep. It bothered him because he knew Katlyn was partly responsible for his success and he knew he owed her big-time for her loyalty and support. For that alone he thought he'd never leave her.

He also knew Katlyn loved him. Not the kind of give and take love he'd known with his mother, but a selfless love. Katlyn always gave and Justin always took. That made him feel secure and he needed that safety net to pursue his dreams. If he failed, he had Katlyn who loved him for him. She was a security blanket he needed at that time.

Now, he was at check in this game of chess. Either he destroyed Katlyn's world or he destroyed himself. The flight from Hawaii landed late. Justin bypassed home and went straight to the venue. His backup singers had already done their sound check and the engineer was waiting for him. Short on time, Justin opted to do the sound check after he got dressed.

Glancing over the green room's guest list he noticed it was loaded with VIPs, and included family, friends and Katlyn. The thought of dealing with her made him cringe. He decided to delay the inevitable as long as possible.

Katlyn was more gorgeous than usual. Her black floor-length, spaghetti-strap jersey knit dress with the fishtail hem fit her like a glove. She'd cut off all her long flowing hair and dyed it jet-black. Though a shocking change, it was stunning on her. People complimented her all night on her liberation. Sistahs who "got it," having liberated themselves a long time ago, gave her the thumbs-up and hugs.

"You go, girl," they exclaimed, motioning to the hair. Those who were yet in bondage admired her brevity, but dared not go there. "Katlyn, that's a drastic change," one well-meaning friend commented.

"I know," she said, not really caring what the well-meaning friend thought.

"So what did Justin have to say?" the friend continued.

"It doesn't matter; it's my hair," Katlyn responded, looking straight at her.

Katlyn had long grown tired of her mane, but Justin forbade her to cut it. The compromise was her hair always snatched back in a ponytail or bun. She realized most of the females they knew had long hair for the same reason. Men; *they* had hair issues and their issues became women's issues. Katlyn's man was no different.

After sound check, Justin stopped by the green room and peeked in to see if Katlyn had arrived. Unaware of her haircut, he overlooked her in the crowd. Feeling comfortable with the absence of his wife, Justin entered and began to circulate. He unknowingly walked up to his wife.

Katlyn greeted him with a chill that would make the North Pole seem warm. Her slight was noticeable to everyone watching. Justin attempted to hug her; she backed away and held up her hand, signaling him to stop! Embarrassed, he reached for her hand, pretending everything was okay. She snatched her hand away and raised her voice.

"Do not touch me again!"

Justin was shocked at her behavior. "Katlyn," he whispered. "Not here, not now. Pleeezzz!" Katlyn knew the way his fans perceived them meant everything to him. She ignored his pleas and threw her drink in his face. The entire room gasped. Next she spun around looking for a weapon, something she could use to hurt him. An opened bottle of champagne was the first thing she spotted. She hurled it at him and missed him with the bottle, but not the champagne.

Looking like a crazed maniac, she shouted, "All right. Every slut in this room who has slept with my husband, get out now!" Guilty or not, women began to scatter like roaches do when the lights are turned on.

Katlyn grabbed a tray of fruit and began to throw apples, bananas and grapes. Justin rushed her, holding her in a bear hug, her arms pinned to her side. "Katlyn, baby, what are you doing?

"Let me go, you let me go!" she screamed, violently thrashing about.

Justin held on, tightening his grip. She closed her eyes and began to sob.

Silently at first; then she began to moan louder and louder, until her moans turned into screams. He picked her up and placed her on the sofa.

"Get out!" he shouted as he wiped the tears streaming down her face.

Security cleared the room. "Mr. Kincaid, you gonna be okay?" Tank, head of security, waited for an answer. Justin waved him off, never looking up.

Katlyn cried uncontrollably. Through tears she told Justin she heard the Hawaii interview and she knew he was having an affair. Justin blotted her tears with a cold towel, hating himself for hurting her. Security stuck their head in the door and informed him it was showtime.

"Katlyn, listen, I gotta go." He waited for a response; she pretended he didn't exist.

Justin felt like a louse and was embarrassed by the green room scene with his wife. But he didn't let that deter him. Always a professional, he mesmerized the audience for two hours and left them begging for more. Energized by the chants of encore, he performed another thirty minutes before calling it a night.

Sitting in his dressing room he thought about what had transpired earlier with Katlyn. Fortunately the number of family, friends and fans in the green room when she lost it was minimal and he hoped what had happened would not make newspaper headlines. Going home was the last place he wanted to go, so he stopped at Carlos and Charlie's for a nightcap.

The next morning Katlyn found Justin sitting in the kitchen at the table, staring into his coffee. He looked at her when she walked in, really noticing her haircut for the first time. He liked it—it was sexy on her. She was beautiful with or without hair. Why hadn't he noticed that before?

Katlyn ignored him and avoided eye contact.

"Are you okay?" he asked. Slowly she turned and looked at him, but remained silent. Her glare made him uncomfortable. "I was worried about you," he offered. Again silence.

"Um, Katlyn, I don't know what to say. I didn't mean for this to happen."

"What did you mean to happen?" she asked sarcastically. Justin, his brain on rewind, tried unsuccessfully to find the words to explain where he'd thought his fling with Nikki was headed.

"I don't know," he said, feeling stupid. Justin's mind was blank. He sat silently, wanting this to be over, trying to figure out how to end it. "I've hurt you and I can't handle that…"

Katlyn jumped in, sounding lifeless. "I lived my whole life believing in the fairy tale. The happily ever after, one love, one time for life B.S. Then you came along, my knight in shining armor on the white horse. You swooped me up in your arms and carried me off to paradise and I believed you loved me, for me." She stared at him.

"Justin, I know I am not perfect, but for you I tried to be. My whole world revolved around you. *Your* likes and dislikes. *Your* expectations, *your* needs, *your* dreams. Mrs. Justin Kincaid, well, just who is that?"

He listened and tried to figure out how to respond.

"Do you love her, Justin?"

"I think so," he answered softly.

"More than me? I mean enough to walk away from us?"

"Katlyn, I am so very sorry…"

She began to cry. Justin waited for her to regroup. "I thought you cared enough to be honest, but you've repeatedly lied to me," she whispered.

"I was scared," he admitted.

"Justin, you put my life at risk sleeping with her unprotected. You gave me Chlamydia," she said just above a whisper.

He had not thought about his actions until now. Katlyn was right, he had put them both at risk. "There's nothing I can say. I f'd up badly. I'm sorry. Sorry for lying, sorry for being unfaithful, all of it!"

"So what now, Justin? You just kiss it all good-bye? Is that what you expect me to do?" She continued, not allowing him to respond. "Was this all a game? Did I imagine you loved me, that we were a team? Did I, Justin?" She glared at him. Justin froze, afraid of a repeat from the green room. "Answer me, Justin," she said calmly. He looked away.

"Justin, I have to know, was this all a lie? Us, our life together?"

He knew the answer would cut like a knife. She didn't deserve that. He stood up and walked toward the door. Taking the coward's way out, he turned his back on her and just before leaving said, "I'm not feelin' this anymore. I want out!"

Katlyn watched him open the door and walk out. She began to shake.

She couldn't breathe and she wanted to die. "Justin," she called out. He turned and looked back.

"I'm pregnant!"

Stunned and not happy to hear this news, he spoke from his heart. "I'll pay for the abortion, let me know what it costs." For once she saw him differently; suddenly Justin looked like someone on all fours with a tail. He left, taking a piece of her with him and leaving his seed behind.

CHAPTER 17

Faced with the truth, Katlyn realized she couldn't handle it. Every fiber of her being hurt and in return she wanted to hurt Justin—real bad. Slowly, she climbed the stairs, each step laborious.

At the top of the stairs staring back at her was one of his prized possessions encased in glass, his first gold record. A blow-up of his face made up the album cover, which was framed and superimposed on his gold album. The sight of his face filled her with rage. Katlyn lifted the framed memento off the wall and threw it down the stairs. It crashed into the wall at the bottom and shattered, glass flying everywhere, the gold album rolling on its side into the kitchen.

Now in anger overload, she headed for his pride and joy—his image. She opened the door to the garage and stared at their luxury autos sitting side by side. The scene from *Waiting to Exhale* where Angela Bassett set her wayward husband's clothes and luxury auto on fire came to mind, but she wasn't that crazy—yet! That's because the two Mercedes Benz sitting in the garage, belonged to her just as much as him.

Heading for their bedroom, she thought about doing the bleach thing, but, "*Every dog* expects the bleach thing," she said and smiled. Katlyn walked over to her desk, opened the top drawer and took out her sharpest pair of cutting shears and headed for his closet.

"Versace great, let's see, you'd look good with stars." She proceeded to cut large star shapes in his $1,100 shirt. "Armani, circles, what do you think?" She paused, as if waiting for the designer to answer. When he did not, she cut circles and ovals in a pattern throughout the suit. One by one she cut shapes in every piece of his wardrobe. Then she neatly hung them back on the hangers in the closet. Flipping over the last pair of pants to reach the leg she had yet to alter, a folded business card fell from the pocket. She picked it up and unfolded it. On the front of the card was a photo of a beautiful, extremely tanned, Brazilian-looking woman striking a model's pose, with the name Nikki and a phone number in the lower right-hand corner. On the back a crimson lip print had been pressed in the center. Beneath the lip print was written in what appeared to be female handwriting, "Nikki, 18455 Fountain Ave, Unit G." Underneath the name Nikki, Justin had written "Nicola" in parentheses. Katlyn assumed this was the ho he had left her for. She tucked the card in her bra—she'd need it later.

Still not satisfied, she turned her anger on his $1,000-a-pair-and-up reptile shoes. "You poor little creatures. Here, let me return you to your natural habitat," she said as she placed all thirty-two pair of gators, snakes, crocs and lizards in the tub and filled it with hot water. The only thing spared was the pair of ostrich cowboy boots, which lay out of view under the bed.

Lost in the drama, she turned her anger on his "ego," which included numerous plaques, trophies and awards. The walls of the library housed Justin's triumphs, the accolades the public bestowed on him.

She slowly counted and named each one of them. Then she picked up her favorites and read them out loud. "Best New Artist." Mimicking Justin, Katlyn turned to the audience, blew them a kiss and waited for the screams to die down before making her acceptance speech. From memory she recited the BS that Justin had fed to the audience that night. She remembered it word for word because he'd credited her for his success and pledged his undying love and devotion to her. "Lies...all lies," she screamed.

Proceeding down the wall, she stopped at Best Male Vocalist and Male R & B Vocalist of the Year. Katlyn humbly lowered her head and feigned wiping a tear from her eye as Justin had the night he received those awards.

Once again, she waited for the crowd to quiet down. She stared at the wall as if it were a large group of adoring fans and blew them a kiss. Raising both plaques above her head as he did that night, she thanked them and then threw them down the stairs.

She took her time gathering the remaining plaques and as if mixing the ingredients of a favorite recipe, she read them one by one, then tossed them into a metal trash can she'd retrieved from the garage. Returning for the pile of debris at the bottom of the stairs, she scooped it up in a shovel and added it to the pot as well.

"Now, let's see," she said, humming as she went back to the garage in search of one main ingredient. "Ah, there it is!" she exclaimed, lifting the can of gasoline as if it were something precious she'd misplaced and just stumbled upon.

Katlyn sat the can in the backyard and returned to the kitchen. Reviewing the "ingredients" in her head, she remembered some "spices" she'd forgotten to add—pictures. Then she poured gasoline over it all and tossed in a match. While her concoction of wood, metal, plastic, paper and glass began to smolder, she smiled. When it burst into beautiful orange, yellow and red flames, Katlyn felt a rush. "F you, Justin Kincaid, I'll be fine, just fine!" she screamed as she backed away from the intense heat and slowly entered her home.

But she wasn't. Blood began to stain the seat of the pants she was wearing. Excruciating pelvic pain forced her to the floor. Crawling, she worked her way to the telephone in the living room and dialed 9-1-1.

Several hours later she was in the emergency room involuntarily aborting the child she'd hope to raise, alone. Her doctor assured Katlyn she'd be able to have more children.

Katlyn began to cry. To give her some time alone her doctor left the room to order something for the pain and sent her home. After an hour and a half the pain medication eased the pelvic pain. But man had yet to make a drug that could ease the pain she had in her heart!

The downward spiral into the abyss was instantaneous for Katlyn. Undressing to put on her pj's she unfolded the piece of paper she'd stashed in her bra and read it again. The area was familiar to her, but she was uncertain of the exact location of the address. Looking it up on a map she discovered it was less than fifteen minutes away. Unable to sleep, angry and curious, she threw on some sweats over her pajamas and got in her car.

During the drive, she replayed in her head what she would do to Justin, and his ho, when she found them. Katlyn had no trouble locating the address but gaining entry was a huge problem. The entire condominium complex was gated and required an access card or code.

Two hours passed before anyone entered or exited the building. When someone finally did, she started her car and drove through the gate before it closed. Having no knowledge of what condo Nikki lived in, Katlyn drove around the parking structure looking for Justin's car. Seek and ye shall find.

Justin's blue Porsche was parked in stall 628, behind a black Range Rover. Katlyn stopped and read the license plate to be sure it was his car. Certain it was, she parked behind it, blocking it in. She got out and tried to enter the building, but you had to know the entry code to get in.

Frustrated, she returned to her car and searched the trunk for a sharp object she could use to key Justin's car and flatten his mistress' tires. That mission accomplished and still determined to wreak havoc on his life and beat the crap out of Nikki, she returned to her car and watched the door like a hawk. The moment she saw it open, she ran to catch it. A beautiful female exited and held the door for her. Things were going so smoothly, Katlyn tried her luck.

"Excuse me, I was wondering if you knew which condo Nikki lived in?"

The beautiful female turned and looked at her, puzzled. "Nikki?"

"Yes, Brazilian, about your height and build…"

"Ohhh, you mean Nicola? Yes, I know her, she's my neighbor."

"Great, I forgot her unit number, and I left…" Katlyn was rambling and the beautiful female was in a hurry.

"No problem, she's in 1102, but I would call her first. Right now she has company. That star, uh, Justin somebody."

"Really…" was all Katlyn could muster and keep a straight face.

"Yeah, I could hear her screaming his name," the beautiful female said, laughing.

Katlyn feigned a laugh and headed toward 1102.

The first kick she landed on the door sounded like a bomb. She could hear Justin and Nikki whispering on the other side of the door.

"Open up, Justin!" she said, almost singing the words. Ignoring her was not the smart thing to do. Katlyn acted even more ignorant.

"Justin, open the door now! Get your tired butt out here and bring that heifer with you!"

One by one, neighbors' doors opened. Each time one would peek out the door, Katlyn would glare at them. Doors quickly slammed shut! She laughed. Katlyn clowned for fifteen more minutes before Justin finally appeared. The moment he stepped into the hall he quickly slammed Nikki's door behind him, preventing Katlyn from sticking the crowbar she had in her hand in the door. Aware of the crowbar Justin darted down the hall with Katlyn fast behind him. Making it safely to his car he locked himself in before realizing her car had him blocked.

Katlyn caught up to his car and threatened to break out all his windows if he didn't get out of the car and face her like a man. With the car still running, he put it in park, got out and slowly walked over to her. The moment he was close enough, Katlyn kicked, aiming for his balls. He blocked her kick with a karate move that left a three-inch gash in her shin. While she writhed on the ground nursing it, Justin used his spare key to her car and moved it out of his way. Leaving it running, he jumped in his Porsche and sped off.

Katlyn hobbled back to her car with blood streaming down her leg. She used a rag out of her trunk to press against the gash in an effort to halt the bleeding. It was daylight before Katlyn was finally able to follow some-one out of the parking garage. By then, her leg was seriously swollen and blue. Instead of heading home, she returned to the emergency room.

Fortunately for Katlyn, neither Justin nor his mistress had any proof she flattened the tires on Nikki's Range Rover or keyed his Porsche. When contacted by the police, she denied everything. And even though Justin and Nikki knew she did it, neither could prove it, so they dropped it.

It was definitely time to move on. To Katlyn's good fortune, Felicia had a long vacation and persuaded her to come to Atlanta for an extended stay. Katlyn was ready for a change. She knew she'd hit rock-bottom and was a stone's throw away from never crawling out of the dark hole. Nothing made sense to her anymore and she cried daily. Her spirit was broken and the pieces no longer fit. She felt like Humpty Dumpty, and "all the King's horses and men could not put her together again."

The miraculous change in Asa stayed on her mind. Life and men had not been fair to her, either, yet she seemed content with the hand she had been dealt. Katlyn envied her positive attitude and outlook on things. In her quiet moments she wondered what it might feel like to be in that space. To be happy and content with who she was and where she was.

Asa knew how Katlyn felt; she'd worn those shoes. She also knew neither Katlyn or Humpty Dumpty's men could fix what was wrong with her.

"Whuz-za uu-uup?" Asa answered in a bubbly voice.

Katlyn laughed. "Hey girl, you on the phone?" Katlyn thought to ask, remembering Asa once lived on the phone.

"Not even, told you I gave up being the Tabloid Queen." Katlyn chuckled as Asa continued. "Girl, when I got a life, I didn't have time to be dippin' in everyone else's."

"Yeah, I know what cha mean," Katlyn said absentmindedly, trying to figure out how to bring up their past conversation.

"So, how you feelin' these days?" Asa asked, trying to get her to open up.

"I'm hangin' in there," Katlyn answered, nonchalantly.

"You been anywhere, gettin' out of the house?"

"No, I'm really not up to going anywhere or meeting men," Katlyn confided.

Unable to handle all the gloom coming from Katlyn, Asa tried to lighten things up. "Oh, so you got your 'I hate men' neon sign turned on and it's in flash mode, I see."

"You know, Asa, I look at you and I know you've been in a similar situation, yet you've managed to get it together and you seem so happy.

How? How do you do it? I mean, I feel so out of it, lost. This is not me—I don't know who I am anymore, and I'm so very unhappy with my life. Everything is in disarray and out of control."

While Katlyn shed tears, Asa spent the next forty-five minutes explaining how she "did it" and ended the conversation by inviting her to church. It had been a long time since Katlyn had been in a church and she felt out of place. She decided to wait in the lobby for Asa.

Religion was not new to her; she had been raised in church. She prayed often and watched her "Gospel Posse"—Bishop TD Jakes, Bishop Eddie Long, Bishop Victor T. Curry, Bishop Charles Ellis, Creflo Dollar, Joyce Meyer and Paula White—on TBN and the Word Network regularly. But she had not made a conscientious effort to really connect with God.

Things were a lot different in church than she remembered. The music had changed, but she knew that from listening to the crossover of gospel music from Christian to secular broadcasting. However, she was totally unprepared for the changes the music had taken inside the sanctuary walls.

In her more sedate church upbringing, the congregation might hit a sway or two, to the upbeat tempo the sole musician, the organist, played. Here, in New Visions, ten-thousand-plus-seat auditorium, the music was moving and energizing. The small orchestra was grouped off to the left of the pulpit playing Gospel music that sounded more like an R & B concert. Observing the massive choir clap, sway, dip and sing in ultimate perfection made her chuckle. Katlyn could not help but compare them to the twenty or so members who showed up faithfully, at Rock Creek back in the day, to sing off-key selections from the hymnals.

Women dressed to the hilt in large rhinestone hats, designer suits and high heels jumped, swirled and shouted. Katlyn watched and wondered what would make someone act like that. She found their behavior entertaining and very unladylike.

After what seemed like an eternity the music and the noise subsided. A lean, tall figure dressed in a beautiful robe approached the pulpit. He stepped to the podium and began to belt out a portion of the song the choir had just finished singing. As he repeated the chorus over and over again the enormous choir hummed it softly behind him. Once again the congregation began to sway. One by one, people jumped to their feet, arms flailing, tears flowing and faces contorted. The higher each round of the chorus went, the more they danced and shouted.

Hats began to fly; a shoe sped past Katlyn's head and one mother's wig flipped into her seatmate's lap. Katlyn's first reaction was to laugh, but as she peered around the sanctuary, it became quite apparent she was one of the few who did not get it!

In need of a breakthrough in her circumstances, Katlyn sat well over an hour intensely listening to the sermon. It was moving, bringing her to tears. Yet, she failed to see where it could help her put back together her broken heart, broken marriage and broken life.

The well-prepared message, "God is an on-time God," from the minister was about perceiving God to be late in showing up to resolve a difficult situation. According to him, God was never late. Whenever He showed up to deal with your situation, it was His timing and His timing was on time, never late. It might seem to the person in need of His services, He was late, "but God's timing is not our timing," the minister informed the congregation. He assured the congregation, no matter how bad the situation might appear, or no matter how desperate the circumstances might be, God is aware of it and is taking care of it. The sermon ended with the scripture, "All things work together for the good of those who love the Lord and are called to his purpose."

Katlyn chewed on what the minister had said and disagreed. "Well… this time, God, you are late, very late and if I didn't know better, I would go as far as to say, *too* late! None of the pain I am feeling can possibly be working for my good."

Bits and pieces of the message left the church with her. Something about seeking God's face and not His hand and seeking first God's Kingdom kept running through her mind. It made her reflect on what her mother had said about "stepping out of security and into significance." She pondered if and how these cryptic messages could possibly be the answer to the dilemma she was facing.

For months Katlyn reflected and pondered on the message, hoping to find some "hidden solution" to her quandary. "Where's the answer to what is wrong with Justin in these words?" she wondered. After all, seeking God's help in fixing her marriage was her entire reason for going to church. Realizing HE may not fix it, frightened her.

"Seek ye first the Kingdom of God," she repeated several times. "Step out of security and into significance," she said out loud, and then wrote both phrases. Katlyn stared at them, clueless as to how important they were in her circumstances and life.

For months the phrases echoed in her head and for months she ignored them. One evening, without thinking, she picked up her dusty Bible and looked in the Concordance for those words "Seek ye first..." Her finger stopped on the book of Luke, chapter 12, verse 31. The explanation of the verse in her study Bible said it meant making Jesus the Lord and head of your life. He must control your work, your play, your plans and relationships. Two things stuck out: the fact that *He* must control and relationships. Finally, the Scripture that had her baffled for months held promise.

Katlyn was intrigued by this information. As she read further, the explanation posed a question—"are you holding back any area of your life from God's control?" She thought about the question for days before realizing the answer was yes—her entire life!

"Yes, yes, yes!" she screamed, filled with excitement about this revelation. She ran to her Bible and began to read more. The last sentence of the explanation said, "As your Lord and Creator He wants to provide what you need as well as guide how you use what He provides!" And with those words, God showed up in Katlyn's life.

Katlyn lay on the floor crying for hours. So much pain had lingered for so long; way longer than it should have and she was to blame. She had baggage, lots of it. Much of it, packed when she was a child, remained unopened when she became an adult. There were a few "oversized" pieces (you know the ones they charge you extra to check at the airport) she'd opened—but found the contents much too overwhelming to deal with, so she neatly tucked everything back inside and stored them in the secret places of her heart and mind, with no intentions of carrying them on her journey. Oh, but she had!

Katlyn began to feel a need to be closer to God, not for what He could do for her, but what He could do in her. Her need for that false sense of stability she called Justin, was no longer tied to who she was and wanted to be. Now she was ready. Ready for God to show her how to step out of the security of a life asphyxiated on what others think, say and do; and into a life of significance, anchored by who she would discover she was.

Finding God excited her and she wanted to share this news with Asa.

"So, I'm listening, Missy," Asa said as Katlyn answered the phone.

"You got my message," Katlyn exclaimed, happy Asa was returning her call. It had been several months since their missed rendezvous at church and they had not spoken.

"Hey, what happened to you that Sunday? I waited in the vestibule for you, but I never saw you. When you left me the message saying how much attending had changed your life, I was so happy to know you made it! Been waitin' for a praise report, so lay it on me." As always, Asa had something flip and funny to say. Katlyn laughed heartily.

"First, let me say, thank you..."

Asa interrupted, "Nuh-uhh! Don't thank me, thank God."

"I know that," Katlyn continued. "Just listen for a minute!" Sensing her seriousness, Asa put all jokes aside and gave her several minutes of her time, uninterrupted.

Katlyn told her God had "showed up and showed out" in her life in a major way. She made sure Asa knew how truly grateful she was for sharing her experience with Christ. She thanked her for not being pushy, but open to her questions as they came; yet allowing her to seek God when she was ready.

"And you know what else I discovered; seeking God did not take away my desire, my yearning, to be with Justin. I still love him. But the more I seek God, the less I seek Justin." Asa fought back the urge to scream, "Amen." "Now that I finally let go of everything, Justin included, I have found an unbelievable peace. Sure I miss Justin, but I don't feel lonely."

Caught up in her thoughts, Katlyn got quiet.

"You okay?" Asa asked.

"I'm fine, it's just amazing when I look back over my life, I cannot help but get choked up. After the confusion and hurt subsided, I was able to hear God's voice. He introduced me to someone I had never met before: Katlyn, the real me!"

Asa began to cry as Katlyn poured her heart out. She admitted it was difficult to accept Justin had pretty much used her love and emotions as a place he could come for a tune-up, take the part of her he needed for that moment, then move on.

Katlyn confided, "At one point, things seemed so unbearable, if it were not for me opening my eyes each morning aware of a heartbeat and still able to see my lungs move in and out, I would have believed I no longer was alive. I would look in the mirror, and see no one. I was totally non-existent."

They both cried a little and laughed a little. Asa, having been there not too long ago, knew this was only the beginning. The days ahead for Katlyn were not going to be all peaches and cream. Far from it! At the onset, she would have more bad days than good, but it would get easier now that she saw the light, *and the truth shall set you free*!

CHAPTER 18

Each season brings about a change. Winter, life takes a respite. Spring, new life begins to take root. Summer, life celebrates its birth. Fall, life prepares to make way for new beginnings. It was fall!

Katlyn unsuccessfully tried to leave the bad memories with Justin in Los Angeles. Her miscarriage, then the well-publicized (thanks to Justin) breakup, were more than she bargained for. She had her good days, but her bad days far outweighed them. While she had faced her past, it continued to haunt her at odd moments. One moment she was strong enough to throw Justin and all his BS in the dumpster. The next moment, she was frantically digging in that same trash bin, trying to pull him out.

Tears of guilt and shame caused this quintessential drama queen to cry, snot, act up and act out—and once done, she started all over again. No one was invited to these outings but a box of tissues and the twins—pity and party.

After months of stressing over Justin and her circumstances, Katlyn decided to tell herself the truth. As she separated fact from fiction, the Ping-Pong of emotions, misery, confusion and despair subsided. The clouds gradually lifted and she began to see life without the rose-colored glasses. As she did, things became clearer. She understood life was something she could not control and Justin was not someone she could change.

Reflecting on her choices, she was forced to admit she had walked into and remained in her relationship with Justin with her eyes wide open. Although she loved him, that love was not the first thing that drove her to him. And if truth be told, love had nothing to do with it.

Old fears held her to the vow she'd made as a little girl. Future doubts about the vow being fulfilled helped her see Justin as an insurance policy to the good life. Like in the past she once more became a chameleon, wrapping herself around her man, conforming and molding her life and personality around his.

Her marriage, though filled with all the right external images of intimacy, was shallow. Justin had issues, but she knew that and chose to ignore them. It didn't take a rocket scientist to figure out they were unequally yoked spiritually and mentally, but she didn't want to deal with that reality. Katlyn chose to surrender everything she was and wanted to be in life to obtain the one thing that continued to elude her—wealth and fame.

When she finally got both, it did not fulfill her and neither did her marriage. Not happy where she was, she was not sure she wanted to leave. Hanging on, not wanting to hurt herself or Justin, she lived in denial, choosing to believe what she had was worth it. Only now was she willing to admit that it was not!

Quieter and more accepting of herself and the people and things that were a part of her life, she began to work on her yet untitled manuscript with hopes of completing it soon. Writing gave Katlyn solace. Her "implosion" utilized every ounce of time, energy and brain capacity she had to wade through and then work through what she needed to do to get her life in order. Her pain and drama gave her the substance to draw from. Sorting through this process took time. With each line written, a new outlook was unveiled. Slowly but surely she was healing.

Katlyn sold her publishing rights to "Who's Kissin' You?" and the other song she'd written on Justin's successful freshman album, "Get Closer," and made a fortune. Settling into a "Minsion" (her dialect for a baby mansion) in an affluent suburb of Atlanta was a refreshing change from her condo in L.A. Her seventy-eight-hundred-square-foot, three-level home was a "coming out" present to herself. The open floor plans; well lit by windows and lots of skylights, lent inspiration to her writing.

Living on opposite coasts, Felicia had not had the opportunity to read any of the excerpts her girlfriend had written. Now that she was a resident of Atlanta and only twenty minutes away, Katlyn gladly made her manuscript available for her friend to read at her leisure.

Felicia found Katlyn's use of nouns, pronouns, and adjectives—the English language, down-right enchanting. She knew Katlyn had talent as a writer; her hit song "Who's Kissin' You?" was proof of that. But when she read her manuscript, it was obvious she was a budding author.

Something in Katlyn sprang forth from her loss and the book took on new life and a new message. She had a story to tell. What she had to say, women needed to hear. She hoped they would feel her pain and learn from her experience. Her mistakes and her scars were battle wounds. If shared, they might help the next woman out of the dark hole.

From the moment Katlyn sat at her computer, the keystrokes began and on most days they didn't stop until she was too tired to go on. And then only the keys stopped; the words and creativity continued to pour out of her.

Getting published was an honor bestowed on very few black authors. More now were recognized for their talent than ever before, but few made it onto the Bestseller list. The list of black authors who made it to the top and stayed there were slim to none. But Katlyn did not let those odds discourage her.

Soon to be the former Mrs. Justin Kincaid, Katlyn's Hollywood connections were suddenly unavailable. She mailed query letters with return envelopes to numerous literary agents and publishing houses and waited for a response.

Nothing happened. Two months later, lounging on her chaise, kickin' it with her "TV girlfriend" Oprah, she had a light bulb moment. On this particular *Oprah After the Show* episode, "O" (as Katlyn called her), did not accept a book from a man in her audience who was desperately trying to push his work on her. Her refusal to accept his merchandise was not because she was not interested; it was because it had to be copyrighted first. The pushy man eventually got her to agree to accept it (after the show) by convincing her he had the copyright.

Katlyn thought of an excellent PR tactic. She mailed query letters to the top talk-show host, newscasters and radio hosts and personalities in the country. It worked! In no time she was getting calls to have her manuscript forwarded to their assistants or directly to them with promises to read it. And even though she didn't get a response from "O," they remained "TV girlfriends"!

CHAPTER 19

Many times the hunt can be more exciting than the kill. Nikki loved chasing the thing she couldn't have. It was her nature to relentlessly pursue her prey.

She knew Justin was married long before he told her. At the time she met him she was looking for some fun, something exciting. The fact that he was married made him more attractive to her. The venue of married men was familiar territory to Nikki. She had successfully dated several—getting in and out with little or no drama. The rewards and fringe benefits were immeasurable. Married men knew they had to pay to play.

She routinely told herself she wasn't doing anything wrong. Not once did she force Justin or any of the others to be with her. The fact that Justin left his wife was proof he made his own choices—something Nikki was now beginning to regret.

Lately things were becoming complicated and confusing. Now that she had what she wanted, à la Justin Kincaid, she no longer found him exciting. Being tied down to one man was rapidly becoming boring. Justin's tour schedule, which kept him away from home eight months out of twelve, helped to amplify her boredom, but he was still Justin Kincaid and that alone held benefits she was not ready to relinquish.

Justin overslept. The call from the limo driver woke him. He looked over at Nikki, still fast asleep and watched her breathe. Although they had been cohabitating for several months, she still was not showing any sign of being "wife" material. She was bratty, a spoiled princess with a cold side.

As long as things went her way, she was loving and caring. Cross her, she became an entirely different person—something Justin had learned the hard way.

Nikki wanted to go on the road with him. Though possible, Justin knew it was not the best thing for his career, or him. He thought Nikki believed him when he gave her a lame excuse about no room on the tour bus. She never voiced an objection and things seemed to be business as usual, until he reached to touch her body. He learned he was wrong, very wrong. No tour, no making love.

He felt less enamored toward Nikki now that they were "playing house" and in each other's face day in and day out. Justin still loved her, but there were lots of things *about* her he did not love. She lived for *her* moment in the spotlight. Whenever the camera focused on Justin, Nikki made sure it was on her as well. She loved being seen with him, loved the attention it brought her.

Something else he disliked was her continuous fussing over her hair. Nikki lived in the mirror fixing her hair and face. And because she did not want to smudge her lipstick and mess up her hair "doin' it," she made little time for him and his insatiable appetite for her.

My, how things had changed! When they first hooked up, she let him kiss her, mess up her hair and even get off in an elevator. Not anymore. Now he counted himself lucky if he hit it once a month.

Significant others had a "place." Nikki knew hers but refused to stay in it. When Justin was approached for an autograph; Nikki took the liberty of accepting the pen and paper and scribbling her name before handing it to Justin. If he said something to her about her it, she punished him with a sex time out.

However, the biggest nails scratching on the chalk board moments for him were when she would amp up the PDA (Public Display of Affection). Not allowed! Nikki knew he did not like her all over him in public, but it got her what she wanted—a photo op with the paparazzi—so she didn't care.

Lazy and self-centered, Nikki kept the housekeeper busy. She seldom hung up the new clothes she'd maxed out his card purchasing, and cooking for him was out of the question. For months he thought she didn't cook because she didn't want to. Later he found out it was because she couldn't.

He had always depended on Katlyn to take care of the things that made their lives run smoothly. She made sure the bills were paid on time, got the groceries, and kept their home neat and clean in between deep cleanings by the housekeeper. The comfort she brought to his life made it easy for him to focus on his career.

Having Nikki around was taxing. She could not balance a checkbook, so his account was always overdrawn. Housework made her "allergic," and "Why buy groceries when you can eat out" was her motto. At times he felt like a parent with an out-of-control child.

A self-proclaimed party girl, Nikki loved the club scene. She knew every hot club that opened, and made sure she and Justin were on their A list. All the bartenders and bouncers were on a first-name basis with her. The beverages she chose to consume were expensive. She often boasted, "Only the best labels touch my lips."

Drinking became her passion. She loved to drink and she could out-drink Justin. After her third drink she would order a stogie and toke on it throughout the night. It made her breath foul and drove Justin nuts.

He was now ready to start a family and expressed that to her, but party girl Nikki had no interest in becoming a mother. A baby would mess up the figure she barely ate to maintain.

Even though he and Nikki seldom saw things eye to eye, Justin routinely told himself he was happy. Making a life with her was a choice he felt good about, despite her faults. On numerous occasions he made excuses for her lackadaisical attitude toward him to assure himself she was still crazy about him. But that Band-Aid would only last a short time.

Nikki's lack of attention toward him and her gradual withdrawal from him sexually caused his past insecurities with his mother to come out and play. Afraid of abandonment, Justin spent unbelievable amounts of money on Nikki, feeding her desire for the finer things in life, trying to make her stay.

Every now and then he had a discussion with himself, in which he admitted he had been thinking with the wrong head when he left Katlyn. However, it would not take long for his close friends Ego and Manly Pride to convince him he did the right thing. Truthfully, he missed Katlyn and the wifey things she did, sometimes, but all in all he considered losing her a fair trade-off for all the happiness Nikki brought him.

Lately, he forced himself to believe his decision to go public with his divorce from Katlyn, was the right one. And maybe it was. In the past months since his departure from her, he had not had the nightmares. That in and of itself was a major relief!

"Yeah, life is good—*real good*," Justin said, fooling no one but himself.

CHAPTER 20

Ruby Kincaid surfaced in Justin's life when he was at the highest point of his career. She'd seen her son on TV, in magazines and on billboards. He'd grown up handsome and "looked just like his dad," she'd tell anyone who listened. Most thought Ruby was lying about being the mother of the renowned Justin Kincaid, but she didn't care.

The soft knock on his dressing room door was greeted with a "yeah... who is it?"

Afraid to say anything when she heard her son's voice, Ruby stood silent contemplating walking away. She'd managed to sneak past the posted security at the stage door. Once backstage, she knocked on the only door that had a star on it.

Barely above a whisper, she responded, "It's me, yo' momma."

Justin's heart stopped beating. Sweat began to cover the palms of his hands and his mouth felt dry. Tears filled his eyes as he slowly rose and walked to the dressing room door. Fear would not let him open it. He reached for the door knob, turned it, but did not open the door.

Taking a moment to gather his thoughts, he leaned his forehead against the fame and took several deep breaths. Where had she been all this time? How had she found him and what did she want? More important, after being gone nearly twenty years, why surface now? Realizing only she had the answers to the battery of questions echoing in his head, he snatched open the door.

Ruby had turned away and was slowly walking off.

"Momma, where you goin'?"

Ruby stopped walking, but didn't turn around.

"Momma," Justin called out, choking back tears.

Ruby turned around, tears streaming down her face. Justin thought she looked good for her age. She was still slim and her skin did not show any wrinkles or signs of aging. But her clothes looked ragged and dirty. He reached out to hug her as she walked up to him and knocked her wig sideways. Her hair underneath the wig was all gray and matted. She smelled like she needed a bath.

The hug he longed for since the day she left felt good. In spite of her odor, he held her tight and cried. Ruby missed her boy and was thankful he still wanted to hug her. Freely she hugged him back and this time she didn't let go.

Justin's bodyguards interrupted their reunion.

"Showtime, Mr. Kincaid."

Justin nodded and waved them off. His mom continued to hold on to him as he gently pulled away.

"Let me look at you, Ma. Where you been? What you been doin'? How you livin'?"

"Boy, you better get yo'self ready to go out on that stage." She pulled away and gently pushed him back toward the dressing room. Justin grabbed her hand and pulled her into the small dressing area.

"Sit down, Momma. You want something to eat?" he asked as he stared at her and wiped away his tears. His staring made her uncomfortable. She reached up and fixed her wig and tried to smooth some of the wrinkles from her clothing.

"What you lookin' at, boy?" Ruby asked playfully.

Justin smiled but didn't answer. He handed her a plate of finger food and a bottle of juice. Ruby got up and grabbed some fruit and a napkin, then bit into a chicken wing. While she ate, Justin went into the bathroom and dressed.

"Curtain call, Mr. Kincaid," security shouted.

"Momma, you want to see my show?" he asked when he came out.

Ruby smiled broadly. Justin noticed her teeth, though yellow were still perfect. He grabbed her by the hand and led her to one of his bodyguards. In seconds she was ushered into the venue and seated in the front row.

Her heart pounded rapidly. She looked around at the large crowd that had gotten all dressed up to come see her son. They were screaming and crying and throwing flowers on the stage. Ruby smiled once more. Pride was something she hadn't felt in a long time. It felt good, so good it made her cry.

One of the hysterical females seated next to her assumed she was caught up in the excitement of seeing Justin Kincaid. She gave her a quick "I know how you feel" girlfriend hug and stuffed a wad of tissue in her hand. Ruby laughed and thanked her.

After the show, Ruby remained seated. Her son's performance was amazing. She knew he could sing, but he actually looked and sounded like a professional. He'd done well with his life, he'd made it, and she was thankful he had.

Looking around the green room, Justin could not find his mom. He frantically ran to the dressing room to see if she was waiting there. She was not. Panic began to set in. Quickly he dialed his bodyguard's cell phone number.

"Hey—where's my mother?"

The bodyguard explained he had seated her in the front row for the concert and had not seen her since. Justin asked why he never went back for her. The bodyguard reminded Justin he hadn't instructed him to.

Justin asked him to meet him in the back corridor of the venue near the stage. Together they searched the back area. Nothing. The bodyguard suggested they check inside the venue. When they entered from the right stage, Justin saw Ruby still seated in the front row, smiling.

"Momma, why are you sitting out here?"

"Where else was I supposed to go?" she asked sincerely. It dawned on Justin the question might not be for just this moment. He wondered if she had a home to go to.

Taking her by the hand, he helped her from her seat and put his arm around her as he guided her to the green room.

Once he knew she was seated and comfortable, he instructed his body-guard to watch her and not allow her to leave. It had been years since he'd spoken to his siblings, who were scattered all over the country. One cousin he had stayed in touch with might be able to shed some light on his mother's current situation. He called him.

"Hey man, Justin. Yeah, it has been a while. You okay?" Justin asked, not really concerned. Justin explained Ruby's sudden appearance and asked if his cousin could tell him anything.

It took nearly an hour, but by the time Justin hung up he knew why Ruby smelled and why she appeared on his doorstep. According to his cousin, she'd been diagnosed with paranoid schizophrenia and institutionalized for more than a year. Justin's oldest brother had had her committed because she'd become violent and wouldn't take her medication.

Plus Ruby had begun to threaten the police with a gun she'd stolen from her deceased father's collection. The gun was never loaded and most of the local cops knew that, but who knew when she'd threaten someone who didn't. So an institution was really the safest place for her.

The treatment she received made a huge improvement. Three weeks prior to Justin's concert, she was released—with nowhere to go. She went from one relative's home to another, sleeping on the streets in between. Justin didn't need any more incentive than that. He had to help his mother. Without calling Nikki first, he bought her a one-way ticket to L.A.

When he told Ruby he was taking her home with him, she beamed like a kid being told they were on their way to Mickey's house. Ruby had never been on a plane before and she'd only seen L.A. in movies. Exhausted from his tour, Justin slept the entire flight. While he did, Ruby ate every-thing they put before her in first class. Not because she was hungry, but because it was free.

Limousines were something only the rich rode in. When they sat down in the silver super-stretch the record label sent for them, Ruby wondered how Justin could afford to pay for it.

"Justin, you think we should just take the bus?" she had asked.

Her son laughed heartily as he held her elbow to assist her as she climbed into the limo.

"Don't worry, Ma, I can afford it."

Ruby smiled nervously. She heard what he'd said but did not believe him. On the ride home he had the driver take them past some of the historical parts of L.A. Ruby sat on the edge of her seat and watched the sights. When he drove them past Lucille Ball's home, she squealed. Justin burst into laughter, glad he'd brought her home and thankful for the reunion.

Nikki was not home when they arrived and he had no idea where she was. They'd had an argument while he was on the road and she had not answered her phone or returned his call in two days.

He settled his mom into the guest bedroom and gave her the things she needed to bathe and relax. She was close to Nikki's size, so he gave her one of Nikki's numerous robes to wear and a sweat suit and T-shirt as well. His mistake was picking Nikki's favorite cashmere one because Nikki never loaned her clothing. Ruby liked the feel of the soft fabric the sweat suit was made from, holding it close against her face. While she cleaned up, he called his publicist and had her arrange for a shopping spree for his mom and a day of pampering at the spa Nikki loved to frequent.

After being pampered, Ruby was very hungry. Justin took her to the spot he and Nikki frequented. The maitre d' seated Ruby and Justin at his VIP table on the sidewalk under the umbrellas. Most of the celebrities seated around them were unfamiliar to Ruby. She sat quietly watching the people as they walked by. When Justin brought Denzel over to meet her, Ruby burst into tears. The sight of someone so rich and so famous standing in front of her, and not on TV, frightened her.

Denzel leaned down and hugged her and told her he'd see her at the barbecue he was having at his home on the weekend before walking away. It took her a minute to get it together. When she did, she simply smiled and said nothing to her son. Justin smiled as well; glad to see she was okay. He was never sure when the "illness" would surface again and he never knew what might trigger it.

Moments after their food arrived, so did Nikki. She looked fabulous in a new designer outfit she'd just purchased. Nikki extended her hand to meet the woman seated with her man. She assumed the older woman had money and it was obvious she had great taste since she was wearing a cashmere sweat suit just like hers.

Justin introduced his mother to Nikki and informed her his mom would be a guest in their home for an extended period. This news did not sit well with Nikki. The last thing she needed was another nut in her space. She tolerated the nut she was currently cohabitating with because he was gone more than he was home. However, she doubted if he was going to take his mother with him and she was not in the mood to baby-sit a fruitcake.

Nikki did not feel like sitting and socializing with either of them, so she faked an incoming call on her cell phone and exited to take the call in private. Justin felt slighted when she never returned, but dismissed it as another one of her selfish actions.

"Friend of yours?" his mom asked.

"My girlfriend," Justin responded dryly.

Ruby was disappointed her son had chosen a white woman to make a baby with.

That was not going to work in the long run, she knew from experience. In her day she'd messed around with the "other color" a time or two. They always slept with her and left. Not one of them made the effort to contact her again.

A secret rendezvous with a married white man resulted in Jason's second older sister. Ruby never knew how to contact him and never knew where he lived. Young, alone and pregnant, she decided to take her secret to the grave. Feeling used and dirty, she found it difficult, if not impossible, to cope with her mistake. Instead of seeking professional help, she sought solace in other men's beds. "Two babies and me make three."

Four more children and six baby daddies later, she was no longer mentally capable of dealing with her repeated relationship failures and tribe of six. She began to lose touch with reality, often hearing, seeing and feeling things that were not there. As the paranoid schizophrenia progressed, she developed delusions of persecution and personal grandeur.

Years of dealing with this mental incapacity Ruby left her children and began to "homestead" in abandoned properties. She'd tear the boards off an abandoned home and fix it up, living in the home without running water and electricity, because she believed both were out to get her.

With no money of her own, hungry and cold, she would eventually return to her children, only to leave again later. The oldest son made the decision to get her some professional help.

Therapy programs and medication worked as long as she kept up the ritual. Unaware she could get assistance to continue the therapy and medication, Ruby walked away from both at the point she needed them the most. Sadly, she never fully recovered and her condition worsened with time.

Nikki never returned to the table. Pissed off and no longer able to enjoy this outing with his mom, thanks to Nikki, Justin suggested they return home. He needed to catch up on some calls and check his bank account. Tired and jet-lagged, Ruby chose to take a nap. Justin called Nikki after his mom retired.

"What is wrong with you? Why you diss my mother like that?" he growled.

"She's *your* mom," Nikki quipped. "And the two of you seem to be getting along just fine without me."

The future Mrs. Justin Kincaid wanted nothing to do with her future mother-in-law. Justin had told her a long time ago his mom was crazy. Okay, those weren't the words he used; more like "mentally unstable," but it meant the same thing to her. Either way, she knew this woman had a problem that could not be fixed with medication or therapy, and the prospect of spending any time alone with her frightened her.

"God knows when she'll appear over my bed with a knife in her hand, thinking I'm some demon out to hurt her," she mumbled.

Ruby and Justin made an awesome pair. They spent lots of time together talking and catching up on life; the life he missed as a kid and was completely oblivious to. Ruby educated him on his past. He never knew his grandparents on either side so she told him as much as she could remember. It was exciting to finally learn who he was and where he came from.

Details about his father were mind-boggling. Justin learned he not only looked like his dad, he acted like him. His father was French Canadian and lived just across the border in Detroit. Ruby admitted it had been years since she'd seen Justin's dad, but the last time she had, he looked good and was doing well.

Singing was genetic. Justin's father was a blues singer in Canada and well known and celebrated locally.

There were twelve or more of Justin's Canadian cousins who were doing some remarkable things in the entertainment industry. Seven male cousins all around his age were dancers, rappers, singers or musicians. Three of his female cousins danced in Las Vegas as showgirls and two were actors. One in particular was doing well as a Canadian soap opera actress and was considering moving to L.A. to advance her career.

Hopeful of a reunion, Justin asked his mom where he could locate his father. She gave him as many details and family member names and numbers as she could, but warned him they were not the most congenial group of people. Justin chose to ignore her warning.

CHAPTER 21

Willa Mae Sanders hummed her favorite hymn, "Jesus Keep Me Near the Cross," as she dusted the cluttered fireplace mantel. She'd turned it into somewhat of a shrine, which she maintained by arranging and rearranging the numerous photos and mementos weekly.

"Look at my boy," she exclaimed, lifting Terrel's third-grade picture and studying it as if it were her first time seeing it. She picked up a few more pictures, studied them and then dusted under them before cleaning their frames and returning them to their spot.

She was an attractive woman. It was easy to see where Terrel got his good looks. Stylish, she spent most of the monthly allowance she got from Terrel on church clothes. Willa Mae was also a proud woman, who'd made a wonderful life for herself without a husband and raised a fine, respectable Black man in the process. Terrel was away at college when his deadbeat dad dropped dead on the factory floor of a heart attack.

It was Terrel's freshman year and Willa Mae was thankful the "Good Lawd" had seen fit that his education was paid for with an athletic scholarship. He excelled in all sports and did well for himself as a professional athlete.

Excited about Terrel's call, she busied herself around the house preparing for him and his girlfriend. *Terrel ain't never brought home no girl! Oh, ain't like he ain't had his share of them, but to bring one home means something,* Willa Mae surmised. She wanted her son to find a decent church-goin' girl who could give her the grandbabies she longed for, before the "Good Lawd" called her home.

Willa Mae got teary-eyed thinking about the prospect of having grand-babies. They'd be good kids, smart as a whip. This Felicia was smart; Terrel had told her that much and she knew her precious son was bright. He was always readin' and learnin' and loved to ask questions. Most times they were questions she couldn't answer so she'd left that responsibility to his teachers.

Out of respect, Terrel rang the doorbell, even though he had a key. Willa Mae hurried to the front door, pausing to get a glimpse of herself in the hallway mirror.

"Hi, Ma," Terrel said, hugging her and lifting her off her feet. Willa Mae giggled.

"Boy, put me down," she said, fixing her clothes when he did. Willa Mae turned to get a look at the beautiful brown-skinned girl standing next to her son. Extending her hand, Felicia smiled and introduced herself. Mrs. Sanders warmly held Felicia's hand in hers and told her she was happy to finally meet her.

Willa Mae liked her instantly. Still holding her hand, she led Felicia into the house.

"You want some of my famous iced tea?" she asked, not waiting for an answer and pouring Felicia a glass. Felicia sipped the tea, which was exceptionally good.

"I love your home, it's very comfortable," she commented, looking around at the eclectic décor. Terrel gave Felicia a thumbs-up; glad she remembered one way to his mother's heart was compliments, lots of them.

"Come on, baby, let me show you around." Willa Mae began at the back of the house and worked her way forward. She explained her color choices, the style of the furniture and accent pieces in great detail, as if she were a curator describing a piece of art in a museum.

The family room housed the shrine, which Willa Mae saved for last. She approached it with pride, pausing in front of it to allow Felicia to take it all in. One by one she picked up each item from its spot and explained its importance before replacing it. Felicia adored her and listened intently, thankful for some insight into who and what Terrel was about.

Hungry, Terrel interrupted the tour. "Ma, what did you cook?"

As proud moms do, Willa Mae beamed.

"That boy act like he's helpless when he comes home." Felicia followed her into the kitchen, where Terrel began digging in pans on the stove. His mother got the dishtowel and playfully swatted him.

Willa Mae laid out her best china, glasses and silverware. She preferred linen napkins over paper whenever she had guests.

"Mrs. Sanders, please don't go to all this fuss…," Felicia offered, reaching to help.

"Baby, this ain't no trouble. I enjoy company."

"It looks good, Ma," Terrel said, pinching off a piece of meat. His mom saw him out the corner of her eye, stopped what she was doing and gave him a disgusted look.

"Boy, go wash your hands so you can bless the food." Turning to Felicia she continued. "You'd think he was raised with no manners." She chuckled and completed setting the table.

Terrel returned and turned his attention to Felicia. "You need to freshen up or anything?"

"I'm fine, just need to wash my hands."

"This way." He motioned for her to follow him. Once in the bathroom and out of his mother's view, he passionately kissed her. Felicia pulled away, concerned about his mother catching them. He laughed, pleased with her respect for his mother and her home. "You're a class act," he said, smiling.

"Thanks," she said, looking for a towel to dry her hands. Terrel grabbed the mauve one that hung closest to the sink and handed it to her. Felicia took it with her left hand and flicked the dripping water from her right hand in Terrel's face. They both laughed.

Willa Mae's voice whipped them back into shape. "All right, you two, come on and eat. Food's gettin' cold!"

Terrel blessed the food with a very eloquent prayer. It impressed Felicia, but everything he did impressed her. Her cell phone rang before she could take a bite. It was Katlyn; she excused herself from the table to take the call.

Willa Mae watched her leave. "Terrel, she's delightful. So pretty, and smart, too. I like her," his mother whispered.

"Me, too, Ma."

"You known her long?"

"Awhile, Ma, why?"

"Just wonderin'now, is that her hair or is all those curls somethin' else?"

"They're hers, Ma." Terrel laughed at his mother's question.

Felicia rejoined them at the table. "Sorry about that, it was Katlyn," she explained, her eyes focusing on Terrel.

"Is she okay?" he asked.

"Yes. She's fine. Finally getting out."

Surprised, Terrel asked if she was dating. Felicia's "sort of" answer told him she was not going to share details and his intuition told him she'd rather not discuss it in present company.

CHAPTER 22

Two years had passed and Katlyn was still apprehensive about dating. Dinner with a man other than Justin made Katlyn nervous. Although it was business, Kyle suggested they take in a movie first. She wondered how the two fit. Fighting the urge to figure it out, she decided to wait and see.

He arrived on time in a rag-top Hummer, dressed like a modern-day lumberjack. Katlyn was glad she'd wisely chosen to leave the sparkles at home, opting to wear rhinestones only on her belt buckle. When Kyle dropped the top, she smiled; pleased she no longer had hair to fret over.

The movie caught Katlyn completely off guard. It was a romance that ended with an unexpected twist and left her guessing about the point the writer had hoped to make. Again, she pondered Kyle's motive for taking her to this movie and she found it impossible to connect the movie to the meeting.

"Well, what do you think?" he asked her as he opened the car door for her.

"I'm not sure what to think. I enjoyed it, I guess," she responded, looking at him, bewildered.

"I apologize if it bored you. This was business for me. One of the writers I represent wrote the screenplay. Of course I am obligated to see it and I thought you might benefit from seeing it as well." He stared at before starting the car.

Again, she looked at him strangely. "How so?"

"Don't be coy, Katlyn."

She stared at him and waited for an answer.

"You're not going to let me off the hook, are you?"

Tired of this child's play, she shifted in her seat, angled her body toward him and answered, "No," with a sistah-girl edge on it.

Kyle found her demeanor and lack of desire to "play tag" humorous. "It should be pretty obvious. You have talent—talent that can go beyond writing songs and books. Why not shoot for the stars?"

"What do you mean?" she asked, completely dumbfounded.

"Katlyn, why not have your book turned into a movie?" They pulled into valet and waited for an attendant. Flowers filled the entry and the foyer of Muse. There were several small rooms off the back of the restaurant that reminded her of villas in Italy. Each room opened to its own private balcony with tables that seated two or four. They were seated at a table for two, which was reserved with a bottle of expensive wine chilling.

The wine was served promptly, along with a platter of appetizers. "I brought you here for the ambiance," he joked, but Katlyn could feel the romantic atmosphere and it made her uneasy. Kyle could see she was uncomfortable.

"Listen," he said, sipping his wine. "I don't bite, relax." He made eye contact with her and held his gaze there.

Kyle was a powerhouse who wore many hats and had the ability to make things happen. He knew the moment he read the excerpts from her novel *Stumbling Into This Place* that she was talented and immediately requested the manuscript. That was a week ago and now they were meeting to discuss a possible deal.

"So, is Atlanta growing on you?"

"It's an adjustment, but I like it," Katlyn admitted.

Kyle nodded in agreement. "I know what you mean. It took me awhile to adjust. How long have you been writing?"

"Years, but just for fun," she said honestly.

"Always lyrics to songs?"

"No, poetry also, but like I said—it was something to do."

Curious about why she chose to switch from writing lyrics to writing books, Kyle continued to question Katlyn, hoping to get more than one-sentence responses. He motioned for the waiter to refill their glasses, which were nearly empty.

The wine made Katlyn feel more at ease, and as Kyle had hoped, she did open up.

"Songs are an abbreviated version of books. They both tell a story, but one limits the time and quantity included in the finished product. Writing a book, telling a story from beginning to end, is awesome." Her mouth formed a broad grin as she thought about her writing.

Kyle smiled, and probed some more. "How did you end up writing *Stumbling Into This Place*?"

She let out a long sigh and thought carefully about her answer. Kyle watched her deep in thought and regretted broaching the subject. Thanks to Justin and the tabloids, everyone knew, Kyle included, about her legal separation and messy pending divorce.

"Uh-hh, you know, on second thought, I'm sorry. My question was inappropriate," he said apologetically.

She could see he was struggling for the right thing to say.

"It's okay, Kyle. I'm a big girl," she said. "It's like this…I gave all I had to a relationship I believed in, and in the process I lost me. Writing about that part of my life was healing. Those thoughts I wrote in my journal birthed this novel."

"That is an excellent synopsis, remember it—you'll need it when the press begins to hound you with the same question," he informed her, winking to reassure her he meant what he said.

"My turn," she said.

"Shoot!"

"Why me? Why my manuscript?" She leaned closer to hear what he had to say.

"This is a woman's book, filled with painful realities women experience when dealing with men and love."

Katlyn jumped right in. "You're so right! I know tons of females who have lived what I have. Some made it, some didn't. As a matter of fact, I have a schoolmate who is institutionalized right now because a man broke her heart. I have been there, done that, hated it and made it. Women need to know they can, too!"

Kyle sat forward, looking in her eyes. He knew she would do well on a book tour. Her pain was real, you could see it, hear it, and, most important, feel it. The stuff good movies were made of. When she spoke about what she had endured, he was drawn to her and she held his attention, making him want to know more.

As she ran on, he noticed her natural beauty and was taken aback by it. "You know, not many women can wear their hair like that." Katlyn blushed, uncomfortable by the observation. She avoided eye contact and focused on the view.

"Tell me about you, Mrs. Kincaid," he commanded.

She started by telling him she was a former flight attendant and he interrupted, wanting to get to what was really on his mind.

"You seeing anyone?" She was caught off guard by his bluntness.

"No and I'm not looking," she answered emphatically.

"Ouch!" he said, chuckling. That made her smile.

Since he opened the door, Katlyn, somewhat curious about his personal life and his availability, walked in. She asked if he was attached and whether he had kids. He was very forthcoming about his failed marriage and she gathered from his tone he regretted it. That made her think for a moment about Justin. She had not cared before, but suddenly she wondered if he had days like this, where he sat and thought about how he'd blown it. When Kyle admitted he and his ex were cordial and saw each other regularly for the kids, she digressed once more wondering if she would ever be *cordial* with Justin.

"My former wife found our lives together empty. She started seeing someone else and told me about if after the fact." Katlyn nodded her head empathetically. She could relate to being dumped, traded in for a newer model.

Kyle continued, "I know—or should I say, I read about your situation. For the record, I think he's a fool." In total agreement with him, she laughed a very hearty laugh.

"You're very attractive and quite talented. You can have anything and anyone you want." He stared at her, waiting on a response. Katlyn finished her glass of wine, and then made eye contact. Kyle rested his hand on hers.

"I like you. I'd enjoy doing this again sometime, Katlyn Kincaid." She pulled her hand back to safety. "Listen, I am over fifty and done chasing skirts."

"So what do you call this?" she asked boldly. Her frankness caught him off guard.

Kyle looked at her for a while and said, "I'm not sure!" She appreciated his honesty.

Flabbergasted by this turn of events, Katlyn finished her glass of wine and had Kyle fill it again. Kyle Russell, the star maker, voted one of the sexiest men in America, was pursuing her. Most would consider him nice-looking; Katlyn considered him exceptionally good-looking. He was bald and distinguished-looking with strong masculine features; the Michael Jordan type. And even though he'd lived in Georgia forever, he still had that East Coast thing happening.

Two bottles of wine and six hours later, Katlyn had told him about growing up without a mother, being goal-oriented, and her painful breakup. No stranger to bestsellers (books or movies), Kyle knew the making of one and she was sitting across the table from him.

Momentarily he discussed business, setting a future date to have her review a contract. The last hour of their evening was spent discussing what it was like being a Black male in an industry that was just beginning to recognize Black talent.

"You're a wonderful person, Katlyn. Like I said, your soon-to-be ex is a fool." She smiled in agreement. "I'm not just saying that, I mean it. Can I see you again?"

Katlyn looked away, needing a moment to think. The fact that he was very busy and committed to his children might allow her to have a casual relationship with him, on her terms.

"I only want to talk," he assured her, putting her at ease.

"Sure, *talk* would be nice."

❖❖❖

Justin sat waiting for Nikki at their favorite spot. She was late, which had become her modus operandi. Her constant tardiness aggravated him, and aggravated his current bad mood.

The new CD was not doing well. His record label was hopeful, telling him to "give it more time." He knew they blamed his recent marital shake-up and his public display of his relationship with Nikki as the reason. In secret, he did, too! The timing was wrong. Justin was rapidly approaching his mid-thirties—a questionable age in the entertainment industry, especially for someone who wanted to take his career to the next level and break into acting. His plans for his career and life with Nikki were huge. By now he should be riding on top, but instead, success was slipping from his grip. He felt like the walls were caving in on him.

He needed to talk to someone, someone who understood him. Katlyn had always been his sounding board, but he knew better than to call her. And of course he couldn't talk to Nikki about it: that would be like an adult trying to talk about adult things with a child. While he contemplated his circumstances on the tree of woe and absentmindedly played with his keys, Nikki pulled up in the new Benz convertible Justin had bought her, with the top down.

She was wearing a DKNY form-fitting, low-cut white dress—no underwear—strappy sandals and Gucci sunglasses. He saw her arrive and watched her walk toward him with her usual sexy sway.

"Hey sweetie," she said, leaning down to kiss him on the nose. Justin pulled back, not wanting her lipstick on him. "What is your problem?" Nikki grumbled.

The hurt tone in her voice made him check himself. He paused, and took a moment to correct his attitude. He really was glad to see her, but did not appreciate her tardiness. *He was the star* and she still had not recognized that.

"Sorry, I just need to eat," he offered as his explanation. "You ready to order?"

Nikki glanced at the menu, intentionally ignoring his question. "I'll have the usual," she snapped, promptly excusing herself from the table. That angered him more causing him to slam his keys on the table. He felt like a minion, hoping to be graced by her presence. Nikki's ungrateful attitude and refusal to show some appreciation for what he'd given up to be with *her* pissed him off!

Over time he had become suspicious of Nikki. Lately she was unavailable by phone and spent quite a bit of time away from him. When he asked to join her, she made excuses for him not to, which exacerbated his insecure feelings.

By the time she returned, Justin was almost done eating and her food was cold. She pushed her entrée to the side and nibbled on her salad.

"I'm going to Europe in the morning," she informed him, never acknowledging his presence.

"What do you mean you're 'going to Europe'? For what?" Justin said angrily.

"To see my dad."

"Nikki—why?"

She cut him off, sick of his whining. He had done a lot of that lately and it was getting on her last nerve. "My dad is getting older and I missed his last birthday, I don't want to miss this one."

Justin felt his temper escalating. Nikki had found lots of reasons to be away from him and their home lately, and he was beginning to wonder why. His tour had been cut short and when he arrived home she was "on vacation." She had yet to say with whom!

"Is there a reason you didn't ask me to go?" He stared at her, wanting to smack the smirk off her face.

"Didn't think you could or would want to, I mean with the CD sales stalling and all."

She had to bring that up, just had to go there! Justin began to boil. Before he knew it he was enraged, screaming and shouting obscenities at Nikki and having a full-blown temper tantrum, unaware of the paparazzi nearby.

Humiliated by his outrageous behavior, Nikki picked up her cold entrée and threw it in his face. She grabbed her purse, picked up the keys from the table and ran to her car in tears. The key did not fit the door lock and the remote failed to open the door as well. Flustered, Nikki tried to force the key into the lock and in the process dropped her purse, which popped open and spilled out most of its contents into the open storm drain below. As the paparazzi clicked away, this situation moved quickly from a mere spat to front-page news.

In her Jimmy Choo stilettos, Nikki stomped back to Justin and demanded *her* keys, figuring she'd taken his by mistake. When he told her he didn't have her keys, she threw his into the street. *Plop!* They plunged into the drain joining hers, which had fallen from her purse. Unable to stand being near him any longer, Nikki caught a cab to a girlfriend's home. Justin paid to have a cab take him across town to his condo.

His manager's third call to his home phone successfully woke him from a one-too-many-beer sleep the next morning.

"Justin, wake up, what were you thinkin'?" Sherman yelled.

"Man, why you hollerin'?" Justin mumbled groggily.

Certain this would be a total disaster and really expensive to fix, Sherman told him to hang up and read the morning gossip columns.

Starbucks coffee will wake the dead. Justin was wired and headed to search for a paper when he passed a tabloid lying on a table. He froze, unable to believe what he was seeing: a photo of him and Nikki on the front page.

Sitting down at the table, he read the entire story and then tried to call Nikki. She had not come home and had never told him what time her flight would leave. No answer on her cell, so he walked to a nearby sidewalk magazine stand and purchased a copy of every tabloid and newspaper there was.

At home he carefully scanned each one to find any and all articles that talked about his public display of SOS—stuck on stupid. He blamed Nikki for this catastrophe, and as usual she was nowhere to be found.

He needed someone with wisdom and sound advice to help him think through this mess he called life. Ruby had settled into L.A. and his home quite nicely, but she was no one he looked to for life advice or guidance.

Fatherly advice would be good here. Even though he didn't know his father, he wanted to find him so he purchased round-trip tickets for himself and Ruby to Detroit. Justin decided to take his mother with him so she could help locate and meet his relatives on his father's side.

Leyton Shreeves was a strikingly handsome man with the same chiseled bone structure of his son. His alto voice was sensuous and easy to listen to. Justin felt a rush as he watched his dad work the audience.

Justin's father was the main draw and the house act at the Ritz Carlton-Ontario. All table seating was gone, so Justin and Ruby sat at the bar to watch the show. The dimly lit room helped shield Justin from the eyes of adoring fans in the audience. Confident no one noticed or cared he was in the room, he took off his designer shades and ordered a beer.

After Leyton's set ended, Justin gave him time to chill in his dressing room. He and Ruby had a game plan: she would approach Leyton first and then introduce his son to him.

Leyton smiled broadly when he saw Ruby. She looked fabulous (Justin had made sure she would) and he really was happy she did. Leyton knew he hadn't done right by Ruby. When she told him she was pregnant, he was excited about being a father. He moved to Detroit and shacked with Ruby for five months, working hard to take care of them. He would have gladly married her, but she already had four other mouths to feed and a struggling musician's salary could not feed them all.

Justin grew up without his father's presence after Ruby threw his dad out. Leyton didn't know about the schizophrenia, but he knew she had to be nuts to pull a knife on him and order him out of their home half-naked, in sub-zero temperatures for no reason.

For a while he sent monetary support to Ruby for Justin. But after a couple months the envelopes began to be returned unopened, with no forwarding address. Since he had no idea where Ruby had gone—and it was obvious to him Ruby didn't want to be found—Leyton just opted out of the whole thing.

"Ruby, you look great!" Leyton reached out to hug her, but stopped short as his clone stepped inside the door. Both Leyton and Justin froze, and then stared at each other. It was eerie, like looking at oneself in a mirror. Thanks to a bottle, Leyton's natural gray hair was jet-black, just like his son's. They looked like twins, partly because Leyton hardly aged and partly because Justin had aged tremendously since he'd left Katlyn.

Instinctively Leyton knew Justin was his son. Without saying a word, he walked over and hugged him. They held each other without making a sound. Tears began to slowly find their way down Justin's cheeks. He let go of his father and grabbed some tissues. Neither said a word. Ruby smiled, pleased at this reunion.

Leyton was quite familiar with Justin Kincaid, but was totally unaware this was his son. He often thought they resembled, but people said that about him and Billy Dee and they were nowhere close to being related. A sense of pride overtook him when he realized this handsome and talented phenomenon was from his genes.

With so much to catch up on and so much to learn, Justin booked a two-bedroom suite for himself and his mom. Leyton offered his spare bedroom to them, but Justin felt they would be more comfortable on neutral turf since his dad was now married and had a family.

Once they settled into their room, Justin called his father, who invited them over for dinner to meet his other half-siblings. Leyton had five children and two grands he wanted his son to meet.

Justin accepted the invite, but Ruby didn't want to intrude on the reunion. Not wanting her to be in Detroit alone, Justin ordered a limo for her and paid the driver handsomely to escort her wherever she wanted to go.

Meeting his half-siblings and cousins was a big thrill. All of them favored and all of them were attractive. As the night progressed, word spread of Justin's arrival. More and more relatives stopped by his father's home to meet him. One cousin in particular stood out from the rest.

Tracee was extremely attractive. Her chocolate fudge complexion was flawless, as were her perfectly aligned white teeth. Every curve was in the right place on her five-foot-seven, one hundred-twenty-five-pound frame, with no fat in sight. She wore her hair jet-black, cropped short and spiked on the top, which drew attention to her beautiful, light-brown doe eyes. She reminded Justin of Katlyn.

The two of them hit it off immediately. Tracee was a soap-opera actress famous in Canada, but her show didn't air in the States. She wanted to take her acting career to another level and that required moving to L.A. The soap paid well, but not well enough for her to afford to live as she would like. Not willing to go west and struggle like so many actors she knew, she'd put her plans to take her career to the next level on hold—until now!

It took Tracee no time at all to settle into Justin's home and the groove of L.A. Ruby had decided to stay in Detroit and get her life together, which freed up her room for Tracee. Carless, Tracee depended on Justin to show her L.A. and introduce her to the power players. With Nikki still gone, he was happy to oblige.

When people met Tracee they loved her. Men reacted to her the way they did Nikki. Justin enjoyed the attention being with Tracee brought him. He knew people assumed Tracee was his piece on the side and his ego said let them. She was all that and being all that made the press take notice. With his career on the down slope, any press would be better than no press (which was what he was experiencing right now, with the exception of the fight with Nikki).

Nikki saw a picture of Justin and his new "beau," Tracee, in one of the gossip columns in a newspaper in Brazil. It infuriated her. Nine weeks had passed and she had not made plans to return to L.A. That quickly changed when she saw this hoochie on *her* man's arm.

Suddenly the sistah came out in her. Miss Thang called Justin with every intention of going off. She reached his voice mail, but that didn't deter her. Head moving and finger waving, she threatened to castrate him when she returned. Having recently retired his cell phone and purchased a new Blackberry, Justin never got the message and never returned the call.

A witch on a broomstick had nothing on Nikki when she returned home. She'd had a wonderful time in Brazil and had not planned to be back this soon. This intrusion into her vacation was inexcusable and she intended to make the two of them pay for messing up her good time. Being away from L.A. and Justin had allowed her to clear her mind and relax. Everyone had called her to tell her about her infamous moment in the headlines, and she hated Justin for causing her to make a fool of herself.

When she walked into her home she became irate. It was very apparent she wasn't the only one who'd had a good time during her nine-week absence. Their condo was in complete disarray and smelled like week-old garbage.

Upon entering the front door she found Justin asleep on the sofa with days of razor stubble on his face and several empty liquor bottles scattered about. The sight of him lying there, half-naked, snoring and drunk, made her want to puke. A picture of her was clutched tightly in his hand, which rested on his chest.

Nikki hated the way he smothered her and allowed her to walk all over him. She wished he would stand up and be a man. But the nastier she treated him, the wimpier he acted. Tired of the whole thing, she planned to leave soon. The tenant subletting her condo was moving in two more months. Up to now she had been counting the days, but since it was obvious Justin was creepin,' leaving was put on hold.

Justin woke to pee and stumbled over Nikki's luggage. "Nik, you home?" he called out. The sound of his drunken state annoyed her.

"Yeah, I'm in here," she said softly, hoping he would go back to sleep. He stumbled into their bedroom and stood there, staring at her. Crust surrounded his mouth and eyes, and he stank. When he tried to hug her, she broke away from his embrace and sat on the bed.

Justin sat next to her and gently rubbed her thigh, enjoying the feel of her smooth skin. Touching her once again made him hard. The bulge rising from his boxers repulsed her. Nikki stood up and moved away from him, opening the window.

"It stinks in here," she barked. Hurt by her slight, Justin sat quietly for a moment searching for something to say to make her respond favorably to him.

"Baby, I been gone." His words were slurred and Nikki had a difficult time understanding him. That made her even angrier. Why was he drunk in the middle of the day?

As she walked into the living room she noticed things, feminine things, in places that had not been there when she left. "Oh, hold up…wait just one minute! What is this?" she shrieked as she picked up a makeup pouch off the cocktail table.

Justin, still groggy, walked in the living room to see what she was holding. It took him a minute to focus on what it was and remember why it was there. Before he could gather his thoughts and explain it belonged to Tracee, Nikki lit into him.

"Save it, Justin," she said curtly. Her tone told him she was about to say something bad; he suddenly felt queasy.

"Who is the heifer you been parading all over town with? Does this belong to her?" she screamed as she waved the makeup pouch in his face.

Before he could answer, Tracee walked through the front door, dropped her overnight bag and stared at Nikki as if she'd lost her mind.

"What's going on?" she asked, addressing the question to Justin, but looking at Nikki for the answer.

"Who are you?" Nikki demanded.

"My name is Tracee; who are you?"

That was it; Nikki lost it. She threw Tracee's makeup bag at her and charged. Tracee moved out of her way and Nikki broke her fingernails as she ran into the wall. Justin jumped up and attempted to hold Nikki, but she was not having it. Miss Latino Heat scratched his arms with her remaining fingernails. When he let go she charged Tracee again.

This time Tracee darted into her bedroom and locked the door behind her. Nikki kicked the door several times before she realized what she was doing. Backing away from the bedroom door, it dawned on her Tracee had not gone to *their* bedroom. Turning to Justin, she asked one question.

"Who is Tracee?"

"My cousin who moved here from Canada to pursue an acting career."

Feeling every bit of the fool she'd just acted, Nikki slowly walked to their bedroom, slammed the door and locked it, not wanting to deal with any of this.

After several minutes of calmness, Tracee poked her head out the door. Justin motioned for her to come out.

"Is that your woman?" she asked guardedly. Justin nodded yes, but said nothing. Tracee continued in a whisper, "Did she not know I was here?"

"I haven't heard from her in more than two months. How was I supposed to tell her?"

Tracee sat next to her cousin and stared at him. He looked bad. She'd gone home to Canada for a couple days and he seemed fine before she left. Maybe he was coming down with something.

"You okay?" she asked, sounding worried. Justin nodded, but still had nothing to say.

"Want to talk about it?" Tracee offered.

"No."

Unable to face the recipient of her ill-timed tirade, Nikki remained in the bedroom all night with the door locked. The next morning she left early with hopes of avoiding Tracee.

Tired of playing taxi and tour guide, Justin had traded in one of the two Mercedes he'd purchased for Nikki for a Land Rover for Tracee. Of course, Nikki didn't know that. And Justin hadn't thought about it until she burst through the door screaming, "Call 911! My Mercedes is gone!"

Justin took her by the arm and pulled her down next to him to explain the car had not been stolen, but traded.

Strike one! Sure he'd bought the car, but it was Nikki's. Next he told her Tracee had moved into his mom's room because his mother had gone back to Detroit. Nikki waited for him to say when Tracee would be leaving. He did not. Strike two! Finally, Justin revealed that he was giving Tracee a monthly allowance to help her out while she got on her feet. Strike three! Now the cow was cutting into Nikki's spending change? That was so not going to work!

Tracee had to go! Nikki sat on the chaise in their bedroom trying to figure out how to make that happen. First thing she needed to do was get control over the situation, which meant get control, once more, over Justin.

While Tracee was out for the evening, Nikki ran a bubble bath and invited him to join her. Justin, horny and in desperate need of some personal time alone with the love of his life, did not hesitate. They finished making love for the third time just ten minutes before Tracee arrived. The sun was up!

That morning Nikki put the second part of her plan in action. She apologized to Tracee for attacking her. Tracee graciously accepted her apology and assured her she wouldn't hold it against her. She chalked Nikki's behavior up to stupid and went about her business as usual.

Not long after Tracee left, Nikki set part three of her plan in action: creating doubt and distrust. Justin barely knew Tracee and Nikki believed she had a past that she was running from in Canada. Several phone calls later she still had nothing on her, but she was not going to give up.

Tracee felt the same way. Nikki had to go! It was obvious Nikki was a gold digger with a capital G and she was not about to let her cousin and *her* meal ticket get used!

❂❂❂

Katlyn sat at her desk, reviewing the messages on her machine. A couple were business, the remaining were pleasure. Three suitors were inviting her to dinner and two suggested a movie. She weighed the invites and decided to stay home. Conquering her fear of dating thrust Katlyn into demand, but none of the suitors stood a chance of getting past the first date. Katlyn actually enjoyed being alone.

Kyle was proving to be a valuable friend and business confidant. He'd negotiated a lucrative book deal for her and they were close to finalizing the details. He schooled her on investing her money and making long-term plans for her future. His extensive knowledge of tax loopholes and shelters helped her ensure her money would remain tight.

The phone rang. Not interested in a date, Katlyn allowed the machine to take the call. She heard Felicia's voice and picked up.

"What cha doin', girlie?"

"Avoiding the phone," Katlyn replied.

"You that much in demand?"

"Hey, when you're good, you're good," Katlyn boasted, sounding quite confident. Felicia laughed, glad to have her old girlfriend back.

"Why are you calling? I thought you were supposed to be on lockdown!" They both laughed.

"Terrel stepped out. Guess where I was last night!"

"Don't have a clue," Katlyn answered. "Where?"

"At a Justin Kincaid concert."

"You lyin'," Katlyn answered quickly, anxious to hear the details.

"Not even—he performed at Cheri's graduation celebration." Cheri was a friend of Felicia's, who Katlyn had met once or twice. She had obtained her master's degree and had planned an extravagant celebration.

Katlyn listened to the details, which Felicia gave step by step. Cheri hired Justin to serenade her and her friends. In need of money, Justin agreed to do the show live to track, which both made him affordable for Cheri and meant he didn't have to split the proceeds with his band.

In spite of what the press said about him being a has-been, he still knew how to make the women scream, Felicia informed her. Everyone enjoyed his hour-long performance. The Hollywood buzz was he could not get a recording deal and hadn't had a hit in two years. However, if last night was a barometer on his popularity, he had not missed a beat. His hits were hot then, and still sizzled.

Katlyn was silent for a moment. Felicia knew what she wanted to ask, so she volunteered the information.

"Yessss, I spoke to him. He seemed genuinely happy to see me."

Curiosity got the best of Katlyn. "Was *she* there?"

Felicia could not wait to tell her this tidbit of information. "Sit down—rumor has it they broke up!"

Katlyn stood up from her desk and unconsciously began to pace the floor.

"Nuh-uh, you lyin'!" she screamed.

Felicia let that register before she continued. "And, Mr. Kincaid's popularity has taken a dive. Those in the know say his album has fizzled and Miss Thang is to blame. Looks like making the front page of the tabloids hurt his image and he could not buy a new one. That's how Cheri got him at bargain price."

They continued to discuss Justin, Felicia making sure to tell Katlyn he only had made $7,000 on the gig. Astonished, Katlyn tried to comprehend how he could work for so little money, when he had made so much in the past.

Terrel came home and broke up their party, so Felicia told Katlyn she would fill her in on the rest later and hung up. Katlyn sat there stunned, holding the phone, wondering if Justin and Nikki really had broken up. Impulsively she dialed their old number. Justin answered on the first ring—sounding like he'd been drinking.

"Justin, heyyyy, it's Katlyn." Silence.

"Aw-ww wow, hey baby," he said, glad to hear from her. "How you been?"

"I'm great—don't know when I've been better."

"You sound good," he admitted, shaking his head in an attempt to sober up.

"Felicia told me she saw you in Florida said you still got it." They both chuckled.

Embarrassed she knew about the gig, he lied. "Yeah, I did that gig as a favor to a friend."

"She said you looked good."

"She looked good, too. Happy is more the word—I almost didn't recognize her."

"She's seeing someone and they're doing well," Katlyn informed him.

Justin saw an opportunity and took it. "What about you? You seeing anyone?" he asked with bated breath, certain she was.

"Not really."

Relieved, he volunteered the next piece of information. "Me, either. You know Nikki and I broke up." There was an awkward silence.

Her question answered, Katlyn wanted to get off the phone. Her feelings for Justin were still intact. She missed him and cared about him. Calling was not the smart thing to do, but she was glad she did. Her only regret was not finding out who dumped whom. Knowing he got dumped by the person he dumped her for would be justice. She hoped Felicia knew and would tell her the next time they discussed the topic.

After Katlyn hung up, Justin sat back on the sofa, very sober, taking it all in. He wondered why she had called and if her calling meant she still cared.

❂❂❂

Terrel went out for bagels while Felicia slept in. He returned to find her sitting on the living room floor watching the morning news. "Hey, Sleeping Beauty has awakened!" He kissed her on the forehead and headed to the kitchen with the bagels. He put plates on the counter alongside the cream cheese and butter.

"Bagels!" Terrel announced. He looked at Felicia smiling, as he held them up.

"Oooo, from our spot?" she asked.

"You know it."

Felicia jumped up and hurried to the bag of bagels. Terrel stood by smiling as he watched her tear into the bag. She stopped long enough to plant a kiss on his cheek, then proceeded to layer her onion bagel with butter and cream cheese.

"Fattening," he warned. Felicia looked at him and winked, enjoying each bite.

Terrel and Felicia were happy with each other. They were opposites who were extremely attracted to each other. What they had was serious; each was comfortable with that. Not one to like relationships that had labels, Felicia was excited about the one she had secretly given Terrel. "Her man" was a godsend. She knew she cared a lot about him and for once looked forward to being in a committed relationship.

Terrel liked the way Felicia was "working" him. She was available, but not all the time. She let him know she liked him, but kept a cool detachment. He liked her enough to weigh taking what they had to another level. She had all the criteria needed to be the one, but he wasn't quite ready to turn in his playah's card.

❂❂❂

Kyle's phone call had left Katlyn with a weird feeling. He had asked her to meet him at his office, but didn't say why. She was so anxious to find out what he wanted to discuss with her, she arrived a half-hour early.

"I'll let Mr. Russell know you're here," his secretary said, motioning for her to have a seat.

When she entered his office, Kyle was staring at his computer screen and did not look up. Katlyn spoke first. Looking up to acknowledge her presence, he paused and smiled.

"You look wonderful."

"Thank you," was her reply. She smiled and waited for him to offer her a seat.

"Oh! Forgive me, please sit down."

Kyle joined her on the other side of his desk. He engaged in small talk for a few minutes, which only heightened her curiosity. She wished he would cut the crap and get to the point, but she remained calm.

"I asked you here to discuss some things." *Finally*, she thought. Her posture and demeanor changed. She leaned toward him and made eye contact.

"We've been in each other's company a lot over the past months." Katlyn nodded and continued listening. "Lately, I find myself wanting to see more of you. Is that possible?"

She looked at him as if he had spoken to her in Greek. This was not at all what she expected to hear and was not sure how to respond.

"I can tell from the expression on your face, you were expecting something else. Forgive me; I should have gotten business out of the way first. Let me back up. If you are wondering about your book deal—don't! It's a done deal, I have your completed copies of the paperwork right here." Kyle stood up and lifted a stack of legal documents from his organizer bin and placed them in her lap.

Flabbergasted by his "opening," she did not and could not focus on the mound of papers resting on her lap. She knew she was not ready for a serious relationship, but Kyle would be a wonderful diversion. He was safe—still legally attached and dealing with his own issues.

From the moment they began seeing each other; Katlyn decided she enjoyed having Kyle around. He was fun to be with and easy to be around, "smooth" would be the adjective of choice.

Most weekends she made the hour-and-a-half trek to his place on the water because she loved the ambiance. A fire was always burning in the fireplace and he always had a good book and a glass of wine waiting. Not one to take in the nightlife, Kyle preferred to stay home with her and spoil her. An excellent cook, he prepared her favorite meals while she relaxed by the fire.

Some weekends, he gave her a massage after he let her soak in a warm tub of her favorite bubble bath, milk and honey. Other times, he washed her short curly hair and brushed it dry. In turn, Katlyn played board games with him or read one of his favorite books, out loud.

Kyle threw a surprise get-together at his home and only invited Felicia and Terrel to help celebrate the sale of Katlyn's first book. He had not met either one of them, but had heard lots of good things from Katlyn.

Felicia liked him immediately and made a mental note to tell Katlyn she approved. It was very apparent they were much closer than Katlyn let on. Kyle was not shy about showing affection toward her. Whenever possible he held her hand, kissed her nose, massaged her shoulder and neck or gently rubbed her back. Touching her felt good to him and he did a lot of it. PDA was something Katlyn liked, but was not accustomed to; it made her blush, but she never resisted his touch.

"Things seem to be pretty hot and heavy with those two," Felicia commented, observing Katlyn and Kyle from his deck.

"She seems happy," Terrel interjected. Never one to interfere in someone's relationship, he preferred to stay out of it. He also preferred his woman to stay out! One time too many he had been the victim of someone not minding their business.

"I want her to be but I don't know about this. I think it's too soon," Felicia said.

"Your bed ain't empty at night," he said sarcastically. "Old dude is swept, leave it alone and let her do her thing."

Felicia took offense at what he said. She knew her girlfriend and knew she wasn't a loose person and she didn't sleep around. If Katlyn was sexually involved with Kyle, it meant she really liked him.

Attempting to mellow the tension in the air, Terrel made a comment in jest that was not the least bit funny to Felicia. He burst into laughter; she did not. The expression on her face let him know he had hurt her feelings. He reached out, pulled her close and apologized, realizing he was heaping his anger from the past on her.

"She's a big girl. I think she can handle her own life," he offered, trying to minimize Felicia's concerns. But Felicia continued to analyze the situation.

"I hope I'm wrong, but I don't think she is over Justin," Felicia confided.

"So, you think she still got a thing for Pretty Boy?" Terrel asked.

"Don't know…," was all Felicia said.

"If you suspect she still got it bad for Pretty Boy, she needs a mature man, one who understands where she is right now. No pressure from him, know what I mean?"

Felicia looked at Terrel, amazed at his wisdom. He was right; Kyle was mature and unattached. Perhaps he'd be the cure for what was still ailing Katlyn.

"Come on, gang, it's time to toast the author," Kyle shouted from the lower level. Terrel walked ahead as Katlyn and Felicia lingered at the top of the stairs.

"Okay, Miss Thang, what is going on here?" Felicia whispered.

"He loves to spoil me and you know what? I love that he does." They hugged, Felicia relieved to see her best bud so content. As they entered the game room, Felicia pinched her. She could not believe how much effort Kyle had put into decorating the room.

Katlyn's eyes sparkled as Kyle handed each of them glasses. Terrel worked on opening another bottle of Cristal while Kyle offered the toast.

"I adore you, Katlyn. You are a breath of fresh air and now the whole world will get a chance to breathe!" Kyle kissed her gently on the lips as Terrel and Felicia shouted, "Here, here!"

Kyle motioned for everyone to join him at the bar. A superbly decorated buttercream cake sat in its center, a slender gift box next to it. Before Katlyn cut the cake, Felicia picked up the card from her and Terrel and handed it to her. She opened it and read it silently. A broad smile let Felicia know it hit home. Katlyn passed it to Kyle, who chuckled and handed it back to her. Lifting the slender box, she shook it and then carefully opened it. A loud squeal from Katlyn was followed by a "stop the madness" from Felicia, who grabbed Terrel's arm to brace herself.

The box contained a custom-made platinum necklace with a rare blue diamond in the center. Kyle took the necklace from the box and gently fastened it around Katlyn's neck. Tears filled her eyes; she stood silent for a moment to gain her composure. Felicia reached out and squeezed her hand in support.

"It has been a long time since I have felt so blessed and so very happy." A tear fell; Katlyn paused and Kyle kissed her nose.

"Kyle, you are the reason I remember to smell the roses. Thank you, Terrel, for making my 3 G's, Felicia, so happy. Felicia..." Katlyn could not continue. They hugged each other.

Terrel lit a stogie Kyle had given him when they arrived and moseyed out to the patio. Kyle, sensing a need to leave the girls to themselves, followed.

Felicia was concerned about what Katlyn was doing, so she asked. "Girlfriend, you know he's got it bad, don't you? You sure you got this under control?"

"Not to worry," Katlyn responded confidently.

Felicia pressed the issue, certain she was right. "Friends don't give friends gifts like this," she said, touching the extravagant necklace.

"They do when they got it like that," Katlyn answered matter-of-factly, admiring the necklace in the mirror behind the bar.

"You do realize this thing cost a fortune, don't you?"

Pleased with her gift and certain she owed an explanation to no one, Katlyn ignored her. Without saying one word, she looked at Felicia, smiled, grabbed her by the hand and led her to the patio to join the men.

Kyle and Terrel were seated at the patio table, enjoying the bubbly.

Felicia studied Kyle, trying to figure out what he wanted from Katlyn. Although Katlyn deserved to have someone like him, he could have anyone he wanted. He had class and long pockets and it was apparent he was at ease with his "ruling class" status.

A gut feeling told Felicia Katlyn was not yet over Justin *and* on the rebound. Her fear was she might fall head over heels for this man, who may not be as serious about her. Yes, anyone could see he liked her, but did he have her best interest at heart? Felicia realized her psychic skills had not worked in predicting the future for her own life, so she decided to leave Katlyn's life alone.

❁❁❁

Stumbling Into This Place was number one on the bestseller list. The book tour was nothing like Katlyn had imagined; she longed for home. Six weeks on a national tour from the East Coast to the West Coast was draining.

"I hate this," she told Felicia, as she stretched out on the floor of her suite to unwind.

"It's almost over," Felicia offered reassuringly, for her benefit as well as Katlyn's. Seniority carried benefits and Felicia was senior enough at her airline to bid whatever trip she wanted. So she always selected trips that allowed her to get all her hours logged in the beginning of the month. The first three weeks of this four-week hiatus, she'd spent on the road with Katlyn. Suffice it to say, she, too, was ready to go home.

They arrived in L.A. very late. Katlyn had an early morning so she went to bed. Terrel was in town on business and had agreed to meet Felicia at La Spree. Working her way through the packed room, Felicia saw several stars she had met when Katlyn was still on Justin's "campaign." She thought about reintroducing herself, but felt she'd come off like a groupie. Instead, she acted just as "don't you know who I am" important as they did and said nothing.

Heading back to her table she noticed a beautiful woman she was sure she knew, seated at her table with Terrel. She stayed back, camouflaged by the crowd, and tried to place the face. Terrel appeared to be enjoying their conversation a little too much, so Felicia decided to interrupt them.

"Oh, hey babe, you're back!" Terrel said. Felicia waited for the stunning beauty to get up and move, which she took her time doing. Momentarily face-to-face with her, Felicia remembered who she was: Nikki, the home wrecker who had caused Katlyn so much pain.

She became instantly angry with Terrel for consorting with the enemy!

"What was that cow doing here?"

"Baby, shame on you. You not trippin', are you?" he asked, feeling and sounding guilty.

"You did not answer my question." Felicia made eye contact with Terrel, letting him know she was serious, and waited for an answer.

"Aw babe, she remembered me from the Pebble Beach golf outing. Remember the…"

"Trust me, I remember," she said dryly.

"Felicia, she didn't want anything, just makin' small talk."

Agitated with his insistence she was harmless, Felicia gave him a piece of her mind.

"You know, Terrel, any other time I could care less who you talk to, but that ho broke up Katlyn's marriage."

Here we go again, Terrel thought. He found Felicia's belief that Nikki was to blame for Pretty Boy's decision to leave his wife foolish. Grown people make grown-people decisions. Nobody forced a gun to Justin's head and made him sleep with the woman, and then leave his wife for her. He'd chosen to do that.

Still disgruntled, he told Felicia, "It takes two to tango."

Wrong thing to say when your woman expects you to be in her corner. Felicia sucked her teeth, rolled her eyes and looked away. Terrel, uncomfortable with where this was heading, shifted in his chair and focused on the dance floor. After ten minutes of dead silence, he asked her to dance.

"Not now, Terrel, I'm not feelin' this."

"You ready to go?" he said. She answered yes. Terrel helped her to her feet and grabbed her hand, leading her through the crowd to the exit. Once outside, he waited for valet to bring his car, holding her in his arms. He looked her in the eye.

"I know you know I'm crazy about you. No need to start actin' jealous."

"Jealous is not my style," she said, hating herself for lying to him. She *was* jealous. She'd seen him look at Nikki in "that way" at Pebble Beach and she'd watched him look at her the same way tonight. Nikki's presence made her feel insecure.

Terrel dropped her off at the Ritz-Carlton, declining to come up. Tired and not over the Nikki episode, Felicia was glad he didn't. Terrel, not sleepy, headed back to La Spree.

Katlyn's interview on "AM-LA" went well. Patricia Henry, a well-known local newscaster and former friend of the Kincaids, conducted the interview. Despite the break-up, she liked Katlyn and really pushed her book. After the taping they hugged, exchanged numbers and agreed to stay in touch.

Felicia slept in. Katlyn had a three-hour break before her next interview. She decided to take a stroll on Rodeo to unwind and, of course—shop. Heading down a side street, she noticed that the restaurant that had become infamous during the O.J. era was gone. A cute little bistro had taken its place.

She admired its architecture from across the street and decided to stop in and check out the menu. Inside, while admiring the interior, she saw a gorgeous woman, well tanned with a fabulous copper-colored mane. Looking briefly at the man seated with her, she then focused on the woman once more.

Simultaneously, she recognized the woman—Nikki—and the man—Terrel. Katlyn froze, her heart pumping wildly and her knees shaking. She had always hoped for this moment, minus Terrel, of course. And now that it was happening she felt like running in the other direction. Taking a deep breath, she exhaled and walked right over to them.

"Terrel, hi!"

"Katlyn, hey," he said, looking around for Felicia. "How's your book tour going?"

Nikki suddenly looked up, staring at Katlyn as if she'd seen a ghost. She recognized her from seeing her on posters that were promoting her book. It didn't take long for her to realize this was *the* Katlyn Kincaid. Up close and personal, Nikki thought she was prettier than in her photos. That bothered her; she would have preferred to continue to believe she was just okay-looking.

"You wanna join us?" Terrel offered nervously, pointing to an empty chair.

Katlyn declined his offer without taking her eyes off Nikki. Nikki was everything she'd heard she was, but it didn't bother her like she thought it would.

"I've gotta get back. My next interview is in forty minutes," she told him.

"Wow, look at you interviewing and stuff," Terrel teased her, hoping to ease the tension in the air.

"Felicia will be at the station for my next interview, I'll let her know I ran into you."

"Uh, yeah cool," he said nervously. "Tell her to call me when she's free."

"I'll be sure to do that."

Felicia was waiting in the lobby of KJLA when Katlyn arrived. She broke into a smile when Katlyn walked up. "Hey, girl."

Katlyn grabbed her by the arm and pulled her into the ladies room.

"I ran into Terrel at a restaurant," she blurted, out sounding winded.

"Really?"

"Yeah, guess who I saw him with?"

Felicia's heartbeat picked up its pace, anxiety setting in. Something told her the answer would be Nikki. Katlyn could tell from the expression on Felicia's face she knew who it was. They were both quiet for a moment. Felicia broke the silence.

"Let me get this straight. You just saw Terrel, *my* Terrel, at a restaurant with Nikki?"

"You got it!" Katlyn answered, and then waited for a reaction. Felicia leaned on the wall and replayed the night before.

"Katlyn, I would be the first to chalk it up to mere coincidence, but I know better. Last night at La Spree, Ms. Thang was seated at my table when I came back from the ladies room. Terrel blew it off as nothing. Supposedly, she remembered him from the golf outing at Pebble Beach."

"Pebble Beach?" Katlyn repeated, with urgency in her voice.

"Yeah, she was there with Jus—" Felicia, with her mouth still open, stopped talking and stared at her best friend.

Katlyn's eyes filled with water. Felicia knew the tears forming were not because of Justin's infidelity—it was because of a trusted friend's silence!

CHAPTER 23

Justin flipped through the pages of the latest *Billboard*, not really interested in seeing what number his now defunct album had plunged to.

Upstart artists, though less attractive and less talented, were skyrocketing to the top of the charts. Music was changing, the industry standards were changing and Justin was not comfortable with the changes.

Beats, sampling, more beats and no talent paved the way for these studio artists who could not hold a note to him live. But the hip-hop generation cared less about God-given vocal ability. Money, money, money, *mon-nay* drove the industry and hip-hop was where the Benjamins were made.

The reality of it all was a bitter pill to swallow. Justin knew he'd blown it. His hands were too full of his own agenda, his mind too full of his own greatness to see the value in what he really had. While he had the world by the balls, he should have capitalized on it. Instead he gave up his "image" of being a happily married man with the belief he could re-invent himself. He'd proudly paraded his mistress around in public and thought his fans would get over it. When they turned on him and decided to hang him from a tree, he was lost. Sherwin wasn't around anymore to fix things: in the middle of negotiations for a huge movie role, what was supposed to be his debut on the big screen, Justin fired him because he was sick of him telling him what to do.

His new management team had yet to yield positive results and funds were coming in slower than they were going out. Money now tight, Justin sold the five-bedroom luxury condo and downsized to a plush but more affordable two-bedroom.

Justin tossed the magazine on the pile with the other outdated issues, and sipped his gin and juice. He examined his life. At first glance he was a success. It was both satisfying and alarming, particularly because he'd grown up with so little. Success had always frightened him. If he made it to the top, he was not sure he had what it took to stay there. He always felt he was living someone else's life and that in the blink of an eye, it would all be taken away.

He'd spent so much time and energy creating and maintaining the illusion of who he was supposed to be, he'd lost who he really was. Not knowing himself made him afraid to peel away the layers of self-doubt to find out his true identity.

Thinking back, he believed Katlyn knew his whole persona was a lie. She had a knack of always making him feel secure about himself and his career. With her by his side, he could do anything; with her gone—well, his downward spiral was a testament to that.

CHAPTER 24

Terrel, on the West Coast again for a business trip, ran into Nikki at the same restaurant. He'd hoped she would be there and was pleased to see her.

"What's up?" he said. Nikki slowly looked up from the menu and smiled.

"Sit down. What are you doing here?" she asked, looking around for Katlyn.

"Just stopped in to get a quick bite."

"Where's your guard dog?" she quipped, getting in a dig. Terrel didn't laugh.

"Hold up, I don't have no guard dog and if you're referring to Katlyn, she's a friend. I don't take well to you puttin' down my friends!" Nikki's comment not only angered him, it killed any thoughts he had of hooking up with her.

His take-no-prisoners approach caught her off guard. This time when she looked at him, she really checked him out. He had on an expensive hand-tailored suit, hand-made Italian shoes and a watch that cost more than most folks earned in a year. She found him cocky and very sure of himself. That turned her on.

"You staying near here?" she asked.

"At the Four Seasons."

"We should do dinner."

"Some other time." Terrel looked at his watch. "You take care of yourself."

Nikki, dazed by his indifference, watched him walk away, even more attracted to him.

Terrel could understand Justin leaving his wife for Nikki. She had that certain *something* about her that made a man lose his mind. Few women had it; Nikki had it and then some.

On the way back to his hotel, Terrel made the decision not to find out what that certain *something* was, now that he was going to ask Felicia to marry him.

❂❂❂

The six-carat diamond took on a life of its own in the sunlight. Felicia smiled as she looked at her hand; thankful she'd forced herself to abandon any thoughts of Nikki and Terrel getting together. Planning her engagement party with a vengeance, she went all-out, hiring a party consultant, a jazz quartet, caterers and a DJ.

Terrel's list of friends and relatives paled in comparison to hers. A minimalist, he'd kept the same friends most of his life. They were an interesting mix—some high school and college teammates, a boyhood friend or two, and a gal pal from the hood.

Full of excitement, Felicia flitted about making sure all their guests were comfortable. Terrel's friends individually whispered compliments and congratulations, making him a bit uncomfortable. Although he was happy about his decision to make a commitment, he was not yet comfortable with the idea of it becoming public knowledge. He wished Felicia had discussed this with him before calling his mother and moving forward with these plans.

His mother was beside herself. The thought of her boy "settlin' down" and making some grandbabies she could spoil made her want to cry. She knew he was doing the right thing—she liked her future daughter-in-law.

Katlyn arrived solo, newly detached from Kyle. It was tedious dealing with his inability to move past his marital limbo. He professed to be okay with his wife being a close friend, but didn't handle well her choice to date younger men. At first she didn't mind listening to his problems and sharing her thoughts when asked. But when she saw he was becoming dependent on her for advice, she stopped offering it. "I am not raising another grown man," she declared, and meant it.

Still carrying scars from his wife's abrupt departure, Kyle took Katlyn's decision not to voice her opinion as an indication that she was tired of him. Protecting his pride, he let her go. Kyle Russell was the dumper, not the dumpee.

Felicia hugged Katlyn, handed her a drink and pulled her into the bedroom to talk.

"You okay with this?"

"With what?" Katlyn asked puzzled.

"Justin! He's here!" Felicia informed her. "I did not invite him, he kinda just showed up!"

Katlyn knew Justin had probably heard about Felicia's engagement through the grapevine, but never expected him to attend. The thought of seeing him after all this time made her nervous. She took a big swig of champagne while she absorbed the information.

"Don't do too much of that, I need you to keep your eyes and ears open. Never know what those well-meaning friends of Terrel's might say behind my back!" Felicia winked and they giggled as they admired her rock.

As Katlyn suspected, Justin had heard about the engagement and the celebration through mutual acquaintances. He wanted to see Katlyn, so he invited himself. Not on the guest list meant risking being turned away at the door or worse yet, he might be asked to leave, but he wasn't concerned. He knew Felicia well enough to know she was too classy to allow that. If he was brave enough to show up, she'd let him stay.

Hoping to see Katlyn before she saw him, Justin stood off in a corner, charming a group of women gathered around him. He noticed Katlyn the moment she walked in the room, as did several others. More beautiful than he'd remembered; she'd changed a lot and the change was for the better. Before he could excuse himself from the groupies, a relatively handsome man made his move.

Justin lay in wait, like a panther sizing up his prey. He felt a twinge of jealousy as he watched the man flirt with Katlyn and even more jealous as she flirted back. No numbers were exchanged between them that he could see, and that gave Justin hope.

Standing near the bar working on her second glass of champagne, Katlyn casually looked around the room and saw Justin standing on the outer rim of the dance floor. Seeing him for the first time in two years made her stomach flip. He'd aged tremendously, but he still had the same beautiful smile and he was still—fine!

Feeling her gaze, Justin turned around and looked at her. They both smiled. He walked to her and extended his arms to embrace her. She hesitated, and then allowed him to hug her. Justin gently kissed her cheek and pulled away to look in her eyes.

"Wow, you look good."

"You, too," she said. An awkward moment of silence forced him to loosen his embrace.

"So, this is some party, huh?" Justin said finally, making small talk.

"You know Felicia," Katlyn responded, looking at the elaborate decorations throughout the room.

"Did you see her ring?" Justin asked, wondering what Katlyn had done with the six carats he had given her.

"What ring?" Katlyn asked, facetiously. "Are you talking about that big boulder she's wearing on her left hand that needs a brace to help hold it up?" Laughter followed her comment and put them at ease.

"You here with someone?" Justin asked, looking around the room, not really wanting to hear the answer.

"No, I came alone."

"By choice?" he asked apprehensively.

"By choice," she affirmed, looking him in the eyes. Justin wondered if she and Kyle were still an item.

Terrel and Felicia danced and mingled with their guests, she relishing in splendor, he dreading every minute of it. He was having second thoughts. Felicia was pretty, not beautiful; definitely not what he thought he'd end up with. To her credit, Felicia had more goin' on than anyone he'd ever spent time with. Her extreme stance on being self-sufficient and independent was a plus. And the added bonus was their future living arrangement. He could not give up his office in Florida and she could not be based there, so theirs would be a commuter marriage, which was fine with him.

He found a quiet spot away from the crowd, nursing a glass of brandy and thinking hard about what he had done. His fiancée was a wonderful person, honest and hard working. It was of no consequence to him that she'd not be the mother of his seed, they could adopt. No doubt, his mother would be disappointed, but she would eventually get over the disappointment and readily accept any child they adopted.

Tired of playing the field, Terrel wanted to be with one woman, come home at night to a well-cooked meal and unwind with her and the kids. He believed Felicia was that woman, yet he couldn't shake the uneasiness he'd felt ever since he'd given her the ring. He always assumed that once he made a commitment, he'd feel content. He wondered if he was making a mistake.

Katlyn walked around the party, casually mingling with a number of former coworkers. Most of them were coupled off, living the life she once lived. The majority of them greeted her warmly, complimented her haircut and carried on as if nothing had changed. Others, those probably having marital problems of their own, shied away, afraid they'd catch her social disease called divorce!

A year ago their demeanor would have hurt her, but now she could laugh at them. They were clueless, caught up in a make-believe world.

An entire hour had passed and Katlyn had successfully avoided Justin and a repeat of what she'd felt in his presence. As if reading her mind, he appeared carrying another glass of champagne for her. Against her better judgment, Katlyn accepted number three.

"How's it feel to see all those people from home?" he asked.

"Reminds me of that game show, *This Is Your Life*." She laughed, tickled by her own humor. Justin loved to see her laugh; it was infectious as was her presence. He moved a little closer to her, something she missed by being one drink closer to drunk.

"What happened to that guy you were seeing?" he asked, now directly in front of her and close enough to kiss her, resting an arm on the wall she was now using for support.

"Um, I don't see him anymore," she answered nervously.

Justin, relieved to hear they were not together, tried to hold back the big grin forming on his face. Katlyn saw it and knew he was pleased with that tidbit of information. It pleased her to see he was still interested.

They stared at each other for a moment, both aware of the electricity between them. Justin gently lifted her chin and held it. He softly pecked her lips then pulled away, staring in her eyes. Katlyn slightly parted her lips wanting more. He leaned in and fully parted her lips with his tongue, which she met with hers.

In each other's arms, they spent the night remembering what Katlyn had worked so hard to forget.

CHAPTER 25

Terrel never wanted to hurt Felicia. He loved her. But he knew if he married her, he'd hurt her more than he was about to. He'd flown to her home to break the news. He figured she'd be near her girl for support.

"How you doing, sweetie?" she cooed, kissing him as he walked in. He stood in the doorway and stared at her.

"You look beautiful," he told her.

"Thanks, babe. You hungry?" She grabbed his hand and led him to the kitchen.

"No. Listen, we need to talk," he said, trying to get her to meet his eyes.

"Okay, but don't you want to take your things upstairs, unwind a bit?" she asked, looking around for his noticeably absent luggage. Finding none, she finally focused her eyes on his. The pain she saw in them caused her alarm.

"Baby, we gotta talk." He took her hand in his.

"Sure, Terrel, what is it?" Anxious, she spoke just above a whisper.

Terrel inhaled deeply, trying to figure out how to tell her what he knew would devastate her.

Sensing the worst, she opened the conversation. "Terrel, you can tell me anything—it won't change the way I feel."

He sat on the sofa, pulling her left hand with his right hand. She resisted, fear beginning to consume her.

"Terrel, listen, you're scaring me. What is it? Just tell me, please!" she begged.

"Babe, I would do almost anything to keep from having to say this to you."

"Say—what...," Felicia began.

Terrel shushed her. "I need you to understand, I love you." Felicia's eyes filled with tears. "But I can't do this, we can't get married."

Felicia wanted to ask why, but she couldn't control her body involuntarily jerking as she fought back tears. She let out a wail and began to sob uncontrollably. As her head fell to his chest, he closed his arms around her and held her firmly wishing he could avoid hurting her more.

She managed to recover slightly, grabbing tissues to blow her nose. She inhaled deeply and the sobbing subsided, but the tears continued to fall.

Terrel could tell she was coming around so he took another deep breath, in preparation for the second bomb he had to drop.

"Felicia, I messed up, real bad! In the two years we've been together, I've never strayed; I loved you too much to do that. But a couple months ago, Bay...I, man...baby. I've been exposed to HIV. You need to get tested," he blurted out.

Numb, Felicia stared at him. Her breathing halted. She passed out and hit the floor before Terrel could catch her. Scared to death, he checked her pulse for a heartbeat first and then made sure she was breathing again. It took several minutes, but she came around and when she did she slapped him with all her might.

Guilty or not, he did not take kindly to being slapped. That told him she was feeling just fine, so he got up to leave before she laid any more abuse on him. She took off the ring she was still wearing and threw it at him. It ricocheted off the door. He picked it up and sat it on the table near her door.

"Why?" she screamed and cried even harder.

Relieved she didn't ask the other three Ws—who, when and where— Terrel opened the door and left. He couldn't bear to tell her he had slept with Nikki the last time he was in L.A.—unprotected.

With Katlyn's help, Felicia did well in recovering from her broken heart. Her life in balance once again, she set out to sever all ties with the painful memories left by Terrel. However, that choice was taken away when she tested negative for HIV and learned she'd need to be retested every six months since the HIV virus has the ability to lie dormant for ten years.

CHAPTER 26

When you dig one ditch, you'd better dig two! Nikki's diabolical plot to get rid of Tracee had finally borne fruit. A friend of a friend of a friend located a paper trail that connected Tracee to possible embezzlement and money laundering.

Nikki had the newspaper article sent to Justin's management. By the time this revelation had arrived, Tracee had become real comfortable living large at her cousin's expense. Searching for acting jobs sat on the back burner while she tooled around town in her Land Rover without a care in the world.

Every time Tracee took a chunk out of Justin's account, Nikki kept track of it. In time his accountant began to question Justin's spending. Once questions arose, Nikki helped push things along by ordering a charge card in Tracee's name on Justin's account. When she was certain Tracee was in town, Nikki charged on the card and signed Tracee's name. Not long after a pattern of spending was established, Nikki began to use the card as a debit card, requesting large sums of money as cash back. Finally, the day of reckoning arrived.

Justin's management team informed him of his financial dilemma. His money was dwindling fast, his spending was out of control. Of course, none of this made sense to him. Aware of his declining popularity and slow-selling CD, he had cut back tremendously on his spending. And the last time he checked, which was four months ago, Tracee was not going over the budget he had her on.

Two aspirin and a Pepsi did little to quiet the throbbing in his head. As Justin carefully looked at the ledger his accountant handed him, his head ached more. Tracee had been playing him big-time. She was spending way past her limit and the spending was usually for two or more. This was a blatant disregard for the ground rules he had set (and she had agreed to): Justin would take care of Tracee's expenses, but her friends and acquaintances would be on their own.

While he made an effort to digest this deception, a copy of the article was placed in front of him with a picture of Tracee being arrested along with two other guys. According to the article the jury had dead-locked and was unable to come up with a unanimous verdict. Tracee had walked as a result of that hung jury.

Unable to handle this information, Justin got up and left without saying anything to anyone. All the evidence proved to Justin Nikki was right. Tracee was using him. In the past he never acted on her suspicions because he knew Nikki wanted Tracee gone. However, with all the proof he'd just seen, he could not continue to deny what he had overlooked for months. Putting Tracee out would be hard. He really cared about his cousin. She was smart, sassy and great company.

The bar in the lobby was his first stop. Alcoholic stimulant became his pacifier over the months Nikki was gone. After Tracee moved in, it was his survival mechanism. Being around the two of them was unbearable. Like alley cats they were constantly battling and Justin often found himself stuck in the middle.

The credit card statement addressed to Tracee came in the mail on the rare day she happened to be home and up when the postman arrived. Pleased to see her, he handed the mail to her and then lingered long enough to flirt and ask for her number. Tracee refused to give him any information other than her name. A mailman did not make nearly the funds she needed to keep her in the lifestyle she was now accustomed to.

Closing the door behind her, Tracee leaned against it and thought about her last conversation with Justin. If she didn't know better, she'd think he was jealous of the guys she chose to go out with. She knew he was lonely, little Miss "Gold Digger" was gone *all* the time, but she hoped he was not growing dependent on her to fill that void. Although he took good care of her and was extremely generous with his money, he was her cousin and she had needs his money could not take care of.

Tracee tossed the mail on the cocktail table and poured herself a glass of juice. The pile of mail landed on top of the television remote. While searching for the remote, she noticed the envelope from Chase Bank with her name on it. She assumed it was a credit card invitation. With her past credit history, there was no way she'd qualify. Without a second thought, she tossed it in the trash and retreated to her bedroom to take a shower.

Even though she'd allowed the water to run for a few minutes, it was cold when she stepped into the shower. Soaking wet, she climbed out the shower and wrapped a towel around her. Thinking back, something about the way the credit card envelope was addressed bothered her. Tracee had not used her middle name since high school and yet there it was: "Loraine."

Water still dripping, Tracee ran to the trash can and retrieved the envelope just moments before Nikki walked in. Behind the safety of her bedroom door, Tracee opened the envelope and stared in disbelief at the documents inside. Her butt was in big trouble and she knew who to thank.

No price was too high to get rid of that scheming B. Tracee paid a private detective to follow Nikki, something she felt Justin should have done a long time ago.

Thankfully it only took a week of surveillance to come up with the dirt she needed to cut this cow's throat.

Tracee anonymously mailed the photos of Nikki with her lover to Justin's accountant's office. The day she came home and found him overdosed on pain killers was the day she knew he'd seen them.

Tracee accompanied him to the hospital in the ambulance, stood by while they pumped Justin's stomach, working frantically to save his life. When he opened his eyes twelve hours 1ater, Tracee was at his side, holding his hand and patting his head with a cold compress.

Nikki learned about the entire episode as it unfolded on the evening news. The report failed to disclose Justin's whereabouts or his condition, which drove Nikki crazy with fear. Uncertain what to do in a crisis like this she panicked and burst into tears while pacing in a circle.

Certain Tracee was with him, she tried to find a number to call her. She had never asked for Tracee's number and Tracee had never offered it. Frantically she called all his friends. When she finally thought to call his management team, their offices had already closed for the day. Every few seconds she speed-dialed Justin's number, hoping he or Tracee would answer. She needed to be by his side assuring him everything would be all right. In her absence, Tracee did just that.

Returning home to Nikki was hard. Justin could not get the image of her and the other guy screwing out of his head. Thankful he was still alive, he regretted his decision to try and end his time on earth. Rather than die, he'd made a huge mess of his life, which ended up in the national news. Thinking about how stupid Katlyn must have thought he was made him want to die all over again.

Unaware of his release from the hospital, Nikki was not home when Justin and Tracee arrived. Tracee took advantage of her continued absence by fixing Justin's favorite meal and setting the table for two. After he ate she ran him a hot bath and put fresh linen on his bed.

Tracee busied herself cleaning up the mess she'd made cooking. She'd done a great job endearing herself with Justin. Hopefully he'd see how valuable she was to have around.

Glancing at the clock, she realized time was not on her side. Nikki would walk through the door any minute. Tracee wanted to be in her room when she did arrive and hoped her stay would be short.

Little did Tracee know, the moment Justin opened his eyes at the hospital and saw her and not Nikki at his side, he'd decided that if anyone left the condo it would be Nikki. Checkmate!

Two weeks passed and Nikki was still a fixture in *their* home. Certain she'd cooked this goose well done, Tracee had a difficult time accepting Justin was stupid enough to keep her around. She wanted to confront him and slap the stupid out of him, but she was wise enough to leave it alone. Nikki, on the other hand, was not.

Justin had yet to mention the newspaper article about Tracee or the lack of funds, and Nikki was certain he was aware of both. She'd seen the two of them interact over the past weeks since his overdose and grew quite concerned. Many of their actions were much too close—too touchy-feely—for her taste. If she did not know better, she would easily believe they were sleeping together. Cousins didn't do that! But then, she was never convinced they were related.

Living one more minute with Tracee was an option that had run its course. Nikki decided to put her foot down. Tracee was tucked away in her bedroom when she did.

The conversation began civilly. Nikki expressed concern for Justin's well being and their financial status. Justin listened intently. It had been weeks since they'd spoken to each other. To his surprise, he welcomed the communication.

Things progressed smoothly for over an hour. When Nikki thought it was safe to broach the topic, she asked Justin to put Tracee out. The moment Justin began to defend why she should stay, Nikki issued an ultimatum.

"This isn't working for me!" she announced.

"What are you talking about? What isn't working?" he asked, sounding alarmed.

"You, me, her—this threesome!"

"Hold up, Nik, what are you telling me?"

"Man, just how stupid are you? What, you need me to spell it out?" she shouted. Full of venom, she did just that. She informed him she suspected he and Tracee were not really related and might be involved. Next she told him Tracee got on her nerves and she wanted her out, immediately. When Justin shook his head no, Nikki informed him she would pack her things and leave.

Angrier than ever Nikki began to yell at him, continuing to make demands and innuendos. Devastated by her suspicions, Justin began to cry. For the first time in his life he'd been committed to a relationship and being accused of the opposite hurt. His spirit was crushed as was his pride. He still loved Nikki and despite her infidelity, he did not want to lose her.

The yelling woke Tracee. She tipped out her room and planted her ear to their bedroom door to listen.

Nikki heard Justin sniffling and stopped talking. Seeing him cry pissed her off. Although her intentions were not to leave before Tracee, she decided at that moment he and her nemesis deserved each other.

"I can't take this anymore. I'm outta here!" she shouted.

Ripped to shreds by her verbal beating, all he could muster was, "I thought you wanted to marry me." She stared at him, certain he had lost his mind. He stared back, hoping to find reassurance of what he *thought* they had.

In a flash he realized he'd never really known her. At that moment, he felt foolish for having been so blind. Sitting on the edge of the bed, he silently watched her grab her keys and leave.

"Now I know how Katlyn felt," he mumbled. A failing relationship brings up your stuff—the skeletons you hoped would stay dead and buried. Alone for the first time in years, he was faced with the mess he'd made of his life. After a six-pack and a nap, he sat pensive and thought about what had happened. The reality of it all—Nikki, Katlyn, his waning career—hit him hard.

Needing something stronger to dull the pain, he stumbled over to the bar in the living room and pulled out a bottle of whiskey. He poured two drinks, one for him and one for Whiskey Man. Lifting both glasses, he tapped them together and downed one, then the other, hoping to forget his success at failing.

Not long after Nikki was gone, reality set in for Justin. It hurt him to know she had used him and when she got everything she wanted, she had dumped him. The Katlyn he knew was nothing like that. She was a person of integrity and substance. The life they shared had never been based on what he had or did not have. She'd always accepted him for him, and he was still Justin Kincaid, in spite of his problems.

He wondered if there was a possibility of them getting back together.

CHAPTER 27

While with Justin in L.A., Ruby had done well in getting her life back on track. The therapy sessions Justin personally escorted her to *had* helped her to sort through her demons. His insistence she take her medication on time every day also contributed to her fresh start. For the first time in her life she knew someone loved her and that gave her a new outlook on life.

Detroit, however, was where her demons roamed freely. Painful reminders of her abusive childhood were around every corner. Although a strong woman with a strong spiritual background, Ruby was ill equipped to deal with the torment she faced after returning to Detroit and remembering her father had repeatedly sexually abused her as a child.

In her entire adult life she'd failed to recall what sent her over the edge in her early teens. Then one night she began to dream about the visits to her bed from her father when her mother was gone. Ruby was thirteen at the time. Every night Ruby's mother left for church and every day Ruby prayed she would not. Then she discovered she was pregnant and her father beat her with his fist, intentionally landing blows in her abdomen trying to force her to abort.

A God-fearing woman, Ruby's mother didn't believe in abortions, or premarital sex for that matter, and would never have allowed Ruby to get rid of the child, even though it was conceived by her father.

Before Ruby ran away from home she tried to tell her mother about the abuse and the pregnancy. "Blasphemy!" her mother screamed and slapped her across her mouth. While her mother prayed to God to forgive Ruby for her sins, Ruby ran for her life. She never looked back, never returned home and never shed a tear upon hearing of her parents' death.

The home for unwed mothers readily opened its doors to Ruby. She gave birth to Justin's oldest sister at the home with the help of a midwife. Night after night she dreamed about her father's violation and grew increasingly paranoid of the opposite sex. Eventually she retreated into a shell and was misdiagnosed as being clinically depressed.

Of course society felt a clinically depressed new mom was incapable of taking care of her child. In time a social worker met with her to discuss placing her daughter in foster care. Ruby sat and listened for a few minutes and then excused herself from the conference to use the restroom and never came back. She and her baby girl made a living on the streets of Detroit and in the beds of strangers.

Then the trick beat her so severely, Ruby drifted in and out of consciousness for days in an alley with her baby lying next to her. Fortunately a passerby heard the baby crying and called the police. As Ruby recovered in the hospital, her baby was placed in the foster care system she had run from.

During her hospital stay a staff nurse observed Ruby's strange behavior and associated her actions as being related to those of schizophrenia. Well aware of the dangers involved with a person in this mental state, she informed the doctors of her concern and testing was done to confirm she was indeed paranoid schizophrenic. The day she was released from the hospital she was carted off in a straitjacket.

Months later Ruby's darling little girl wound up in the home of a loving family with strong religious ties. They made a genuine effort to keep Ruby an active part of her daughter's life. With the promise of continuing her medication and therapy, the courts granted supervised visitation and she kept her promise until she met the father of her second child, a boy, two years later. Thus began the pattern of emotional and sometimes physical abuse that would yield seven children with six baby daddies.

With no support from her sperm donors and no money to pay for therapy and medication, Ruby eventually slipped from reality back into paranoid delusions. She resorted to squatting in an effort to keep a roof over her family's head when she was in between men.

Now almost twenty years later and once again penniless, she was forced to resort to her old survival tactics. Unfortunately, she chose a vacant home in a neighborhood that had been subjected to recurring burglaries. A neighbor called 911 when they saw the boards missing from the windows. When the cop shone his flashlight inside, Ruby reared up pointing an unloaded gun at him. The cop opened fire, killing her instantly.

Katlyn's support at the funeral meant more to Justin than he could say. Seeing her seated in the family section along with his aunts and uncles warmed his heart. He smiled when their eyes met. Katlyn gently nodded and smiled reassuringly.

The service was short and simple. Ruby did not have many friends and with the exception of her offspring, most of her relatives had given up on keeping in touch with her years ago. A few kind words were spoken by the minister before the service was concluded. Afterward her body was laid to rest at a local cemetery with just Justin, his siblings and a couple family members present.

Before returning to the limousine, Ruby's brother invited those at the gravesite to return to his home for dinner. Not willing to be subjected to an inquisition by Justin's nosy aunts Katlyn declined the invite and followed Justin to his limo to say good-bye. She approached his side and stuck her head in. He was happy to see her and asked the driver to wait while he stepped out to speak with her.

"You coming by Rose's house, aren't you?" he asked. Katlyn shook her head no and then crossed her eyes and made the silly face she and Justin used to make when they spoke about his aunt Rose. Nosy, messy, opinionated and a wannabe diva, she got on any and everyone's last nerve. Although she could cook, Katlyn decided if eating meant dealing with her, she was not that hungry.

Justin understood, but he wanted to spend some time with her. He hoped he could convince her to accompany him. Taking her hands in his, he leaned forward and kissed her on the forehead.

"Ple-ee-zzz!" he begged playfully.

"No, I'm tired. My flight from Atlanta was delayed and I really would like to get out of this suit and these pumps." Katlyn tugged on his grasp in an attempt to free her hands. No luck, Justin tightened his grip, which made them both laugh.

"When are you going back to Atlanta?" he asked.

"Tomorrow, I really would like to take my father out to dinner this evening and catch up on his life."

Tears formed in Justin's eyes. He wished Ruby had gotten to spend time with him and Katlyn.

That evening Justin stopped by to see Katlyn's dad. He had decided at the cemetery he would not let someone else he cared about leave this earth without telling them. Fortunately, Katlyn had just returned home from taking her father to dinner. The moment her dad saw Justin he hugged him tightly. Justin needed this; it felt good to be held by someone he admired and respected so much. Still emotional, Justin broke down and cried—a cry that was long-overdue.

Dealing with Ruby's death was a fete Justin could not conquer. With his life in complete ruin, he'd hoped to return to Detroit and spend time with her. Learning his mother's life had spun out of control when he stopped sending her money because his finances failed to support them both, drained the life out of him. He could not help but blame himself.

Fortunately he and his father had formed a bond that allowed Justin to open up and share his feelings. Leyton was in town to pay his respects to his son and meet his son's siblings. His timing could not have been better: he needed a strong shoulder to lean on and his father could finally meet Katlyn.

It took a lot of begging and pleading, but Katlyn relented and accompanied Justin to meet his father. Leyton took them to one of his favorite Detroit spots and sat in with the band. He had the same charm and charisma that Justin exhibited when in front of a crowd.

A stroll down memory lane caught Katlyn off guard. Shifting in her seat she crossed her leg and squeezed in an effort to ward off the tingling sensation between her legs.

"Wow," she murmured. *He still got it*, she thought to herself as she glanced at Justin across the table. That old familiar thang between them was alive and well. To her surprise Katlyn found herself reminiscing about the good old days when she and Justin first met and dated.

Bad move when you're still a recovering addict!

CHAPTER 28

Stillness is a wonderful thing. Only in still water can you see your reflection. Katlyn saw hers and recognized her ghosts. Believing in the fairy tale, the ideology of oneness, she had spent her life shaping who she was into someone else's oneness. That someone, Justin, was caught up in his own oneness; incapable of loving or being committed to anyone.

A lifetime of self-doubt and the inability to be true to herself allowed her to live her life as a mannequin dressed up and perfectly posed in the windows of everyone else's world.

Confused and frustrated because she never received what she *thought* she wanted from any man (Justin included), Katlyn lost her way. Disconnected from herself, she developed an unhealthy and unworthy dependency on Justin; a harsh piece of honesty that showed how much she underestimated her self worth.

The Kincaids' failed attempt at a reunion forced Katlyn to reevaluate things. In doing so she had to move beyond shame and old wounds and tell herself the truth. Once she did, she figured out how to end being miserable and unhappy. It was simple. All she had to do was stop including in her life those things or that someone that create the misery and unhappiness.

Spending time with Katlyn stirred up old feelings in Justin as well. He had convinced himself he wanted her back, but he really only wanted her around. Not wanting to be tied down, he hoped to make her a close friend at least until someone else showed interest in her. His life was still a revolving door that Katlyn finally chose not to enter.

Thankful she used protection when she "tripped" and fell back into the past, Katlyn was not the least bit affected by Justin's recent visit to inform her he may have contracted HIV from Nikki. He had just been tested and so far his results were negative.

As the story goes, not happy with Justin, Nikki hooked up with an old flame long before she dumped him. He was a "nobody" who had nothing going on, which made him available whenever she wanted him. She felt free with him, no expectations, no responsibilities, nothing (sound familiar).

On the pill and with no regard for her health or Justin's well being, Nikki never asked "Mr. Nobody" if he were HIV positive and they never used protection. Just weeks after she broke up with Justin, her old flame tested positive for HIV after taking a physical for a new job. Without hesitation, Nikki was tested and her results were positive as well.

Fortunately she only needed to inform two men they should be tested, Justin and Terrel. Afraid to face Justin and ashamed of what she'd done, Nikki chose to inform him by phone. Thankful he did not answer she left him a detailed voicemail from a pay phone eliminating any possibility of him contacting her.

Locating Terrel was not as easy. She had not heard from him since they'd slept together and his cell phone number had changed. Although it took some work, she tracked him down at his corporate office and left an urgent message for him to call. When he did she informed him she had tested positive and he needed to be tested. Her plan was to hang up before he could react—he beat her to it!

Things had not fared well for Justin. His faltering album sales resulted in his being dropped from his label. The downward spiral into the dark hole does not discriminate. Unable to cope with his failures and the fear of one day being HIV positive, his own demons awoke and kicked his butt. He retreated so far into himself he drank away his pain, morning, noon and night.

For quite some time he successfully hid his addiction to this liquid painkiller. But in time the pain grew to like the alcohol, forcing him to seek something stronger to make it go away. Driving under the influence for the second time landed him in jail, which was a blessing. The court ordered him to complete a year in jail, during which time he would undergo treatment for his addiction.

Katlyn took advantage of this opportunity to tell him about God. She pointed out he had already tried, unsuccessfully, to fix the pain and all the things that were wrong with his life. She let him know nothing he was dealing with was too hard for God to fix and encouraged Justin to turn his life and his problems over to Him.

The fact that Justin found humor in what she said told Katlyn all she needed to know; his journey out of the dark hole was going to be a long and difficult process. She prayed for him (and Nikki) and released the whole thing.

No longer searching for a hero—a man to validate her very being, Katlyn filed for divorce. The process was lengthy because of an uncooperative almost ex-husband, who had previously filed and not completed the divorce.

The former Mrs. Kincaid had graduated summa cum laude from the Justin Kincaid School for Naïve Women. With God as head of her life, she found living exciting. Few things bothered her and any piece of the puzzle that did not fit, was no longer viewed as earth-shattering. A welcome positive outlook on life empowered her to anxiously pursue her dreams, accepting each challenge as a rewarding adventure.

Katlyn had befriended her ghosts and confronted herself, the self she neglected and placed on the back burner. The material things and the good life she once craved were still desired, but no longer possessed her. The cost was too high a price to pay for the peace and happiness she now enjoyed. This metamorphosis, though difficult and painful, was necessary. She became a woman fulfilled, not because of a man doing life for her—but because she finally "did" life for herself.

The divorce proceedings were amicable. Clean and sober and looking quite well, all things considered, Justin lingered outside on the steps of the courthouse. He watched in awe as Katlyn walked out of the building and past him with an air of confidence he'd never seen. She appeared to be someone he didn't know, and she was.

As she walked away, shoulders back and head erect—no lingering on the steps and no attempts to stay in touch—Katlyn felt immense peace. With some divine intervention she stepped out of the security of Justin and into the significance of her own self-worth.

It's been said, "If you don't place value on yourself, don't expect others to raise the price." Raising one's consciousness requires some deep soul searching. The process may be painful, but it is worth the *ouch!*

Justin was right, *this* Katlyn he did not know. She was a wiser woman, who had accepted her faults, gained strength from the truth, leaned on patience and stepped out on faith—one foot at a time—until she emerged, on the other side of through.

AUTHOR BIO

Born in Detroit, Michigan, Marsha D. Jenkins-Sanders is a writer of novels and songs. She received acclaim in the music industry for lyrics written for Keith Washington's freshman album project, *Make Time for Love*. Both "Kissing You" and "Closer" introduced her writing talent and she received award-winning recognition from ASCAP for Writer and Publisher in the R & B genre. "Kissing You" was certified gold and went on to be featured as the background music for love scenes on ABC's soap, *General Hospital*. Her crossover into the literary field began when she decided to transform personal writings from her defunct marriage to Keith into a fictional contemporary romance novel. In 2005 she completed *The Other Side of Through*. Shortly after submitting her manuscript to *New York Times* bestselling author and publisher Zane, she was signed to Strebor Books/Simon & Schuster. Her next novel, *Jealousy: A Strange Company Keeper*, will follow in 2008. Events and tour dates will be posted on her website: http://MarshaJenkinsSanders.homestead.com. Marsha resides in the suburbs of Detroit with her husband and two sons.

A READER'S GUIDE

QUESTIONS FOR THE AUTHOR

1. Having lived the "Hollywood life," what aspects of your own experience did you draw on to write *The Other Side of Through*?

2. Who is Katlyn Kincaid? Is she a figment of your imagination or someone you know? How much of Katlyn do you identify with?

3. In conforming to modern-day trends, cursing often appears in novels as an acceptable form of communicating—keeping it real! *The Other Side of Through* omits the use of profanity and yet skillfully captivates the reader from beginning to end. Was the omission of profanity intentional? How challenging was it to write in this manner?

4. The title, *The Other Side of Through*, is unique and catchy. Where did you get it? Is there a dual meaning?

5. We know men will identify with Justin and his challenges. How is Katlyn's journey identifiable to men?

QUESTIONS FOR DISCUSSION

1. Describe Katlyn. What kind of person is she? Is she likeable?

2. What is your first impression of Justin? Myles? Is he likeable? Do you feel the same way toward him by the end of the book?

3. Which of your emotions does Felicia stir up? Same question for Katlyn, Justin and Myles. Recognize these characters in anyone you know? Why?

4. Discuss Katlyn and Justin's relationship. Any surprises? Any disappointments? Same question for Felicia and Myles.

5. Discuss the importance image plays in Katlyn's life and why. Same question for Justin.

6. How does Katlyn's relationship to God change her? Did you like the transformation? Why?

7. What is (are) the life lesson(s) in *The Other Side of Through*? Is it relevant to you or someone you know?

8. How would you describe *The Other Side of Through* to a friend?

9. Which character(s) did you personally identify with? Who do you like the most? The least? Why?

10. Which character would you change? Why? How?

IF YOU ENJOYED "THE OTHER SIDE OF THROUGH,"
BE SURE TO LOOK FOR

Lawd, Mo Drama

BY TINA BROOKS MCKINNEY

AVAILABLE FROM STREBOR BOOKS

LEAH

I was sick and tired of being sick and tired! My energy was drained. For the first time in my life, I could understand why some women killed their children before turning the guns on themselves. Not that I'd made a conscious decision to do harm to my children. I was beginning to feel that it was the only way out of my current situation.

My mind wandered as I sat at the kitchen table shuffling through a mountain of bills. I arranged the bills in order of importance and then by amounts. Any way I stacked them, I didn't have the money. I picked up the phone to call the mortgage company to request an extension and sighed. I hated making "begging calls," but this time I couldn't put it off. A foreclosure notice was tacked on the door for the entire neighborhood to see. We didn't have anywhere to go, so I had no choice but to grovel.

A bored switchboard operator answered the phone.

"I need to speak with someone about the status of my mortgage," I said, trying to get mileage out of humility.

"Hold on," she said.

I waited through seemingly endless country melodies. Just once, I would have liked to hear a song I could sing along to while I was placed on ignore. I was prepared to stay there a while longer when the line clicked over.

"This is Mrs. Turner. May I help you?"

"Hello." I took a deep breath. "My name is Leah Simmons, and I need to speak to someone about a notice that was posted on my door yesterday."

"What is your account number?"

I could tell by her voice that Mrs. Turner was a sister. I felt like I could be real with her. I read her the number, then held my breath in anticipation.

"What is the name on the account?"

"Um, Kentee Simmons," I mumbled.

"And you are?" She was all business, dashing my hopes for sympathy.

"I'm his wife." I drew another deep breath.

"Mrs. Simmons, I cannot speak to you about this account since your name does not appear on it. You need to have your husband contact this office to discuss the account."

"That's the problem." I began to explain my situation, and I did not bother to hold back the stress and fear I was feeling. I sounded like an imperiled cartoon character to my own ears.

"Mrs., um, Simmons, calm down, please, I can't understand what you're saying," she said with more kindness. I was truly babbling and could not stop my anguished moans.

"My husband left me with three small kids. My oldest is five and the twins are two. We have no food, no money, and now this! I don't know where the hell he is, and I can't wait on him to correct this. My family can't be put out in the street!" I cried. As if slapped, all three children started crying in the background. I rose from the table and stumbled into the bedroom so I could hear what Mrs. Turner was saying. I didn't like leaving my children in a distressed state, but I wasn't able to hear anything above their chorus.

"Hold on," she said, placing me back on hold and forcing me to listen to that awful country music.

While waiting, I tried to compose myself. I absolutely hated having to make that call, and loathed Kentee for putting us in that situation. Before I met Kentee, I had a good job and was doing fine. He talked me into quitting my job and having babies but, at the first sign of trouble, he left our asses. *I wish I had listened to Marie!*

The phone line clicked. "Mrs. Simmons, I need to get a number so I can call you back. I'll try to help you, but you have to understand our rules. If I discuss this loan with you, I'll be terminated. The bank monitors any call over three minutes, so I need to go. I'll phone you on my break," Mrs. Turner said.

Relieved, I gave her my number and prayed that she would call before the phone was disconnected.

Kayla, my oldest child, was banging on the door demanding to be let in. She was my drama queen. I could not have a pity party unless she joined in. Ever since Kentee left me, Kayla cried every time I shed a tear. Even when I snuck into the bathroom for a solitary cry, her radar detected my distress, and she sought me out.

"Lawd Jesus," I lamented. "Can't I have five seconds of peace?" I yelled, hoping Kayla would get the message. It was a silly thought, since Kayla was only five going on six. She understood nothing outside of her own wants and needs.

She had matured since the birth of the twins but still required special attention.

The twins were another story. Malik was a dream child and almost a loner. He was content to sit in his room or in the living room playing quietly. He did not like a lot of noise and preferred to do everything himself. Mya, on the other hand, was off the chain! The twins were born two weeks early. I had an emergency C-section because Mya was not in birthing position. She kept getting in Malik's way, so the surgeons had to go in and get them both at the last minute. Malik came out first and they had to fight to get to Mya.

Although the doctors assured me that neither of them had suffered any brain damage, I was beginning to have doubts about Mya. She was not developing as fast as her brother, and she had these inexplicable tantrums that I couldn't understand.

The noise level on the other side of the door was deafening. I opened the door and left the bedroom, realizing that peace would not be found there. Kayla was curled up in a ball in front of the door. I wanted to step over her, but I did not. I helped her up, wiping away her tears. When Kentee left, Kayla had reverted to wetting the bed and her clothes. To avoid embarrassment, I had resorted to putting diapers on her. I needed a conveyor belt to wipe all their butts and keep them clean. I should have also been receiving a residual check from Pampers for all the money I had spent with them.

"I'm hungry, Mommy," Kayla whined.

I glanced at my watch and realized that I had missed fixing their breakfast. It was already lunchtime. The whimpering that normally grated my nerves only shamed me this time. She was right and I was wrong. I led Kayla to a chair and went to look in the cabinets to see what I could fix.

"Mommy," Kayla whispered.

"What?" I mimicked her whisper.

"What's wrong with Mya?"

I was floored. I could not think of a response that would satisfy her. I didn't know my damn self.

"Honey, Mommy doesn't know."

It was not much of a response, but it satisfied her curiosity for the moment. I continued pulling things out of the cabinet. The pickings were slim. I would have to go to the grocery store soon but it was too big of an ordeal; requiring planning and money. Kayla and Malik would be yelling out the things they wanted added to the cart and Mya would scream if anyone looked at her. Because of her heightened sense of smell, she hated all cleaning products and would toss them out of the cart every chance she got; leaving liquid spills up and down the grocery aisles.

I decided to wait on the store until after I dropped the kids off at my mother's. My mind was spinning, and I found no relief. Kayla was right, there was something wrong with Mya and none of the doctors I had taken her to had offered a reasonable diagnosis. I attributed that to not having insurance. The emergency room could only handle so much. Kentee decided to cancel our insurance after the children were born. He claimed he made enough money to pay his bills and that insurance should be called "just in case" because most folks did not use it and never got their money's worth. Although I didn't agree with his premise I could not make him spend his money on things he didn't believe in.

Unlike her brother, Mya still did not sleep through the night. At times during the day she would have these little fits; constantly screaming and kicking. Her fits were not tied to any particular situation; she fell out for no reason. How was I supposed to explain that to Kayla when I didn't understand it myself?

Like a robot, I fixed lunch on autopilot. I did not even remember cleaning up the kitchen. I was worn out and, despite all the love I had in my heart for my children, I had nothing else to give.

I shoved the pile of bills onto the floor and lowered my head to the table. My mind wandered again. I thought of putting an end to all of the pain and frustration. Too tired to think, I waited for the phone to ring and end the suspense that had been building up all day.

Yesterday, while my mother watched the kids, I went to different churches and non-profit agencies trying to get some assistance. I managed to scrounge up $125 from the Salvation Army, $750 from St. Vincent de Paul, and another $500 from various churches. Families in Need was also reviewing my case to see if they could assist me to cover expenses like my light and phone bills. But if I lost the house, I would need that money to cover rental expenses somewhere else.

I felt the tension knot that had formed in the top of my head move closer to the center as I tried to hold back tears. My eyes were already so swollen I doubted they would ever return to normal.

For the life of me, I could not understand how my relationship with Kentee had taken such a drastic turn. Flashes of my life—before and after the children—ran through my brain. *Sure, things were different since we had kids, but I thought he would expect that.* "Was I living in a vacuum where he couldn't see what I was dealing with?" I questioned the walls, but I did not get a response.

I used to greet Kentee naked—or damn near naked—when he came home from work. As long as Kayla was bedded down, I would sit on his lap and feed him his supper. I kept a spotless house and took special care of my appearance.

But that was then, and this is now. After the twins' arrival, Kentee normally came home to find my hair standing on end and the house turned upside down, with no place to walk, let alone sit. And forget about a home-cooked meal. I assumed he understood but, obviously, he didn't.

The shrill ringing of the phone interrupted my musing. A quick glance at the clock told me that I had lost an entire day and had no idea where it had gone.

"Hello," I answered, my voice shaking.

"Mrs. Simmons?"

"This is she."

"This is Mrs. Turner from SunDale Bank. I spoke with you this morning. I did some checking to be certain I relayed the proper information to you. I discovered that I was the loan officer assigned to your husband's account when he first applied for the house you currently reside in. I need to make sure you understand that I have risked my job to call you. I'm doing this because I can relate to your situation. If you tell anyone where you got this information, I'll deny it. Is that clear?"

"I understand. Thank you," I said.

"This isn't the only loan that your husband has with our bank. He has another house over on the south side of Atlanta, and those payments are current."

"Excuse me?" Unable to comprehend what she was trying to tell me, I was fighting the urge to get an attitude with her for bearing the bad news.

"He bought that house a little over six months ago. If I had to guess, I would bet he has set up another household there."

I was so stunned I could not speak.

"Mrs. Simmons, are you there?"

"Uh, yes. I'm sorry. I just caught a curve ball aimed straight at my stomach. Is he aware that his children are about to be put out on the street?" I asked, as if she knew the answer. I felt exactly two inches tall, asking a stranger what was going on with my own husband. But since he wouldn't return my pages or phone calls, I was grasping at any straws I could reach.

Mrs. Turner was feeling my pain. "This is difficult for me to say, and I'm sorry to be the bearer of bad news. When I questioned him about the loan on the house you're living in, he said that you were a renter and he couldn't care less whether you were evicted or not because you weren't paying the rent as agreed."

Well, I'll just be damned. How the hell was I going to pay rent when he forbade me to work after I had his kids?

"He's saying that shit because he feels guilty that I caught his lying ass. Now he'd rather avoid me than face me."

I flashed back to a conversation with my old friend, Marie. She had warned me to think twice before I committed to a relationship with Kentee. Lord, I wish I had listened to her. I might not have been going through the current changes. Hindsight is twenty-twenty.

Still stunned, I could not move my lips to ask the questions I really needed the answers to. Realizing that the lady would not stay on the phone with me forever, I grew angry and plunged ahead.

"Renter, my ass! I'm not a renter; that's my husband!" I shouted, my fear turning into unadulterated rage.

Speaking louder and enunciating clearly, as if she were talking to a child, Mrs. Turner said, "I know this, and you know this, but he spoke to me like that wasn't the case. I informed him that if he allowed the house that you're living in to be foreclosed upon he'd permanently damage his credit rating."

"And what did he say?" I demanded, sure that he would at least try to protect his credit rating; if not his own children. I hoped he had said something that would keep us from winding up on the street.

"Hmm...I don't recall," she said, clearly lying, maybe trying to spare me further embarrassment. She changed the subject, putting the focus back on me.

"Look, I don't believe, based on my conversation with your husband, that he's going to be your knight-in-shining-armor. I'm speaking to you woman to woman. My own husband left me high and dry, and to this day, I don't know what happened to him. He could be dead for all I know, and to be honest, I hope he is. Don't waste precious time sitting around waiting for his ass to come back, or for the other shoe to drop."

Mrs. Turner's words hit me like a plank of wood against the forehead. She was right. I was the only person who could rectify this situation, and finally I understood.

"Hey, I appreciate your advice, but I'm still stuck between a rock and a hard place. I have three kids still in diapers. I can't get a job 'cause I can't afford day care. I have less than a thousand dollars to my name, and most of it I got from begging at the local churches here in Peachtree City. What am I supposed to do?" I wailed, no longer able to hold back my feelings.

"Mrs. Simmons, I don't have an answer for that. I wanted to make sure you weren't holding out false hope that your husband's going to fix this. You need to make a way for you and your children because your man isn't going to be there."

I glanced at my watch and realized that we had been talking for over thirty minutes. I needed some time to think about this new information.

Taking a deep breath, I said, "Thanks for everything."